Behind

the

Clouds

Behind the Clouds

Victoria Mae

For Laura G, Helen F, and Suzie B.

Prologue

Of all the great love stories, how many of them start with the leading lady curled up in a heap by her front door, too devastated and exhausted to move any further? But maybe that's just it: it's not the beginning, it's very much the end.

Under the naïve assumption that I knew what my long-term partner was thinking, I predicted wrongly and ultimately, the person I left standing in front of our favourite restaurant was not the person I thought I was in love with at all; I was standing across from a complete stranger with suddenly no idea who he was or who I am without him.

As I lie here, crying so hard it feels as though my soul is splitting in two, I wonder if we were ever really happy and if it's at all possible to truly be happy again.

Chapter 1

Three hours earlier

Evan leaves his chair and bends down on one knee, taking my hand in his and gazes deep into my eyes, while saying four unexpected words: 'I'm so very sorry.' His voice is almost a whisper. 'But…we've drifted apart. You can't deny it,' he adds quickly.

Six years flash before my eyes in the matter of moments that it takes for my heart to hit the floor. 'Can't I?' My voice matches the feeling of being punched in the larynx. 'I thought you were going to propose.' How can two people in the same relationship be on such completely different pages?

All sympathetic eyes are on me, and dull whispers start to fill the air as I feel the heat of my face starting to match the red of the chequered tablecloths. I need to get out of here. I stand up abruptly and make for the exit as quickly as my four-inch strappies will allow me.

'Melanie, wait!'

The veranda has no direct exit so, short of hitching my leg over the flower beds, I have to power-walk back inside the restaurant. Fighting my way through groups of carefree friends — laughing and clinking their glasses — and smiley waiters with trays of fresh, basil-adorned mozzarella, I dash for the door. I can hear Evan somewhere behind me as I weave through tables of loved-up couples; nearly free, I stretch my arm out for the door.

'Ms Butler!' A frizzy-haired, blurry-eyed lady grabs my hand. 'How are you!?' she screeches and gives me a hug that is far too tight. 'What a surprise to see you here.' She slaps me on the arm. 'My gosh, you scrub up well!'

This village is too small. 'Hi, Mrs Thompson, yes, what a small world.' I glance behind my shoulder and see Evan cornered by a waiter who's waving the bill in his face. 'I'm sorry, I really must be...' I side-step but she mirrors me, once again blocking my path.

'Now tell me, how *issssh* Casey doing?' She sways as the ruby coloured liquid sloshes, attempting to make its escape out of her glass.

'*Um*, wonderful,' I say hurriedly and chance a glance to see Evan holding a card machine. 'Just like I wrote in her report. If you could excuse me, I have to go.'

'Oh *yesss*, of course my dear.' She slaps me on the bum this time. 'No work, just play tonight?!'

'Indeed.' I make for the door as she raises her glass to me before being pulled backward by a muscly curly-headed man, and explodes into a fit of giggles.

Into the warm summer night's air again I head in the direction of the solitude of my flat, thankfully only five minutes away.

'Would you stop running?' Evan is suddenly behind me.

Damn parents, and damn these shoes.

'I need you to understand!'

I turn my head but don't stop. 'Understand what? That you've wasted years of your life? *My* life?' My pace picks up with my adrenaline. 'And what sort of an insensitive moron breaks up with someone in public?'

He has to jog to keep up with me now. 'Well, I didn't want

3

you to make a scene after what I was about to tell you. And you didn't let me finish. I don't want to marry you, Melanie.'

'I know; you made that abundantly clear back there.'

'No, I mean I *can't* marry you because I'm going to marry someone else. I'm going to marry Daisy,' he almost yells at me. I stop in my tracks. 'Did you hear me?'

I turn violently. 'I've always hated that; why do you constantly ask if I've heard you?'

'Because quite often you're not with me,' he says calmly. 'You're in a daydream, replaying a previous conversation or obsessing about something or...'

'You're going to marry Daisy?' I interrupt his list of my negative habits.

'I am,' he nods defiantly. 'Now, this is going to sound horrible, but for a while now I've felt that there's been something missing with us, you know? And Daisy, well, she just seems to complete me. I'm sorry for the way this has turned out. How are you feeling?'

'You've insulted me, erased the life we've built together and to top it all off you're marrying your work colleague who you hardly know, and you want to know how I'm feeling!?' The end of the sentence comes out quite hysterically as I give his arm a couple of swift bashes with my overstuffed clutch, launching the entire contents everywhere. We both bend down to pick everything up.

'No, leave it, I don't need your help,' I bark at him, gathering my things. 'I *knew* something was going on at that Christmas party,' I say to the floor then stand and square up to him. 'So that's what? Seven months?'

He stands silently and my heart plummets. 'How long has this been going on, Evan?'

He sighs. 'A few years.'

My eyes widen with outrage. 'How many?'

'About three and a half,' he says quickly then leans backwards to avoid a further bashing, but I'm the one who's been mentally slapped. Tears are trying to make their way out of my eyes, but I force them back.

We stand in silence for so long all I can hear is the pounding of my broken heart, which has somehow managed to lodge itself into my throat. He comes closer and positions me numbly into a hug, his face now inches away from mine.

'Come on, let's just go back to yours and talk this through.'

Then like a lightning bolt, the realisation hits me, and I look into his eyes. 'This is why you wouldn't move in with me.'

He nods his head. 'I've been living in between mine and hers for a while now; we're going to sell my place though.'

My eyes finally admit defeat and well up. 'You've been lying to me for over half of our relationship.'

With his arms still around me, I take in the person I'd allowed to become the single most important being in my life; the leading man I'd put all my future hopes and dreams into. I'm amazed that only a single tear leaves my right eye.

I leave Evan standing in the street whispering an apology as I walk away without a goodbye. The instant I'm home I shut the door, throw my shoes and collapse into a heap in the hallway, curling my body up into a ball. Through the walls I hear Michael Bublé serenading my neighbour with, 'You'll Never Find'.

Time evades me as I sob silently and somewhere between questioning what it was that I did wrong and berating myself for being so stupid, I fall asleep.

Chapter 2

A warm, fuzzy feeling fills my entire body as I stare at my reflection; I am the world's most beautiful bride. As Mum enters the room, she's practically glowing with happiness. She gives me a huge bear hug from behind and I turn my head to face her. But as I turn back to the mirror my teeth are black and the beautiful sunny day has turned cold and dark. Suddenly there's cackling coming from somewhere and spindly fingers come out of the mirror and rip the veil from my hair. Everything becomes distant and foggy as I throw my arms to my head and touch what seems like an envelope.

Brushing the post to one side I release a huge sigh as my recollection floods back: I'm single; alone; broken. Pushing myself up to a nearly seated position proves to be quite difficult with both hands still fast asleep and I slip back down, smacking my face on the lino floor. Finally seated, I realise a chill has engulfed me. Rubbing my arms, I unsteadily stand up and head towards the living room to grab a blanket. On the way I catch myself in the hall mirror: not quite the blushing bride of my dreams. My gorgeously GHD-curled hair from last night has transformed itself in an electric-shock, meets gone with the wind, sort-of-fashion. I let out a short hoot of laughter. My eyes are so puffy from crying it looks like I've been punched, and now, from my little fall, the right side of my face is bright red; I lean in for a closer inspection and see what looks like the start of a bruise.

Stumbling into the living room, I grab a blanket. Wrapping it around myself makes no difference to the chill I've caught or to the coldness of my heart and so, pulling it tighter, I head to the kitchen to make some coffee. I glance at the Baileys bottle sitting on the counter and swoosh it up into my arms on the way to the coffee maker. As I wait for a latte to appear, I take a swig from the bottle. It feels good so I take another one, longer this time. The tepid milky texture soothes me somehow and I look at the coffee, all steaming and ready to be consumed. After a momentary ponder I turn and leave it sitting. I could have it after.

But I don't. After the first two shots it only really makes sense to carry on; a lot warmer with each unladylike gulp, I sway around the living room, flicking my blanket around me like a wrap. 'I need some music,' I declare to the empty flat. Waltzing over to my Alexa, I stop for a moment, waiting for inspiration to hit me. 'Alexa: play something awesome.'

'OK. Playing Evan's awesome playlist, from Spotify,' she responds to me in her mechanical voice.

'No!' I yell with impatience, as Eiffel 65's 'I'm Blue' blasts through my speakers. 'Bastard!' I yell at the music. 'Alexa: STOP!' The room returns to silence, and I sigh. *When did he make a playlist?* Then the perfect song comes to mind. 'Alexa: play, Kings of Leon, 'Sex on Fire.'

'OK. Playing Kings of Leon, Sex on Fire, from Spotify.'

As the intro starts, it's far too quiet, 'Alexa: volume on full, please.' Jumping on the spot, I break free from the blanket and join in with all the grace Cameron Diaz had in *The Holiday,* singing 'Mr Brightside,' only with absolutely no grasp of the lyrics, 'OOOOOOOH! AND SOMETHING BLAH BLAH BLAH!!'

I continue bouncing and then go for a delicate spin but miss my footing and splat onto the floor with a not-so-graceful belly-flop; the room continues to swirl around me.

There's a buzzing sound coming from somewhere; my phone. *Bollocks, where did I leave you?* I scramble along on all fours, woozy in my search. *Ah! There you are.* I snatch my mobile from the coffee table and see Mish's smiling face flashing at me. We met on the first day of secondary school. Billy Burns was emptying my lunch into a bin and Mish came over and smacked him square in the face. She got detention for a week, but we've been best friends ever since.

'*Helloooo*!' I answer in my tipsy manner. I'm trying to work out why I can't hear her when it dawns on me that the music is still ridiculously loud. 'HANG ON,' I yell. 'I'M JUST GOING TO TURN THIS OFF.' Heaving myself up, phone in hand, I stomp over to the system and press pause. '*Sssssory*, I was just listening to some music,' I slur.

'Are you pissed?'

'Well, I was going to have a Baileys latte and I never actually got around to the latte part.'

'Bravo,' she says without judgement. 'So, tell me everything, then.'

'*Huh*?'

'About the proposal...' she prompts slowly.

'Oh, yeah.' Suddenly everything isn't funny anymore. 'No Mish, he, *um*, didn't propose.' I'm sobering up with each word.

'Oh.' She's taken aback. 'Just moving in then?'

'Yes, actually, but not with me.'

'What? What do you mean?'

Like pulling off a plaster, I try to say it as quickly and painlessly as possible. 'He broke up with me; he's been cheating on me with the girl from the Christmas party, who he's moving in with, before *they* get married.'

'Oh shit.' I hear some scrambling on the other end. 'Give me ten minutes to cancel my weekend meetings—'

'Oh no, no, don't cancel anything and haven't you got an event later?'

'Clive can handle everything; it's only a small do. See you in fifteen.'

I hang up and prepare for her arrival by whipping out the champagne I'd secretly put in the fridge to celebrate my engagement. *My engagement.* Hot tears prickle my eyes and overflow onto my cheeks, as a cacophony of questions and crappy thoughts cascade one after the other through my mind. How could I have been so oblivious? Have I been in a constant daydream? He must have put a lot of effort into seeing us both and keeping it a secret for so long. I wonder if his friends know. I sit down slowly at my dining table and stare blankly; tears become more urgent. I bet all his horrid friends have been laughing at my expense. Brushing away the tears, angrily, I stomp over to my cupboards. Instead of reaching for two delicate champagne flutes, I pull out two I-mean-business steins; a present from Mrs Thompson from her last visit to Oktoberfest.

I live in a small but perfectly awesome one bedroom, ground-floor flat a stone's throw from Blackheath. I would have never been able to buy this on my teaching salary alone, but my Nana passed away three years ago and left me and my two sisters enough money to set up a home. Although saying that, my big sister didn't need the money and my little sister hasn't touched hers yet. My mum's mum was my hero. She made everything all right with a hug and a large slice of the world's best home-made cakes. I was her number one taste-tester; unfortunately, that contributed to my nickname at school: Belly-Melly.

Mish lets herself in with the key I gave her for emergencies and flies into view, pausing momentarily in the living room doorway to assess the damage. My eyes meet hers and with a sympathetic head tilt my slow, silent tears transform into violent and rather loud sobs. She leaves a day bag and a wine carrier at her feet before running over to me for a hug.

'Well, you look lovely,' she says into my hair, and I break away to look her square in the face. 'The *dress* is lovely,' she corrects, then looks closely at my face. 'Did he hit you?!'

'No, I fell this morning; apparently I'm beating myself up physically and mentally.'

'Let's get you into something more comfortable.'

All I can manage is a nod.

'OK.' She switches from best friend mode into drill sergeant events manager. 'I'll go and grab some sensible clothes while you,' she goes over to the day bag and starts unloading onto the table in what seems like one fluid motion, 'take your make-up off,' handing me Johnson's Sensitive wipes, 'tie your hair up,' gives me a hair band, 'eat some of these…' Lindt Lindor chocolates; my favourite in a family-sized box, which I fear may not be big enough today. She walks over to the wine carrier, 'I'll put these in the fridge,' the bottles clunk happily together, 'and I'll be back in a moment.'

She's gone all of two seconds before returning with my plaid pyjama bottoms and a light baggy jumper.

An hour later I still feel like I've lost a limb, but there's a warm glow appearing inside of me, making me feel almost normal; perhaps that's just the alcohol. Collapsed on the sofa, with my legs over hers, Mish grabs simultaneously for the next bottle of pink goodness and the corkscrew. The cork pops and she declares, 'I always thought he was a bit of a shithead.'

Suspended in mid-air, I pause from putting the next treat in my mouth, but don't reply. This isn't news to me; I always knew deep down that she and Evan didn't get on. He thought she was a crazy, control-freak and she thought he was a pompous arse with no sense of humour.

'But it wasn't anything that I could quite put my finger on, you know?'

I love how she can be incredibly polite and protective sometimes and other times completely forward and inappropriate; it makes her unpredictable and exciting — you never know what's going to come out of her mouth, and that's the thing I love most about her.

I sigh and bring myself to tell her what I haven't wanted to acknowledge myself.

'I haven't even told you the worst part yet.'

'How can it get worse?' She fills our glasses back up.

My voice wobbles slightly. 'I found a ring.'

She puts down the wine and takes my hand.

'Turns out, I'm not crazy and he was ready to propose after all.' I look at my friend with progressively welling eyes, 'Why wasn't it to me?' Burying my head in her lap, she strokes my hair gently.

'I don't know, hon.'

'What is so wrong with me that he couldn't comprehend spending the rest of his life with me?'

'There's nothing wrong with you; I plan on spending the rest of my life with you.'

I want to laugh but my body won't let me. 'What have I done to deserve this?'

'You wanted your happy ending; there's nothing wrong with that. Listen.' She continues to stroke my hair, 'If Poppie were here right now, you know what she would say?' I don't respond so she continues, 'She would say that everything is an experience that we're meant to learn from. Right now, nothing makes sense, but it will. It will, I promise.'

Chapter 3

Mish stays with me all weekend; she says for support, but I know it is more akin to suicide watch. Finally, Monday morning decides to rear its ugly and hung-over head and I'm startled with Katrina and the Waves', 'Walking on Sunshine,' with mocking-cheeriness singing away to me from somewhere. 'Really!?' I yell at the innocently chipper alarm coming from Mish's phone and I swing my arm violently to silence it; with a crash, it smacks the floor but still continues.

Slithering out from the foetal position, I then sit up way too quickly and fall straight out of bed with my face next to the merry phone. I feel like I've been hit by a train. I fumble my heavy hands over the iPhone to find the snooze, but my eyes can't focus so I throw it to one side at the exact moment Mish walks in with a plate in one hand and a mug in the other. She sways and trips over but manages to somehow stay upright and hold on to both items.

'What the hell?' Splattered by freshly brewed coffee, Mish momentarily looks furious before we both burst into giggles. She bends down to pick up an escapee half slice of toast and I grab the warm black brew and savour the aroma. 'OK,' she says, swaying slightly, from a weekend that consisted of only liquid and junk food. 'We're running a bit late with exactly forty minutes to get you fed, washed, dressed and relatively human for school. Are you up for the mission?'

I slowly sip and ponder this thought. God, I wish I could

Victoria Mae

call in sick but then again, what would I do? Mope around? Get pissed? Generally, drown myself in self-pity? Yep, sounds perfect. 'Nope, calling in sick!' I say positively, meeting her eyes. 'I don't think I'm ready to be a professional educator just yet.'

'Bollocks,' is her reply, with a snatch of my coffee. 'You've got three days to suck it up before you sit on your arse for two months—'

'Six weeks,' I correct.

'Now,' she gets back on track. 'I've ironed your short-sleeved pinstriped shirt and your cute pencil skirt is hanging up on the back of the bathroom door.' I open my mouth in protest, but she takes this opportunity to shove in some toast. 'Eat that and I'll get the shower going and pack your bag. I'm half way through marking the kids' Shakespeare essays—'

'*Oofh sshit,*' I interrupt, still chewing.

She puts her finger to her lips to silence me. 'I'm going to mark the rest while you…' She searches for the right word, 'Get it together.'

God, she's good.

Relatively human is an overstatement but it is amazing what a little caffeine, several heavily buttered slices of Hovis and a shower can do. I start the fifteen-minute trot to my school with a route directly through Blackheath Village. When I was doing my PGCE at Greenwich University I loved to hop on the bus to Blackheath and wander around with a coffee and daydream about living here. Although back then all I could afford was the odd treat from a charity shop. The owner of my favourite one told me once when I was browsing the book section, 'You won't find true love with your nose in a book. A pretty young thing like you should be out there with her eyes and her heart wide open.' I remember the song

14

'Belle' from *Beauty and the Beast* came into my head.

I realised then that maybe I could try a little harder to meet someone and the next week, as fate designed it, I met Evan at my student union bar. He was studying business at Cambridge and was visiting an old school friend, who happened to be in the same student accommodation as me. We did the long-distance dance for almost a year and when we both graduated that summer, he moved to London to start work at Marigold Enterprises and to be with me.

As I reach the towering black gates of McCarthy Primary, slightly sweaty, I weave my way through the sea of hyper students and tutting parents; it never does look too good to arrive after your class. I have all of five minutes to leg it to the staffroom before the morning's meeting with our ghastly Head Mistress, Ms Crawley. Creepy Crawley, as I refer to her as, is a smidgen over five feet with tottering heels included. Her jet-black hair is forever swept back off her razor-sharp features, glued down to her head and explodes out in a straw-like bun or ponytail.

She always has a way of making me feel the size of an ant as I am constantly being undermined and criticised by both her and Shirley Dagmire, her second in command. My speed is now up to a sprint as I sign in at warp speed (at '8:10'), throw down the pen and whizz through the dining room doors, the Year One corridor and finally, I'm outside the impending door. I allow myself three seconds to catch my breath and compose myself before entering the dragon's den that is the staffroom.

The smell of intensely-strong freshly brewed filter almost knocks me over — Violet from the reception class must be on coffee duty again. Briskly and as casually as I can manage, I slip into the last seat around the table and as soon as I have, the staffroom door flies open; I can just about hear a pantomime villain's theme music, 'bum, bum, BAAA!' complete with a crash of thunder as Creepy Crawley pauses in the doorway for maximum effect. A cold shudder runs through the room.

'Let's begin.' Her voice is hard and laced with distaste.

'And a good morning to you too!' whispers Dave, the only other Year Four teacher, one of my closest colleagues, and best friends; I smile and giggle internally.

'Miss Butler.'

Gulp. 'Yes, Ms Crawley?'

'Do you think I am stupid?'

I feel I should go with no. 'No.'

'For the entire year, we have had the same conversation about your tardiness, and running past me in the corridor…'

Whoops.

'It doesn't bode well for you, I'm afraid. There are three remaining days of this term, are there not?'

I nod mutely.

'I expect you to sign in at 7:30 a.m. and not a moment after. If this is beyond your capability, then I am sure we can find a replacement for you, effective from September.'

Nod from Shirley as she literally makes a note and a smug know-it-all smile slithers across her round face.

'No, that sounds more than acceptable, Ms Crawley, I will—'

'I have no interest in what you have to say Melanie, but Mr Wright…' Her eyes slide slowly across to glare at Dave and her icy tone continues, 'I am at the end of my tether wondering what smart comment you have to grace me with today.'

We sit like naughty school children as she continues to tell us that we are the reason the school is not excelling and after we've had our egos, once more, severely bruised, we exit with our heads hanging and walk with my other two closest friends, Jill and Gracie, to my classroom.

'What a complete bitch.' Jill sits on the window ledge with an e-cigarette.

Dave laughs. '7:30? That's when you get up isn't it?'

'I just want to know how Shirley sleeps at night,' chips in Gracie, patting down her already perfectly ironed plaid dress.

'With a very big sleeping pill and a cold empty void in her bed — did you hear she's finally going through a divorce? Glad that poor, walked-over husband of hers finally sucked up the courage to get shot of her,' says Jill, vaping away.

Jill and Gracie came to my rescue when I first joined McCarthy as a Reception Teacher. I was sitting on the floor amongst an explosion of toys after my first day had finished. Red paint splattered my face and highlighted my hair; sand glittered my new dress; two of my fingers were super-glued together; and tears filled my eyes as I mentally wrote out my resignation, when they swept me off of the floor and landed me in the local pub. That's where I met Dave for the first time. I can still remember his face as the three of us marched through the door of The Fallen Willow. He had already bought three bottles of wine and four shots of Sambuca, each of which he lit and handed out, while declaring, 'Welcome to hell!'

We say our goodbyes and wish Gracie luck for her assembly later. Alone, I sit down at my desk, close my eyes and enjoy the thirty-second stillness.

'What's up with you today, Butler, you look like shit.'

I open my eyes to see Dave standing in the doorway. He glances at my left hand but doesn't say any more and pushes his CK black-rimmed glasses up a smidge on the bridge of his nose — they're not prescription, he just thought they looked

17

cool. I swallow hard to attempt to get rid of the thick wedge that has lodged in my throat and then sigh.

'Evan told me that he's been having an affair, they're moving in together before they get married and have ten thousand beautiful babies and generally live happily ever after, while I am going to die a sad and lonely old fart with only cats for company.'

'Don't be stupid, you're allergic to cats.'

'That's the only point you're picking up on?'

'Oh, Butler, come here.'

He glides across the room in three powerful strides, whips me out of the chair and up into his strong arms. His lips lightly touch my ear as he whispers, 'I'm really sorry, Mel; I know you loved him.'

'*Ooooooooh!*'

We break away, blushing like guilty teenagers as my class file in and continue to whistle and cheer.

I raise my hand to silence them — a trick I've always been very proud of — and the commotion simmers down to a light murmur with a hint of giggles. 'I want everybody in chairs, and I don't want to hear another word.' I direct at the class with a much stronger voice than I thought I could muster.

'We'll talk at lunch; we're all here for you.' Dave flashes me his winning smile and a little sunshine fills my heart.

Chapter 4

Finally, the last day of the year arrived in all of its wonderful and completely overdue glory. Sweaty children fled the gates like wild animals released from captivity and teachers practically skipped their way to the pub. The sun is shining brighter than ever today and it's the perfect temperature for a glass of something cold in The Fallen Willow.

'Cheers,' we all call in unison.

I sigh deeply and everyone turns to face me with sympathetic expressions. Opening my mouth to apologise, I get cut off by Gracie,

'So, when are you heading off, Mel?' She sips her Pimm's through a pink straw and waits patiently for my answer.

I scratch my head trying to remember. 'Tomorrow lunchtime-ish.'

'Oh, it will be so beautiful; I've always wanted to go to Wales.' Gracie takes another delicate sip.

'Me too; it will be nice to finally see it,' I admit.

'Good of Poppie to let you stay at hers; I wouldn't have wanted to stay there alone either. Did you get any money back from the hotel?' Jill asks as she reaches for the peanuts.

'Yeah, Mish rung for me as she had to cancel her reservation too.' She's going to Paris at the last minute for a meeting and she knew I didn't want to stay in a deluxe room that I'd originally booked with Evan. 'No idea what she said but they've refunded the full amount.'

'Next round on you then,' Jill clinks my glass.

Dave snags the peanuts. 'Is Poppie's house all done then?'

'*Nearly finished*, were her words on the phone yesterday. I'm amazed she and Michael have managed to plan a wedding whilst renovating.'

'I'm amazed you're still friends with someone from primary school; I've lost touch with everyone from mine.' Jill shakes her head and grabs the bag back from Dave.

'Well, she's someone I knew I'd always have in my life. She's kind, funny and bonkers; the qualities I look for in all of my friends.' I smile at myself, proud that I haven't completely lost my sense of humour.

Gracie grins at me, 'Shame none of that seemed to rub off on her brother, *huh*?'

Now I'm frowning. The last thing I need is someone else to point out my flaws and inadequacies. 'Craig is, and always has been, a top-notch arsehole. Every time I see him, I turn into this subconscious mess who can't stand upright, can't say the right thing, can't be the person I think that I am, because his stupid critical eyes are constantly analysing me. I mean, the last time I saw him, I ruined what I'm pretty sure was an insanely expensive shirt because he made me jump; I swear he does it on purpose to make me look stupid.'

'Clearly, he brings out the best in you.' Dave winks. 'But your clumsy nature makes you adorable, Butler. I personally look forward to you making an arse out of yourself; it brightens up my day.'

'Well, it's different around you lot, it doesn't matter if I fall on my face, you won't point out how big my arse is while I'm down there — he would. Anyway, the focus is on Poppie, Michael and their beautiful, unique and quirky special day.' I sigh again as I think of Evan and what never was. 'And maybe one day I'll meet someone who actually embraces my quirks rather than uses them as an excuse to not marry me.'

When I'm back home and packing, I think about how I've always looked at the relationships that my family and friends have and compared myself to them. Evan and I never had the same spark of electricity that Poppie and Michael had when they first met. They locked eyes at a wellness convention. In between 'table top' and 'reverse dog', a spark of electricity travelled between them and they fell in love — there and then — no questions, no reservations, just pure, unquestionable love at first sight; soul mates for life.

I go to the bathroom and gather my toiletries, and my back pocket announces the arrival of a text; speaking of the lady in question:

"Are you ready to cleanse your aura and lighten your mind, surrendering negative energy and thoughts and to release them into the universe, where they shall dissolve?"

Bonkers, bonkers, bonkers.

***

I arrive at frantic, furrow-browed Paddington Station late afternoon the next day. As a teacher, I forget that not everyone is suddenly on holiday from mid-July until the beginning of September. Feeling a tiny bit smug, I order a refreshing iced coffee and sit on one of the comfy looking sofas to people-watch. Why the majority of travellers have chosen to sit on the hard, cold, metal seats, I don't know. Some people aren't even sitting; my eye is drawn to a businessman with a neatly folded newspaper tucked under one arm, clutching his briefcase for dear life. He's pacing up and down in front of the monitors muttering to himself and stroking what little hair he has left on his head. I smile and take a sip of my strawberries and cream frappuccino whilst my eyes scan the rest of my surroundings. There are backpackers, groups of friends, singletons, families with pushchairs and whiny children, sad lovers kissing each other goodbye — I avert my eyes quickly. I spot an artistic looking middle-aged man, desperately in need of a hairbrush as he weaves his hand through his wayward wiry hair. I take a look at his table and observe three empty coffee mugs, a bottle of vitamin water and several empty plates of food. His eyes are wildly wide, and he trembles from either too much caffeine or an upcoming deadline and lack of ideas to fill it. Two older ladies busily brush past the writer, each holding about ten bags of shopping. 'Oh Gloria, there's one here!' says the frail one, pointing at the sofa opposite me and hurrying over, she sits down with a surprising and almighty thump.

'Oh, my poor feet, Jude, next time, I swear, I'm wearing slippers.'

They each burst into giggles as the other sits down. 'Oh yes, that'll make us more sophisticated. People'll think we're lost and relocate us to the funny farm.'

I wonder if I'll be that much fun and carefree when I'm their age — seventy going on seventeen.

'We're normally not this daft, dear,' Jude looks at me with her baby blue eyes.

'Yes, we are. Don't ever make excuses for being you!'

Huh, how profound. I'll have to remember that, Poppie will love it.

My platform is announced and off I head after a smile at the chuckle sisters. My ticket says 'quiet carriage' so I'm optimistic when I'm one of the first people on and all you can hear is the hum of the engine. I put my small carry-on sized suitcase on the luggage rack at the door, then find my seat and throw myself in it. The train is impeccably clean compared to the tube I was just on. The midnight purple and pale blue base colours blend with the splashes of pink and grey décor.

As the other passengers take their places and we make our way, I'm horrified to find not only what seems to be a Von Trapp family day out but also what feels like the entire cast of *Annie*. Except these children are completely tone deaf, singing a range of both chart and Disney songs. By the time we hit Reading, I'm just about to pelt them all with my M&M's when they bundle out. It's not until then I realise the corporate skyline has transformed into endless green fields: *now it's a holiday*. I wriggle back into my seat and open my book.

When the driver announces our next stop is Cardiff Central, I consult my ticket details; according to my email print out, I have ten minutes to make my connection after we've arrived. Glancing at my watch I see I've got fifteen minutes before we pull into the station, so I start to gather my things together but as I do, I notice so does everybody else. As I move slightly faster, so does the rest of the carriage. Sideways glances and subtle movements accelerate into panicked looks and swiftly, all bottoms in carriage 'A' fly off their seats and the formerly empty aisle is now a neat queue facing the exit. Why is my seat at the very back of this carriage? Maybe I can get out the other way. Turning around I see a big sign on the firmly closed door: *"Staff access only"* it informs me. *Perfect*. I dare to check the time. I still have a full twelve minutes to catch my connection. Plenty of time.

A crackly sound carves the tension in the air and my stomach does a backflip as a frustratingly jolly voice sounds over the tannoy. 'Ladies and gentlemen, this is your driver speaking. We're just waiting for the platform to become available before we make our final destination into Cardiff Central. Should be any minute now. Thank you for your patience. Next stop is Cardiff Central.'

Twelve minutes turns to eight, eight turns to five and panic is starting to set in. Feeling like a caged animal, I shift from one foot to the other then tiptoe to try and see above the heads in front, to calculate how long it will take this many people to move — like a simple maths problem I'd give my kids. If a carriage full of fifty people shimmy at a speed of five seconds, how long before they get their arses off the fecking...

'Excited, *huh*?!' says the snowy-haired man in front of me.

'What? *Um*, I mean, no. I've got another train to catch', I say irritably.

He turns back around, mildly offended and finally we make it out at a snail's pace and onto the platform. It's a lot smaller than I imagined; let's hope there isn't a hidden side that takes an age to get to.

As I weave my way through the crowds it's like being in London: there are still businessmen, backpackers, groups of friends, singletons and families with pushchairs, but the frantic pace has slowed. Not helpful when you've got all of two minutes to find out where you have to go. A group of drunken stags bound their way around me,

'*Wayyy*! Pretty lady, give Gaz a kiss, it's his last day of *freeeeedom*!!'

Shaking him off, I break away and dash towards the screens.

Yes! Right, OK, I'm looking and nothing makes sense. Oh my God, it's in Welsh. I can't frigging speak Welsh!

Ever so painfully slowly, the words morph into English. I see my next train is waiting at Platform 6 and I spot the descending stairs and break into a sprint.

If I was going for graceful, I think two words would sum me up beautifully: *Epic. Fail.* In my leap of faith as the doors are closing, I throw my suitcase and myself into the carriage. Losing grip on my luggage, it flies in the opposite direction, as I rugby tackle the man in front of me. Now, spread-eagled with my nose inches from his, I'm horrified to realise that I'm panting. Not lady-like pants of some marathon-trained beauty, or the gentle breaths of an intimate moment, but huge, sweaty, gasping-for-breath heaves and I really wish I hadn't just had a hummus and falafel wrap with a side of onion rings. Still catching my breath, I push my top half up and attempt a staggered sentence,

'I...am...beyond...sorry.' I scan the face of the stranger below me and am mortified to find that this is not a stranger at all.

'Hello, Melanie.' His lightly stubbled face spreads into that cheeky smile of his.

'Craig? What are you doing here?'

'Well, it is my sister's wedding in a few days — what on earth did you have for dinner?'

I scramble all the way up, my face turning a completely beautiful shade of puce and sheepishly turn to the now visibly angry older lady. Taking my suitcase, I thank her and apologise at the same time before hiding behind it in a very garish snot-green polka-dot seat. A moment too soon after, Craig comes and sits happily opposite me.

'You always did know how to make an entrance.'

I sit up and attempt to defend my free-fall, 'I had to make sure I caught my connection.'

'You could have got any train after this one you know,' he laughs, as I feel stupid not realising that and try to pretend it's not true, 'but luckily now we can ride all the way to Poppie's together.'

'You're staying at Poppie's?' I say, not attempting in any fashion to hide the disappointment in my voice.

'Yes. She told me your plans had changed too.'

'That's right,' I say with more confidence than I feel. His eyes say something his mouth doesn't.

'Haven't seen you since Poppie's engagement party at my flat.' Craig's mouth dares a twitch of a smile.

'Look. I told you I was sorry. My heel caught on the rug after you made me jump, I didn't mean to throw my wine at you, and I did offer to pay for your dry cleaning.'

'You did.' He nods gravely. 'You have a way of displaying your scattiness whenever I see you.'

'You tend to bring the best out of me.' I use Dave's words whilst displaying a fake smile. *Why do I feel so exposed and clumsy in front of this man?*

A lively businessman next to Craig starts talking at us. I think he's speaking English, but I honestly have no idea what he is saying: like listening to my Uncle Connor after several whiskeys in his favourite bar in Ireland. I find in these situations it's best to smile and nod along. Craig gives me a smirk, knowing full well I have no idea what's going on; I leave them to it and gaze out at the window. The valley train creaks its way noisily through a maze of luscious green forest. I shift to adjust my legs and cross them the other way, accidentally kicking Craig.

'Sorry,' I mouth at him as he's still in full-blown conversation. Well, he probably deserved that.

Chapter 5

When we reach Poppie's *ridiculously* small town — a word with so many consonants and only two vowels, I have no idea how to pronounce — it's twilight. As the train pulls into the platform, I see her bouncing up and down, looking in each window, waving manically despite the fact that she hasn't seen me or Craig yet. As soon as my feet have touched the platform she starts clapping and runs over before giving me the world's tightest hug.

'I'm so excited you're finally here!'

'Me too.' I hug her back with gusto. 'Mish asked me to say again how sorry she is that she can't make it.'

'Like I told her, there are no problems at all...oh yay, I thought you might get the same train!' She's clearly spotted Craig behind me and then opens her right arm so we're forced into a group hug.

'Yes, we *bumped* into each other,' Craig says grinning at me with his face far too close.

'Well,' Poppie moves us so we're all linking arms with her in the middle, 'I'm so happy two of my favourite people in the whole world are here! Come! I've made some treats for you both.'

When Poppie invited me to stay, perhaps I should have asked a few more questions.

'Welcome to our beautiful home!' Poppie's face is full of love and delight whereas mine represents a horrified impression of Munch's 'The Scream.'

'Let me give you the grand tour, honey! *Oo,* mind your step — it's a little bit of a previously-loved items ground at the moment. Although we do have a very nice barbecue area set up over there.' I follow her point, but my eyes are distracted.

Craig follows, silently grinning and I'm careful with my every step, not wanting to give him any more ammunition. The roar of a drill or something comes from inside as we mosey our way through an abandoned sink that's been used for mixing plaster, a tyre, window frames, random slabs of wood, bricks, draining pipe, bubble wrap, and pallets all hidden intricately within a rather wild, wild garden.

'I didn't know nettles could grow that tall.'

'Impressive, isn't it?' Poppie beams completely missing my point.

'*Umm.*'

'Nature has a way of making its presence known…honey, come and see who's arrived!!' she yells through the window. 'Just step through here! We're going to make this into a door eventually.' Standing back, she encourages me to clamber through said window with the aid of a rather Leaning-Tower-of-Pisa-esque pile of multi-coloured bricks.

I look from Craig to Poppie with doubt. 'Where's the present door, Pops?'

'Out of access temporarily.' She helps me halfway in with a swift nudge of my bottom. 'There was nowhere else to keep the insulation apart from the old main corridor which leads to the front door. Plus,' she shrugs and grins at me as I'm straddling the ledge, 'it's a bit of fun! Where else do you climb through a window to get in?'

'Monica's apartment in 'Friends?''

'Exactly, nowhere else in real life, *huh*? Now, just hitch

your other leg over.'

Inside, it's far scarier than the outside. Exposed bricks, loose, dangling wires, an explosion of tools in each room and I think it's a property even Kevin McCloud would walk away from. Craig and I sit in two of the mismatched dining chairs around a Black and Decker workbench for our table as Poppie prepares some herbal tea.

'So, almost finished?' I say in the direction of the kitchen before reaching for a home-made flapjack.

'Yep,' Poppie replies, carrying over two mugs and placing them in front of us both. 'Plumbing, electrics, almost all plastering; the rest is purely aesthetic.'

I look around as she returns to get the other two mugs and spot what looks like a damp patch on the wall, woodworm in the floor and I think it may be a little longer to finish.

'Welcome to our humble home, Mel!' Michael appears in a midnight blue boiler suit, and I take in his shoulder-length blonde waves — peppered with building dust — as he makes his way towards me. I stand and give him a hug.

'You're on the home-stretch, I hear!'

'*Um hmm*, I'd say maybe two months more.' He smiles dotingly towards Poppie, who's still in the kitchen.

'Have you thought any more about that extension?' Craig says in a quiet voice to Michael.

He nods and whispers, 'A yoga room as a wedding present.'

Craig quietly replies, 'I'll happily draw up some plans with you if you'd like.'

'What are we whispering about?' Poppie comes back with two more teas.

'Something for you,' Michael says honestly and kisses her on the forehead gently before taking his drink. 'So, good trip?'

He turns to me.

'She had a *spectacular* trip, didn't you, Mel?' Craig chips in and I frown at his sparkling eyes.

'I did,' I say shortly, still looking at Craig. 'Had to run for my connection though.'

'Oh, I do love that part,' Poppie says with big eyes. 'Gets your heart pumping!'

'So how are the final preparations going? Is there anything I can do?' I ask both of them before Craig can draw any further attention to me.

'Poppie's done everything.' Michael says adoringly.

'No, you've sourced some of the furniture for the reception,' she says to him with just as much affection. 'We're all set really. I finished the decorations and my headpiece today. The only thing I'd like you to do is maybe bake a cake for the buffet? I'll show you where everything is in the kitchen.'

'Absolutely! What kind?'

'Whatever you think,' she smiles at me.

After Poppie and I have put the world to rights, and the boys have discussed everything from Craig's night out in town, to building regulations, I stifle a yawn. 'Let me show you where you're going to be staying!' Poppie leads the way carefully along the loose floorboards to a wobbly bannister and up the stairs.

'So, we've given you our room—'

'Oh no, no, honestly I couldn't possibly take—'

'Nonsense.' She cuts me off as we reach the top of the stairs and guides me along the undecorated corridor. 'You are my very special guest who I love dearly, and I thought you might like some carpet.'

I laugh. 'Are you sure?'

'Never been surer,' she says, standing to one side, after opening the door to my new living quarters. The room is a soft magnolia with dashes of deep purple throughout from the paint to the fluffy carpet, lampshade, and duvet. 'This is the only finished room in the whole house and I would be very upset if you didn't stay in it.'

I turn to her with grateful eyes. 'It's perfect, thank you Poppie.'

'You're welcome.' She pulls me into a tight silent hug and then says as firmly as her calm voice will allow, 'He will regret letting you go. Clearly, he never deserved you if he couldn't see just how special you are.' Before I can reply she changes the subject, 'Now the main bathroom is downstairs, so we've had a loo put in up here,' she points down the hall, 'but there's a trick to it: one quick pull then two long ones; it'll go down eventually. Call if you need anything; we're just there.' She points down the hall at the first room we passed.

Finally in bed with just my thoughts, I think about how odd it seems that Poppie can be so happy in a house like this — I guess she can see the bigger picture. If only I had that much intuition about my future. As I'm drifting off, I remember Evan once hired a cleaner called Karolina to 'sort out' my flat without asking me; they moved all of my stuff and I had to keep asking him where my things were.

I toss and turn that night in a flurry of images: Karolina asking me why I'd left a sheep in the kitchen and that she was not going to clean up after it; Poppie in my fridge meditating; Evan standing on top of the table with a baton conducting at me in between yelling, 'No, no, Melanie, stop being so stupid.' Then my nana invites me to make a cake with her, but I try to explain that I can't leave the sheep to its own devices. I ask her to wait but she steps away from me shaking her head.

Suddenly I'm standing on a theatre stage and the weighty red curtain is pulled up to reveal my entire school; Craig is in the front row next to Dave, who's telling me to bow. When I can't move, everybody starts laughing and pointing. 'I can't do it. I'm not strong enough.'

'Mel.' A disembodied voice calls my name.

'Stop making me.'

'You're dreaming, Mel.'

I squint my eyes open and make out Poppie's silhouette.

'Sounded like an interesting dream.' She turns on the side lamp and I shut my eyes tightly again.

'My dreams are as disturbed as I am. What time is it?' I grumble, frowning.

'About 4 a.m.,' Poppie beams with a voice as bright as her name.

Throwing my arms over my eyes I whine, 'Why are you waking me up then?'

She turns off the light. 'You'd rather go back to sleep, I understand. Like I said, it sounded like an interesting dream.'

'*Ugh.*' I fumble and turn the light on again and sit up squinting and yawning. 'Fine, fine, what are we doing?'

'Well,' she settles on my bed next to me. 'I thought we could go for a little stroll, catch the sunrise before a spot of meditation and then you could join my yoga class.'

'How little a stroll?'

'Oh, it's not far at all,' she plays with the duvet. 'Really lovely small — *um* — hill, called Pen-y-Fan.' Unconvinced, I cross my arms; my frown remains. 'You'll love it, she continues, 'the views are not to be missed. Although to start, you'll need this.' Her hands reach behind her back, and she places a hat with a little torch on the front, on my head. 'Beautiful,' she stands up giggling. 'See you downstairs in five?'

I have to smile. 'Sure, how bad can it be?'

***

'As predicted Poppie Fields, you — are a big — fat — liar.' I puff and stumble over loose rocks.

'What are you talking about?' Poppie skips up the "hill" like a mountain gazelle. 'You don't think it's beautiful?'

'I'm not talking about the view; I'm talking about your need to re-evaluate your definition of "little", *AGH!*'

She stops in her tracks, so I bump into her and fall on my arse. Poppie reasons, 'Well, you wouldn't've gotten up at 4 a.m. if I'd said to you, it was the highest mountain peak in South Wales, now, would you?'

I point at her from my seated position. 'Listen, missy, my legs are about to fall off and when they do, I'm going to hit you with them.'

'Oh shush, we're nearly there, see?' She grabs my arm, pulls me up and points ahead. I can actually see our destination, unlike the previous four times where she said we were almost there. Finally, at the top, we sit, and Poppie gets a flask out of her backpack, hands me a cup and pours; I can smell hot chocolate. She fills her cup and places the flask down next to her and turns to me.

'Life is all about decisions, Mel — some of them appear harder to make than others. Take this morning: sure, collapsing back into bed seemed more appealing at the time, and this journey to this point,' she points to the ground where we're sitting, 'was a little bit tough but sometimes, the cosy option isn't the best one.' She takes a sip and admires the sun peaking over the next hill, 'Look what you could have missed out on.'

'Are you talking about this moment or my life, Poppie?'

She shrugs, not taking her eyes off the glowing red ball illuminating the morning's sky. 'It's yours to interpret, honey; it's your life.'

We sit in silence as the sky displays itself in all its colourful guises: pinky peaches with hints of swelling mauve dance around us and explode into a deep red. I sip my sweet drink, taking in each moment before Poppie instructs me that we are going to do some meditation.

'Close your eyes and clear your mind,' she says with her calm and soothing, dream-like tone. My eyes close and I take a deep breath. 'You are the only person here.'

I open my left eye a touch. 'Except you.'

Poppie, still crossed-legged next to me, rests her wrists on her knees, turns her palms to the sky and shuts her eyes. 'Come on, this will help you.'

'OK, OK.' I hold in a giggle, copy her and try again.

'Eyes closed. Take a nice deep breath in.' I do as instructed. 'Now focus on your breathing. All of your thoughts are being blown away as you exhale. You are breathing goodness into your life and ridding your body and mind of all negativity. Just breathe. There is nothing but you and this moment. Feel the breeze caress and cleanse your skin and let the warmth of the sun fill your heart with love and acceptance. Breathe in your new self: a relaxed, confident being. Just breathe and be.'

Do I feel calmer? My mind isn't racing as usual and all I can hear are the birds singing. Suddenly I hear a scramble and Poppie screaming at the top of her lungs. Jumping out of my skin, my eyes fly open, and I turn to see who is causing my friend pain. But there is still only the two of us. Poppie stands with her arms out to her sides, and I continue to stare at her.

When she's finished, she turns and smiles down at me as if everything were perfectly normal. Wide-eyed I ask, 'Are you OK?'

'Never better. Stand up and join in.'

'Absolutely not.' I hug my knees, 'People will think I've lost my mind.'

She makes a point of walking around in a circle. 'What people, Mel?'

'Well, *uh*.' There are no people.

'There is just you and I; and you, my friend, need to jump feet first into phase two.'

'What's phase two?' I crinkle my nose at her.

'Anger!' She says brightly.

Tentatively I find my wobbly legs, stand and open my mouth but then close it again before speaking, 'I feel ridiculous, Pops, I can't do this,'

'Yes, you can, come on, get it out!'

'No,' I say quietly.

'Yes.'

'NO,' I say more forcefully.

'Yes.'

'NOOOOOO!'

'Louder!'

I take a lung full of breath and thinking of the pent-up rage I have towards Evan, I give it my all, '*AGHHHHHHHHHHHHHHHHHHHHHHHHHHHHHHHHHHH HHHHHH!*'

When I'm done, I hear my voice echo loudly back at me — an angry warrior atop her kingdom. I put my hands over my mouth and muffle a giggle. That felt good.

Poppie starts bouncing and shaking her hands out like a boxer preparing for a smack-down. 'Again!'

I spread my arms out to the side, throw my head back and scream once more. This time with much more gusto than before.

'Wonderful! Wonderful!' Poppie applauds. 'And now shake out that tension and stretch up like this.' She puts both arms above her head and flexes her palms to the waking sky around us. 'Take a deep breath for me.'

I do as instructed and feel adrenaline start to replace my tension. Hands in a prayerful pose, Poppie regards me, balanced and clear.

'There is no such thing as stress, Mel, there is only what we create. Why choose to create something bad when all there really is, is this.' She spreads her arms again and looks around. 'Life is beautiful; but you have to make it so.'

***

'Now put your left foot in between your hands and feel the beautiful stretch…' Not even breaking a sweat, Poppie flows so gracefully you would think she was made of water. I, on the other hand, can apparently no longer touch my toes. Jill would say if you don't use it, you lose it. How true, how very true, I think as I now attempt a "triangle" position. 'And now slowly come up to standing, feeling each vertebrae uncurl and lastly lift your head. Place your palms together at your heart and take a deep breath.' She bows appreciatively at her class. 'Thank you, everyone, for coming; *namaste.*'

'*Namaste.*' Her class reply before applauding and I walk to the front.

'You did great!' Poppie hands me a towel and then dabs her face elegantly even though there's no visible sweat present.

I bury my whole face in the towel. '*Ummmmm,*' is all the response I can momentarily muster. 'How are you so bendy?'

She smiles and shrugs, 'Just lucky I guess!' We hop into Poppie's little lime green 1970's Beetle. 'I'm sorry I forgot to tell you before that my brother was staying too.' I give a tight-faced smile but stay quiet; she knows I know she didn't "forget" anything. She gives me a sideways look with both hands still on the wheel. 'Is it a problem?' she asks sadly.

'Well, I don't have a problem. He seems to be the one who never wants to have a conversation without insulting me.'

'I know he likes you, really; he always has.' We pull up at the house and I see his obscenely pretentious black BMW is still parked outside. 'I thought they were going shopping.'

Brilliant. Unshowered and frizzy.

Poppie gets out and skips ahead. 'I'll just check.' She hops through the window with ease, but I think my legs have had it from the mountain climb and the morning's blast of yoga. I get one reluctant leg through and take a moment as I don't see or hear any sign of the boys. I could make a dash for the shower; just need to grab some clothes from my room; *ugh*, what am I stuck on? I bend my top half back out the window. Straddling the ledge, I see my trousers are attached to a nearby bramble bush and it's managed to intertwine itself completely around the material by my ankle.

Poppie reappears, 'They must have walked there — what are you doing?'

'I'm stuck! Can you give me a hand in?' Sticking her head out, she observes the problem.

'Oh, I've been meaning to cut that back, but it produces such lovely blackberries. Let me grab some scissors.'

I try tugging again whilst waiting for her, it gives a little. *Just a bit…more…*

I hear my trousers give an almighty rip and flying backward into the house, I land with a great thump and my legs in the air.

'Looking good, Melanie!' The deep voice chuckles and I spot Craig's smug face glaring at me through the window.

'You really do have a problem staying upright, don't you?' He hops effortlessly through and strides over my head, not helping me up.

'Hey!' Poppie reappears with scissors in her hands, and she floats over to give Craig a hug.

'Here you go, Mel.' He takes them off of her and hands them down to me. 'Maybe you can even out your trousers.'

I sit up, narrowing my eyes at him.

'Or maybe they'll help you sort your new hairstyle out.'

I put the scissors down, resisting the urge to throw them at him and protectively pat down my fluff ball.

'It's called mountain/yoga-chic.'

He crinkles his nose. 'I don't think it'll catch on.'

I ignore him and face Poppie. 'I'm just going to freshen up, Pops, then I'll get started on your cake.' *What an arsehole.* I stomp back to my room, all my inner calm vanishing with each moment. I roughly search in my suitcase for a change of clothes and there's a light tap on my door. *Go away!* 'Yes?'

Poppie pokes her head around but doesn't completely come in. 'Melanie?'

'*Ummm.*' I find some fresh underwear and throw it on the bed forcefully.

'He just likes to tease. He's always been that way, it's his way of showing affection.' I see her one visible bony shoulder shrug.

I truly doubt that. I respond with a disgruntled look: I pity the girl who ends up with him.

Chapter 6

Thankfully by the time I've woken up, Craig has already left with Michael for his stag do at a nearby activity centre, leaving Poppie and me the entire day alone to plan final details for her hen do this evening. Hen dos. What comes to mind when you say those two words? Feather bowers? Banners and tiaras? Penis straws and strippers mixed with a few colourfully concocted cocktails on your last night of freedom? Not so much. Poppie has her own way that she wants to celebrate her final day as a singleton. She stands in the middle of her lounge beaming at her hen party and I sit casually cross-armed on a beanbag, looking around the room to gauge everyone else's reaction to what we're about to do.

Poppie's Grandma Nora is among the hen coop and looks ever so slightly worried. 'Have you done something like this before? I've read that people have died from it.'

'Yes, that was in America,' Poppie says matter-of-factly, 'but this is absolutely safe, trust me.'

Nora still looks unsure, so I add, 'We've checked it out, the tent itself has had tests that prove it's not damaging to your health; as long as you stay hydrated beforehand, you're all good.' I sip my herbal tea, hoping that I've helped.

'Do you keep your clothes on?' A slender, bobbed-cut brunette asks from the corner where she's hugging a pillow.

'You get changed there; they give you a robe.'

We are going to a spiritual cleansing ritual or what is more commonly known as a Sweat Lodge. The rest of the hen party consists of work colleagues, Kiki and Pru, and three neighbours, Jo — the pillow hugger; Cerys who is unbelievably striking with jet black, pixie cut hair; and Angharad, who in contrast has Rapunzel-esque, blonde locks.

When we arrive at the Centre for Relaxation, night has fallen and there is very little ambient light, apart from a few sparse, dull floodlights. There's a wooden building which consists of the reception and changing areas, then neatly lined around it in a semi-circle, are about fifteen little tipis with smoke protruding out of each one. The tents have been sound proofed, we're told, as we file into the main building and meet our spirit guide, Glinda, who I remind myself is the good witch from the *Wizard of Oz,* so I figure we're in safe hands. 'So, whatever is expressed or confessed in the tipi, can only be heard if you are present inside it; nothing can be revealed from without.'

I catch Kiki and Pru's eyes which both look just as doubtful as mine.

'Please come this way, ladies and we can begin.' Glinda walks from behind the tree stump check-in counter and leads us through to the changing area. As we pass through the wooden door, I'm surprised that the room doesn't smell like a pair of half-dried old socks; instead, it's somewhat like the entrance of a spa with soothing music and candles everywhere.

'Please select a locker for all valuables as well as your outer clothing.' She walks over to a cupboard and takes out eight light, white robes with hoods and hands them to each of us in turn. 'You can leave your underwear on if you wish.'

'If you wish? Who else has worn this?' Jo looks on, horrified.

'All robes have been thoroughly washed between each cleanse — there is really no need to worry,' Glinda reassures. 'I shall give you five minutes to prepare. Please all take some water now.' She gestures to the water fountain in the corner. 'And I will see you momentarily.' Glinda glides out of the room and we all start to undress.

Down to my bra and pants, I quickly wrap the robe around me and pull the belt tight. Pru comes over to me still in her underwear — a matching army camouflage set; she has the flattest stomach I have ever seen. 'I'm quite intrigued really, are you?'

I'm intrigued as to how your stomach is that flat, I want to say back to her casual posture — I guess her hobby doesn't involve flour and sugar — but all I manage is a nod and a smile. Nora comes out of the one private changing cubicle and models her robe to everyone. 'How do I look, ladies? Rather fetching, I think!'

Poppie goes over and gives her a massive cuddle. 'Gorgeous!'

As soon as we step into the tent, I nearly fall over with the humidity. It's surprisingly large in here — deceptive from the outside — and I think of the Weasley's tent in *Harry Potter* for the Quidditch World Cup. We all take a seat crossed-legged on the floor in a circle. I can already feel sweat dripping down my back and we haven't even begun.

Glinda takes her place in the circle sitting so straight that it makes my spine lengthen several centimetres. 'I'm so pleased and honoured to be taking the journey with you this evening.' I note with minor irritation that her ageless face is not sweating as profusely as mine. 'Throughout the session I will give you ice and water at the appropriate moments. If you feel at all unwell during this experience, please make yourself known and we will go from there. Now.' She closes her eyes and flexes her neck from side to side before somehow sitting even taller than before. 'We shall begin by giving thanks to our ancestors for this creation of life; the joy of being a part of this glorious world; and one with everything. We are all connected in a line of continuity and endless abundance…'

I hope I can keep a straight face throughout this whole experience. Nora gives me a look as if she is thinking the exact same thing.

'We shall all close our eyes and visualise loved ones who are with us and also the ones who are no longer with us. We connect to their love, their joy, their passions, their want for us to be triumphant in all areas of our lives. We thank them, we bless them, we feel our world is a better place because of them. We are power, we are abundance…'

I open half an eye and see Poppie nodding and swaying slightly in position.

'We are connecting!' Glinda seems to have gone into some sort of trance-like state and begins to hum; a few of the hens join in and I close my eyes again, joining in half-heartedly and finding it difficult to take this seriously.

'Our energies are becoming one with each other and with the earth. Visualise now your favourite tree. You are that same tree! Sway in the wind and feel your power. Feel the strength of the wind but also the intensity of your strength; you are stronger than any element. Do not fight the urge to move; if you feel the need, you can stand and explore the space. You have no rules and no boundaries.'

'I'm sorry my dear.' I hear Nora's voice, 'But are we the wind or the tree? A tree cannot move for its roots so I'm having a little trouble.'

'We are both simultaneous and neither at the same time,'

Glinda says matter-of-factly.

'Well, that's a lot clearer,' Kiki whispers in my left ear.

'We are visualising and feeling now, not speaking. Please mute your voice for a moment to help quiet both your mind and your body.'

I hear Nora huff and clear her throat but say no more.

'You can feel your roots: strong, grounded, firm. No one and nothing can move you from where you are planted.'

I try to see a tree in my mind. A willow comes into my head thanks to the pub, so I go with that. I see its branches and falling leaves, swaying wildly in the wind but the trunk is not going anywhere.

'Just let your mind see every detail, do not question what comes to mind, simply watch the film in your head. Do not try to understand; you are watching, feeling, being.'

I suddenly see lightning strike it but it stands firm. Where did that come from? A robin flies into the film now and sits elegantly on the top of the tree and starts to sing.

'What can you see, hear, taste, touch, smell? Use all of your senses to be in the moment.'

I swallow and move my dry tongue around slightly in an attempt to wake my taste buds. I breathe in; what can I smell? Sweetness. My tree suddenly bursts into soft pink blossoms.

'Now open your eyes.' Glinda says slowly. 'Welcome everyone to your session.' She leans behind her, out of the tipi and reaches for a small bucket that's filled with ice cubes. Standing slowly, she offers the bucket to each of us in turn.

'You may put the ice cube in your mouth, hold it in your hands, touch it to the back of your wrist or place on your forehead.'

As I put the ice cube in my mouth, I've never been so grateful.

'This session is designed for you to reconnect with yourself, cleansing and purifying as we travel on this journey together.'

Glinda sits again after returning the bucket, not taking any ice; I suppose she does this all the time.

'We will go around the circle and I will say a word to you. I want you to say the first thing that comes to mind; it's important that you do not think.'

Brilliant — I'm great at not thinking about things too much.

We go around several times with random words; eat more ice; and then we are told we have come to the confession part of the ritual.

'Anything you want to confess or confide, please do so now; now is the time.' Glinda glances around from one to another.

The heat is starting to get to me and I feel ever so slightly woozy. I'm allowed to suck on an ice cube but not go outside yet; apparently that's literal and mental escapism.

'Who would like to begin?' Glinda says with her eyes closed.

'I'll start!' Poppie says cheerfully, like a school kid ready to receive a treat.

'Well, I guess I would like to confess not completely being there for my husband-to-be as much as I could. Perhaps it's the move...'

I listen but think it's complete rubbish. Poppie and Michael support and complement each other more than any other couple I know. They left Greenwich two years ago because they were ready for a new adventure; he wanted to build, she wanted to do yoga. They were brave enough to choose a different life, together, and honestly, I think they're both better people for it.

'I know I support him and encourage him but I feel that there is always more that I could be doing; I'm just not sure what that is yet. I feel there's a part of me that doesn't want to share everything with him, even though I can't think of a single thing that I haven't shared.' She pauses to wipe her trickling brow. 'I don't want to disappoint him or know that for one moment of my life that I gave him less than I could.'

'You have real passion,' Glinda says with her eyes still shut. 'I sense a good soul and a purity. Life will be kind to you as long as you continue to be kind to it. Do not fear things you can't control but do control the things you fear. Your kindness is true and you have nothing to worry about. You have found what you were seeking; stop looking for something you already possess.'

Poppie seems satisfied with that and nods with her eyes shut. Did we get the instruction to close our eyes? *Oh, I'm going to burst into flames.*

Everyone takes their turn to confess, Nora being my favourite, saying she forgot to put a herb into her soup last time Poppie came to visit. How amazing that that could be the only thing you have to confess. But all too soon, everyone has had a turn apart from me.

I swallow even though I have no saliva left, and decide to say what's actually on my mind. 'I guess I would like to confess that I haven't been very honest with myself. Deep down I knew that there was something not quite right in my relationship, but I had told myself that Evan was the man I was going to marry. I should have looked at the actual situation, not the one that I created in my head.'

Glinda's eyes remain closed and so does her mouth for such a long time, that I wonder if she's fallen asleep. She creases her forehead as if having to concentrate hard on seeing my future — *we share that conundrum.* After the longest pause she breathes, 'You hide behind a wall, blocking yourself from your destiny. You can't see through it, around it, or over it, so you pretend it's not there. Once you find the strength you will walk right through it as if there were a door that opens at your feet. But you have to make that decision to create a door.' She stops and opens her eyes, 'You have the option to stare at a brick wall or to believe that the wall does not in fact exist at all.'

'Get over a mental block you mean?' I venture.

Glinda smiles. 'Exactly.'

Chapter 7

'You may now kiss your bride,' the officiant shouts and holds onto his top hat. The soggy congregation erupts into joyful applause and whoops of appreciation nearly as loud as the torrential rainstorm around us, and I explode into tears; thank goodness people cry at weddings. And thank goodness for the reliable UK summer. Gripping tighter onto the safety of my umbrella, I tremble with sadness as I watch my oldest friend in the world kiss her groom.

Skipping down the aisle, well, slipping I think would be a more appropriate word, Poppie squeezes Michael's arm and they laugh as they hang onto their umbrella, and head for the marquee.

'Here you go, dear,' Nora hands me a hanky.

'Thank you,' I sniff and mop my cheeks.

'Beautiful ceremony, wasn't it?' She misinterprets my tears but I nod. 'Strange setting, mind you.' She glances at the field and then down to our wellies. 'But a beautiful ceremony. Shall we?' She gestures to follow the crowd. 'It's so nice to attend a wedding.' She muses whilst grabbing my arm, linking it through hers as we walk up the muddy aisle together. 'When you get to my age, it's funerals that take up your weekends.'

Brilliant.

The morning went by seamlessly. All the hens woke and partook in some Tai Chi in Poppie's living room and kitchen before leaving to get ready. Craig met us at the venue and was kind enough to stay busy and out of my way. Poppie was the perfect calm bride; she didn't even flinch when we were battling the elements setting up the ceremony space, losing a few roses here and there on the arch focal point, or laying out small rocks in the green-turning-brown grass to create an aisle. She giggled the entire time.

'Isn't this fun!' she beams at me, raincoat flapping in the wind.

'I think it's Mum and Dad's way of giving their blessing.'

'Oh?' I say, brushing my wet hair out of my face.

'Yeah, when it rains on your wedding day, it's good luck and a sign that your relatives who couldn't be here, approve.'

We file-in in our soggy procession, squelching our way to the marquee opening. Poppie's handmade talents have really shone through, from her hippie-chic dress complete with floral headpiece, to the archway altar of ivy and roses — what was left of them. Because I helped set up, I know what's inside the marquee but I'm looking forward to seeing Nora's reaction. We sweep back the door that's flapping away happily in the wind. Fairy lights and lanterns twinkle above us in between hundreds of home-made bunting flags, all sizes and colours, dancing slightly as a small gust of wind weaves its way through the material doors. Instead of steam-washed, covered chairs wrapped in satin bows, there are different sections to sit: from cushions on the floor, picnic tables, wooden stumps, plastic garden furniture, to deckchairs, beanbags, and patch-work quilts; you name it, it's here. It shouldn't match, it shouldn't work, but somehow, it does.

We step completely inside and take in the scene. During the ceremony everyone was hidden under a coat or umbrella but now the dry room reveals just how unique Poppie's extended circle of friends are.

'Oh, my goodness, it's like walking into the Mad Hatter's tea party,' Nora says as her eyes follow a ballerina linking arms with a rather short man dressed top to toe in tails, complete with a cane and monocle. Another guest I don't recognise appears by our side dressed in a tall, thin hat — red curly hair protruding out the sides — and a huge purple bow tie bigger than his shoulders, which matches his velvet suit of the same colour.

'Please take your boots and socks off here.' He gestures to our left with a slight bow. 'Everyone is to go barefoot from now.'

I chuckle as he pulls up his trouser legs slightly to reveal some impressively hairy, wiggly toes. We do as instructed and make our way in. There is one huge wonky and weaving wooden table stretching the entire tent, which displays an array of plastic tubs, saucepans, various tupperwares of all shapes and sizes with wooden spoons in them and a selection of drinks at the far end. I love that she hasn't organised caterers or waiters. They've asked everyone to bring a dish that they would like to eat or like the other guests to try — a mystery wedding breakfast for all.

'Oh, she is so like her mum.' Nora sighs at me but her eyes are bright as she shakes her head and walks off to congratulate her granddaughter.

I pick up a paper plate and start filling. Couscous, beef stroganoff, prawn crackers, *ooh* hummus.

'Eating for two?'

'Yes,' I say dryly to the far too familiar face across the table.

Craig looks at my stomach. 'I thought so, Belly-Melly,' his mouth itches to smile.

'What is your problem?!' I pick up an olive and throw it at

him. 'This is your sister's wedding; can you refrain from being an absolute moron for one day?'

He looks taken aback. 'I was only joking, Mel. This is what we do. I thought you could take a joke?' He picks up the olive I threw at him and eats it.

'I *can* take a joke; it's you and your twisted sense of humour. For your information, no girl likes to be told she looks pregnant, frizzy or any other name that you've called me over the however many years that I've known you. Now, can you just bugger off, please, so I can attempt to have a good time?' I start making my way further down the table, examine the selection and wish Mish was here as my bodyguard.

'I saw you crying during the ceremony.' He matches my pace and picks up a bacon sarnie as I go for a stuffed mushroom.

'Yeah, so?' I say irritably. 'Everyone cries at weddings.' *Arsehole.*

'*Umm.*' He agrees, taking a spoonful of curry. 'But perhaps not so sob-filled.'

I take a cucumber stick, which I point at him. 'Look. They were happy tears. The only thing I'm feeling right now is pure happiness for Poppie.' Even I don't buy that; I take a bite to shut myself up.

He nods slightly and folds down the corners of his mouth, 'Very well. Garlic bread?' He gives me a peace-offering half smile to accompany the wicker basket.

'*Fhthanks,*' I say with my mouth full.

There's a clinking of glass which breaks our eye contact and Michael's voice sounds over a PA, 'Can I have your attention please, everybody?' He looks excited as he holds onto a small crumpled piece of paper, waiting for a hush to fall over the tent. 'Friends and family,' he says warmly,

'…thank you for making our day a special one. Needless to say, all of this,' he gestures to the room, 'was the vision and creativity of my beautiful…' he pauses to emphasise the next word, '*wife* — Poppie.'

I whoop loudly and a few others join in with claps and "hear-hears". The purple-clad, hairy-toed welcomer is walking around the tent putting a glass in everyone's hand. I give mine a sniff and smell perry.

'Poppie, you are the love of my life and I only hope that I bring you as much happiness as you have always brought to me. You're my best friend, partner, lover, you embrace my madness and I couldn't have asked for a more perfect woman.' He raises his glass to the cloth ceiling. 'Can you please raise your glasses, to my beautiful wife, Poppie.'

'To Poppie!!!' everyone calls and claps.

Michael bends down to kiss her and they embrace so sweetly I can feel myself welling up again but I stare ahead in case Craig is looking at me. Poppie stands up and takes the microphone.

'Hi everybody! I'd also like to thank you all for coming and for bringing such an amazing spread. When I first met Michael, I knew he was the person I was going to spend the rest of my life with.' She looks at him adoringly and I feel my stomach fall; I hope the next time I have that feeling, I'm going to be right. 'Yes, to others he seems eccentric but that's why I love him. You are my whole world.' They kiss again to the sounds of cheering and clinking of glasses. 'Can I please invite my brother Craig up to say a few words?'

When I look across the table he's already almost at the front. This will be interesting; he hates public speaking.

He clears his throat. 'Good afternoon.' He clears his throat again. 'Poppie and Michael are a unique couple.' Craig's eyes slice through the room and pierce into mine. 'They have this rare quality where they know exactly what they want in life and they are not afraid to get it.' His gaze is so intense I can feel my face heating up. Then he turns. 'Mike, take care of my big sister always, she is a very special person.' He speaks to the crowd, 'As most of you know we are a small family and if our parents were here today, they would have said that they were so pleased to have another son and they would have welcomed you with open arms. I wish you both all the happiness in the world: out of everybody I know, you deserve it the most. May life treat you well.' He raises his tumbler. 'To Poppie and Michael.'

That was so unexpected and I'm so touched I could fall over. *Good God, I need to get a hold of my emotions.* I take a glug from my glass and my taste buds confirm that it is perry. *I need to sit down.* I spot a bean bag but feel that isn't the best choice for my sundress. I walk further around the room, trying to spot someone from the hen party; I see Kiki and Pru with a group of beautiful looking people on an assortment of benches.

'Can I join you?' I ask tentatively.

'Of course, of course,' says Kiki, her shiny locks bouncing as she talks, 'pull up a pew.'

They all chortle loudly as I literally pull up a pew.

Kiki composes herself and stretches out a lace-clad arm to gesture round the circle, 'Everyone, this is Mel; Mel this is Marly, Jay, Terry, Tim and you know Pru.'

'We all work at the gym with Poppie,' says Terry.

No wonder they all look ridiculously trim.

'So how long have you known Poppie for?' Marly, a buff but manicured man with a tight-fitting suit, asks me as he leans forwards and fills up my glass with more perry.

'*Erm*, gosh let's see.' I quickly calculate in my head, 'Twenty-two years; we went to primary school together.'

'Nice!' He raises his glass to mine.

'We were just talking about Poppie's brother,' Pru leans in to me and whispers.

'He's not exactly like Poppie, is he?' Tim comments.

'I don't know, I can see a resemblance,' says Jay looking around the room for him.

'No, not in looks,' Terry shakes his head. 'He's a lot more reserved.'

'Did you know him as you were growing up, Mel?' Kiki tucks one side of her honeycomb blonde hair behind an ear full of rings.

I dunk my nose in my glass, not sure how much I should reveal to them. Has Poppie told them about her past? 'Yes.' I answer cautiously. 'He was always the protective brother really, acting like the older sibling.' *Nice. Vague.*

'He seems too tightly wound to me,' I follow Terry's gaze and spot him across the room talking to Nora quietly in the corner.

'They're different, for sure; he's fine talking one-on-one or to small groups of people, but hates all the attention on him,' I answer.

I spend the entire evening with the fitness instructors laughing and sharing fun stories about the bride. After everyone has finished eating, we all help to move the table to one side of the tent to transform the space into a mini dance floor. Somewhere in between the Macarena, and the Charleston, I decide to go for air. Slipping on my flip flops that I'd hidden under the table of presents, I head outside.

The storm has passed and it has turned into a truly beautiful evening. The sun is setting and I hug my arms, feeling suddenly really grateful and not entirely sure what for, but it's a good feeling so I don't question it too much. I take in the wisps of pink and dashes of grey-purple bursting together with burnt orange; sunsets are normally reserved for holidays, aren't they? You don't realise that they are there, every day. All you need to do is look up, as Poppie would say.

'Beautiful.' Craig stands suddenly next to me.

'*Um*,' I agree. 'Nice speech.' I look at him but his eyes stay focused on the sky.

'Just your standard wedding garble.' He shrugs and looks at me, 'I found it on the internet.'

I furrow my brow, 'No you didn't. That was heartfelt — who knew you had feelings?'

'I have feelings; they're just a lot smaller than some people's.' He raises a suggestive eyebrow and I slap him round the arm before gazing up at the sky again.

'Well, I liked it.'

'I'm glad.' He mirrors my folded arms.

'I wish your parents were here,' I say suddenly, without questioning if that's appropriate.

'Is that right?' he says emotionlessly.

Don't you? 'Yeah,' I say out loud. 'Your mum said to me when I was fourteen that she was looking forward to doing the can-can with me on Poppie's wedding day; she would have loved this.'

'My dad wanted to walk Poppie down the aisle,' Craig's eyes remain on the sky, '...and Mum wanted to walk me when I got married.'

How unusual for him to share something. 'Do you think you'll get married? I don't. I mean, I don't think *I* will get married. I'm a lone sheep.'

'You mean wolf.' He looks down at me.

'No, I'm in Wales, I mean sheep!' Maybe I've had too much perry.

We watch a pair of seagulls dance together in the sky for a moment in silence.

'So?' I prompt

'*Hmm*?'

'Do you think you'll ever have this?'

'A tent in a field? I hope not.'

'I'd like a beach,' I jump in there, 'at sunset.'

'Ever the romantic, vacant dreamer.'

'Vacant dreamer?'

'Yeah, you were always like that as a kid,' he says in a nonchalant manner.

'I beg your pardon?' I feel my loathing start to return.

'Oh, come on, that's just you — even now as an adult — head in the clouds, internal commentary more continuous than your external one.'

My mouth hangs open. How can he know something I'm only just beginning to realise myself.

'See, too many words in your head; very few of them actually make it out of your mouth.'

'What is wrong with you?'

'Presently the direction of your unnecessary tone.'

'You're so patronising!' I stamp my foot. 'No wonder you're here alone!'

'Do you really want to play that card?' He is as cool as a cucumber.

'If I had a drink right now, I would throw it over you.'

'And you have an inner anger problem.' He's enjoying himself.

I don't have to stand here and listen to this. 'I don't need *you* of all people to analyse me. Have a nice evening, Craig.'

I turn to go but he spins me back around, holding onto my arms quite firmly.

'You need to get a grip, Melanie. All I am saying is that you've always been more in your head than out of it and that's probably why Evan broke up with you. You fantasise about everything instead of going out there and actually doing it. You appear to be a vacant body with this whole other world going on inside that you don't let anyone into and then you complain that what's in your head is not reflected in your reality. You are constantly disappointed because people don't live up to your expectations of how you *think* they should behave.'

We freeze together, eyes locked and I notice his are bottle green for the first time in my life. *I hate this man.* I frown at him and myself. 'Are you finished?'

He looks searchingly into my eyes and then briefly to my lips. I feel naked under his gaze — like he is peering somehow into my soul.

He loosens his grip. 'Stop dreaming and start living, Mel.'

Chapter 8

I wake in the morning to the grumble of bin trucks. Normally I sleep through everything; how strange. Peeking out of the curtain, I watch impressively as a young whipper-snapper reverses the enormous monster up the hill that is Poppie's road, with relaxed ease; holy hell, that's impressive. I remember crashing my dad's Volvo when I was seventeen with the excuse it was too big.

Scratching my forehead, I'm grateful that I'm not hungover. Hangovers seem to be more painful now I'm in my late twenties. Nora informed me last night that it only gets worse with age: that's great news. Swinging my feet round, I wiggle my toes into the slippers that Poppie left for me, before straightening up and stretching. The house is quiet and I hope that Craig has left already. How can he see right through me? Even when we were kids, he always had this disconcerting way of reading me better than I could read myself. I tiptoe past his room but see the door is open and the bed is empty, so breathe a sigh of relief. Poppie and Michael's room is also vacant; they headed off to Swansea last night for a full ten days of surf and yoga.

Downstairs, I prepare a coffee to take outside and make a mental note to leave Poppie's key with the neighbour before I head home with it. Clambering out of the window, coffee in one hand, phone in the other, it's a beautiful day. The valley is illuminated with golden sunlight, and the sky is such a pale blue that the white tufts of clouds are almost undetectable; who said it always rains in Wales? I sit on a reclaimed door bench, sip, and take in the view. Time seems limitless as I gaze at the still valleys surrounding me; I can see now why Poppie loves it here. It is so fresh and clean that my lungs feel happy — an odd concept, I appreciate. I watch as a pair of horses stride slowly together towards the bordering fence in the adjacent field. One with brown and white markings stops and nibbles at the grass at his feet quite happily, his day already complete. The white horse goes a little further and hangs his head over the fence, reaching for some berries; how awesome to have this on your doorstep. I'm definitely going to make more of an effort to visit.

The village is seemingly still sleeping. I can't hear any cars, any mums pushing prams gossiping, any dogs barking or kids playing; the only sound is bird song. At home I guess I just block out the noise; you become somewhat immune to the soundtrack of London. Plus, I've always found it effortless to block out any sound, even the sound of someone talking to me. Suddenly, I see Craig's face and shake him away with a jolt of my head.

My phone rings next to me and I answer it with a smile, 'Hi!'

'You sound positively human, Butler; I'm very disappointed in you.'

'Why thank you Mr Wright. It's nice to hear your voice.'

I can hear him smiling back at me, 'Ah, one wedding and you're getting all mushy on me. So…I have a proposal for you, beautiful.'

'A proposal? You're not getting mushy on *me,* are you?'

'You're home at five, right?' he answers with a question.

I exhale and breathe in the view once more. 'My train

leaves in a couple hours; think it's 5 o'clock when I get in,' I shrug even though he can't see me.

'Don't shrug your shoulders. Can you double check now, please? I'm making a reservation for us for dinner.'

I get up reluctantly, head inside and hunt for my bag. 'Dinner? Why? What for?'

'Don't sound too grateful! Can you go and check now please.'

'I'm looking now, Mr Impatient...right here we go,' I prize the ticket from my bag. 'Yup, 5:05 I arrive.'

'Perfect.' I hear him tapping at his computer, 'I'll see you tonight!'

***

I step out on the smoky, packed platform at Paddington and head to the barriers. Noticing that my pace has quickened with my fellow passengers, I force myself to slow down. It's somewhat like sports day here: there's no shoving yet but you know it's inevitable.

I'm glad Dave's taking me out, to be honest; I wasn't looking forward to walking into my flat all alone just yet. Maybe I'll look into getting a goldfish or take up a hobby to distract myself from feeling lonely? Fumbling in my bag for my ticket, I hear what sounds like a hen party whooping and cheering.

'Come the fuck on, Bridget!' That sounded like Jill; she loves quoting *Bridget Jones*. I look around, ticket now in hand, clearly going mad, and return my thoughts to an activity: maybe something more active? I have always wanted to run a marathon. Then I spot the excited group of three waving in my direction.

'Put your sodding ticket in the machine, Butler!'

I wave back madly at Dave, Gracie and Jill.

'What are you doing here?' I hurry over and hug each of them. 'Wow that's an impressive hat, Gracie.'

'Thanks! Just got it from Accessorize. I need to make sure all of me is in the shade.'

'Has it been that hot here?!' I'm confused.

'Oh Mel, you need to be more panoramic.' Dave points down to four suitcases and each of them grin silently at me; my friends, not the suitcases.

My eyes twinkle. 'Where are we going? Do I need my passport?' I add with some panic.

'Good thing I have a spare key,' smiles Dave, who pulls out a red cased book and waves it at me.

'You packed for me?' I ask in horror, imagining him examining and picking out either the monthly granny pants or something rather sexy but way too uncomfortable that I should have thrown out years ago.

'We all helped,' says Gracie reassuringly.

Jill bends down to pick her case up and hands me one. 'You can shove anything you want from that small case into here when we get on the Heathrow Express and then you've got check-in and hand luggage. Come on, we need to get going!'

I giggle as Gracie links arms with me. 'Go where?!'

They all turn to me and say together, 'España!'

***

'God, I love the airport.' Jill comments, taking her second sample shot in the duty-free lounge. '*Um*, try this,' she hands me a bright blue liquid that looks like mouthwash.

'What d'you think of these?' Dave pokes his head round a

sun-glass carousel and models a pair that cover most of his face.

'Bloody awful,' Jill quips and winks at me when Dave looks offended and disappears into the book section.

Gracie comes over with a basket-full of sweets and chocolates.

'Hungry?' Jill pauses and looks up from the gossip magazine she's picked up.

'Just in case we get peckish on the flight!'

'It's only about two and a half hours hon,' I say but my eyes widen with excitement as I examine the contents, '*Ooh*, M&M's!'

***

Our plane is small and bright yellow and blue. Excited holiday makers settle themselves in their seats, already wearing straw hats, sunglasses and flip-flops despite the fact that it's pelting down with rain outside.

We make our way to row 22, and following Gracie, I wiggle excitedly into my seat. There's something about getting on a plane; it's like you can heave a huge sigh of relief, knowing that you are being transported to an exciting land of possibilities and whisked away from your day-to-day problems; it's the promise of adventure and new experiences.

We take off with ease as the rain lashes hard against the small window. As we continue to soar, we break through the clouds, revealing nothing but blue sky; it would appear that the sun is always shining behind the clouds.

A little over two and half hours later, we fly over mountains with roads so wiggly they look like paint dripping down from a canvas. Tiny white houses contrast with the bright blue of their swimming pools and I gaze down in awe at the moody mauve falling over our home for the week. The captain takes a horseshoe flight path, flying out to sea before returning to approach the airport. The water is so calm it looks static, but white foam the size of houses dot the scene below. Dave leans over me and points, 'So, that's Fuengirola, Benalmádena, Torremolinos and Malaga. My cousin's villa that we're staying in is about…' he contemplates, 'there.' Gracie and I 'ooh' on cue. 'And see all those lights? They're all beach-front bars and restaurants.'

'Ah!' We both giggle.

When the plane lands, we're informed that we have to walk to the main building; I don't think it'll be a problem as I glance out of the window and take in the mountains. We step onto the metal frame staircase leading us to the tarmac and the heat hits my body like a wall — not unpleasantly like the Sweat Lodge, but like sinking into a warm bath where it instantaneously relaxes your every muscle.

'Wow,' I say and take my cardigan off.

'It's about 30 degrees tonight,' Gracie turns to tell me, iPhone aloft and guide book perched firmly in her arms.

'It's blooming marvellous.' Jill links arms with me as we reach the tarmac.

We walk with the other pale Brits to passport control and I take in the line of milk bottle legs and arms, just waiting for their colour definition to be turned up a notch.

'This is so exciting. Thank you.'

Dave puts his arm around me. 'Oh shush, Butler, you would have done this in a second if it were any of us. Plus, we all deserve this: sun, sand, sea and well, who knows!' Dave raises an eyebrow so slightly I'm not sure if I imagined it.

After baggage claim we're met by Dave's cousin's friend

Pablo, who is going to be our chauffeur and guide for the duration of our stay. We all pile into his little Yaris and I'm shocked to be stuck in traffic as thick as central London rush-hour.

'It's always busy but *a-more* so being the first night of the Feria!', Our young, beautiful driver exclaims to us in his rear-view mirror; I notice his perfect teeth match his crisp white shirt and exaggerate his golden complexion.

I furrow my brow as I have no idea what he's talking about but Gracie responds, 'You'll have to take us to your favourite places.'

'Oh, you will *have great* time wherever we go. Feria *is celebration* of our culture. *Evorrybady* comes with *faaamily* and *friennnds* to celebrate. You *like-a* to dance, yes?' Gracie nods shyly and Jill and I exchange a raised eyebrow.

'We've got about twenty minutes to drop our bags and freshen up before we head to the harbour for the fireworks,' Dave tells us. 'The atmosphere is nuts; we can't miss it.'

Pablo agrees. 'We have time; it's still early.'

I look at my watch and see it's just gone 10:30 p.m. — he thinks that's early?

We pull up outside an isolated villa and climb the white stone steps to the front door. There's one security light to lead us up but nothing more, so we all watch our footing. We step inside, into the darkness; it smells fresh and clean and the temperature noticeably drops. Dave hits the lights and a yellow glow floods the space, revealing an open plan living area, kitchen and diner with tiled flooring throughout. There are several doors around the room amidst brightly coloured feature walls and Arabic ornaments.

'Cool taste in décor,' Gracie says as we take in our home from home.

Jill kicks off her shoes at the door and does a running jump for the bright orange sofa.

'Let me show you around ladies!' Dave gestures to us all with a sweeping arm, while Pablo walks to the kitchen to make a drink.

Gracie and I follow Dave but Jill remains sprawled out. 'Oh, just let me lie for five minutes please!' She whines like one of our students, with her eyes shut.

'Well, there's a pool, will that get you up?' Dave says playfully.

'A pool! You didn't say anything about a pool!' Jumping up and running towards us she hunts, running from door to door, revealing in turn as she flies open each one: two double bedrooms; a twin; and a luxurious bathroom. 'Where? Where?!'

Dave leads our excited party around the corner down a wide corridor and reaches a sliding glass door. He flips a switch and the outside lights up like a Christmas tree.

'*Oooh*!' All three of us say in unison.

We step out and see there's a spacious patio with a thin wiry table and two chairs framed by a railing. To the left, steps lead you down to a pool area complete with several deck chairs and shading umbrellas.

'Why haven't you talked about this before?' I gasp.

'Because you all would have made me bring you here each year,' Dave widens his eyes and raises his eyebrows as if to challenge his comment; we find it fair and stay schtum.

'Oh, I could live here,' Gracie looks up and takes in the stars.

'Me too,' Dave and I say together.

'We could watch the fireworks from here, couldn't we?' Jill says as she sits on one of the wiry chairs.

'*Por supuesto,*' Pablo appears behind us, '…but you want to be *a-right* there,' he points downwards. 'Trust me.'

***

Dave and Pablo were right; the only other fireworks I've seen that had come close to that display were at Disneyland. After we park up, we walk with all the excited Andalusians to the 'night Feria'.

'This is the university part. The day Feria is about ten minutes away,' Dave explains loudly over the combined sound of music, and the voices of thousands of friends and family of all ages, greeting each other with so much love you can't help but feel a part of it. Some mothers, daughters and grandmothers are matching in traditional Sevillian dress. Delicious aromas of kebabs and corn on the cob fill the air. We walk through a funfair and music accelerates as we now pass row upon row of individual bars and restaurants.

'Every business in the town will come and create *ah,* how you say, temporary dwelling, to be part of the celebrations.' Outside most of the pop-up rooms are menu lists accompanied by sexily-clad men and women handing out flyers for discounts. Strung above our heads are lights that remind me of a toned-down version of Oxford Street at Christmas.

'You can't help but be in a good mood around this much joy,' I say to them all.

'I know!' Gracie says back grinning from ear to ear, 'I don't speak very much Spanish myself, but joy is a universal language, isn't it?'

'*Alegría.*' Pablo says to Gracie.

'I'm sorry?' She blushes at him.

'*Alegría,*' he repeats. 'That is 'joy' in Spanish.'

65

She imitates him perfectly and blushes even deeper.

'So, where's the best place to start?...*Gracias,*' Jill says, taking a handwritten voucher from a man with more hair on his face then on his head.

'We're heading for the main stage first and then anywhere that has this amazing aubergine and honey dish, followed by more dancing!' Dave grabs my hand and leads me into a mambo as we walk.

'*Ooh*, shake it!' Jill says as she starts dancing on her own with some appreciation from a group of young guys. If we were in London right now, people would think we were nuts but here, it seems to make sense.

***

The next morning, optimism floods through me, and for probably one of the first times in my life, I throw the covers off with excitement, and leap out of bed. Gathering a cardigan to wear over my strappy pyjama top and shorts, I pad through the deserted house: the only thing I can hear is Dave snoring as I cross the living room on my way to the balcony. Embracing the culture and partaking in countless glasses of local wine, I don't think I've ever seen him drink that much in my life. Face-down in the cushions and completely passed out on the sofa, it would seem Dave likes to sleep in his pants. And only his pants. I tiptoe past and giggle quietly as I reach the balcony door and slide it open.

The sun is yet to rise so the air is fresh, bordering on cold, but I wrap my cardigan tighter around myself as I step barefoot over the threshold. The cool textured tiles refreshingly massage my feet as I walk to the railing and breathe in my view. Twenty-four hours ago, I was dreading going back to my empty flat full of memories and now look at me, surrounded by friends and sunshine. I smile at the Malaga Mountains and promise myself that everything is going to be OK. Poppie would say, 'If it's not OK, it's not the end.' Feeling inspired, I decide that I'm going to treat everybody to breakfast. Marching back to my room, I whip off my night clothes, grab some shorts and a vest top to go under my cardigan and leaving a note, I grab the keys. Last night as Pablo dropped us off, we bought some bottles of water from a small store about two streets away, so I head in that direction. I notice how dusty the roads are as I stroll along the deserted street; it's so quiet I feel as though I am the only person on the planet.

When I return my arms are full with a huge paper bag of cold cooked meats including *chorizo, jamon serrano* and *lomo embuchado,* some *manchego* cheese, a crusty loaf of freshly baked bread and some ground coffee for the machine I spotted in the kitchen.

The still, silent house amazingly doesn't stir as I grind the coffee beans and set everything out. Taking care and pride in the presentation, I smile, happy with my display. I'm in no hurry to eat so, I make myself a *cafe solo* and grab a book from Dave's cousin's bookshelf to read, until the others wake up. Settling on a lounger, I raise my cup to the motionless pool in front of me; this is how every morning should begin; no drama, no sadness, no horrible men.

I read a chapter of 'The Black Swan' by Nassim Nicholas Taleb, not really sure that I've understood anything, but feeling smarter for attempting it. Going to grab a normal sized coffee, as a *cafe solo* is really ridiculously small, I stop again in the living room. Dave snorts in his sleep and rolls over onto his back displaying a surprisingly toned stomach. Tilting my head, I observe the definition; quite perfect, if I'm honest.

'What are you doing?' Jill appears behind me from nowhere, quite amused.

'Just looking,' I admit, still not averting my eyes. She joins me and we both examine his chest with our eyes.

'*Um.* Nice,' Jill agrees. 'Who knew? Do I smell breakfast?' She wanders off in the direction of the kitchen.

'*Um hmm,*' I answer, still staring. He has a perfect line of hair tracing down from his belly button to his...I force my eyes away. 'I thought I'd surprise everyone,' I say to Jill.

'Morning!' The door opposite me opens and Gracie appears looking fresh-faced and perfectly bright and breezy.

'How can anyone look that perfect after just waking up?' I ask, adjusting my frizzy ponytail.

She bats a hand at me and walks over ignoring the compliment, 'Sleep well? Oh my.' She spots Dave in all his glory, unconsciously unaware of our presence. He scratches his head in his sleep.

'This is absolutely delicious,' Jill reappears with a mouth full of something.

'Oh yay, food!' Gracie claps her hands, grabs my arm and marches me towards Jill, 'I am absolutely starving despite the amount of tapas we had last night.'

'Shouldn't we wait for Dave?' I ask, glancing back at him now scratching something else.

'Nothing short of an earthquake is going to wake him up. I'm impressed he made it to the sofa last night,' Jill says, still with her mouth full.

Gracie starts piling plates onto her dainty hands in true ex-waitress fashion. 'Let's take it out and eat by the pool.'

'Oh, bloody hell, it's boiling,' Jill says as we walk into the intense sunshine. We make our way to the huge umbrella next to an olive tree and draw a table and three loungers together.

'This is so beautiful,' Gracie sighs looking out at the view.

'I can't believe Dave never told us about this place before now,' I say while making a mini sandwich with as much as I can stuff in, in one go.

'If he always comes here with his cousin there isn't enough room for us too.' Gracie shrugs.

'Plus, he couldn't bring back any women with three already here,' Jill points out with a poke of her *chorizo*.

'So, what shall we do today?' I ask as I stretch out on my lounger.

'This.' Jill gestures around with a slice of cheese this time. 'I have no desire to move anywhere quickly.' She yawns then throws the *manchego* in her open mouth.

'Oh no, come on! I've done some reading up on Malaga, it's one of the oldest cities in the world! There's a castle I want to see and the botanical garden. There are some beaches we should check out and I've heard that you can get five tapas and a jug of sangria for 3 Euros! Be a shame to go somewhere and not see any of it. Plus,' she tries to act casual, 'I think Pablo really wants to show us around.'

'Well, when Dave returns to the world of the living, we'll get him to ring Pablo and invite him up here. There'll be plenty of time to see things, but for now, why don't we all just lie here and try to remember how to breathe?' Jill moves her sunglasses from the top of her head onto her eyes and soon falls back asleep.

The next few days blur into one, beautiful mix of dozing, reading, drinking, sleeping, swimming and dancing. It's not until our fourth day that we actually act as tourists, rather than living it up with the locals, and we visit a few historical sites with Pablo. Gracie wasn't kidding when she said she had done some research; she knows just as much, if not a little more, than Pablo. They have been a double act through the *Sagrado Corazon, Museo Picasso Málaga* and the *Castillo de Gibralfaro*; Gracie's little face has been red with something else other than sunburn.

Jill, Dave and I move past and leave them chatting outside *Alcazaba's* Roman Theatre. As Dave pays for us, I stop to look at the information board and read:

"Alcazaba. Built between 1057 and 1063, this is probably the most important military fortification remaining from the Hispanic-Arabic period."

We walk through mazes of decorative arches and doorways, and continue to climb our way up. A small sign declares, '*Patio de Armas*,' and I step up to reveal a courtyard disguised as a sunken garden. Four topiary hedges with roses surround a small fountain, framed by a large pergola with purple and white climbers. Watching my step, I cross the small water channels that run from one end of the courtyard to the other. Each taking our time, I wonder off a little further from everyone, gazing around and marvelling at the expansive built-up city of Malaga, its backdrop of mountains, and the border of glistening water.

'Can't beat a good view.' Dave joins me and puts his arms around my bare shoulders.

I sigh. 'I could stay here forever.'

Dave squeezes my arm and rest his head on mine. 'Me too,' he agrees, gazing out with me. 'I've come here almost every year since my cousin got his villa; I don't think I've ever been anywhere quite like it. The weather, the people, the food; I even looked at a few apartments once,' he says dreamily.

I break away slightly to look at him, our faces quite close. 'You have?'

'Yeah.' He doesn't meet my eyes and moves a little further away but still keeps his arm loose around my shoulders. 'Not really seriously though.' He brushes off the idea with a shake of his head. 'But I can point out where my favourite one was.' He smiles excitedly at me and moves closer again. 'You see that row of four white and sandy buildings just there,' he points to our left,

'*Um.*' I follow his point but I'm not sure I'm looking in the right place.

'Now see the cream and blue then terracotta building just behind? That's it.' Hard to tell from here if we're looking at the same building but I make an excited noise of appreciation for him. 'It was the twelfth floor, and had a shared swimming pool area. According to the estate agent it's rarely used, as most people just head to the beach after work. Imagine.'

'Why didn't you tell me you'd done that?' I ask, not sure if I'm offended or envious.

He pulls a face. 'It's just a dream, Mels.'

'But a damn good one. I'd come and visit you.'

'You wouldn't leave,' he squeezes me again playfully.

Doesn't sound like a bad idea to me.

Chapter 9

Sun-kissed and rejuvenated, I float from the train station towards my house with a new confidence that I can handle anything. Who cares if one person on the whole entire planet didn't want to marry me? That doesn't mean that *no one* will ever want to. Turning into my road I approach my building; the area around my normally sleepy block is alive with activity. There are people with worried expressions, neighbours flitting about and whispering nervously, an empty fire engine standing by. I spot Nina, who lives a few doors down, sipping from a mug and sitting on a wall, facing our building thoughtfully.

'Hey. What's going on?' She stands up as she sees me approaching and her expression is grave.

'I tried calling you.' She gives me a hug then holds me at arm's length.

'I've been in Spain. I didn't bother charging my phone when it died about five days ago,' I say, scanning her face. *Has someone died?*

'There's been a fire in Jack's flat. They're not sure of the cause yet, but, *erm*,' she pauses and considers her words, 'I overheard them saying there's damage to the whole area.'

It's bad. Really bad. Even having the news delivered to me by a tall, undeniably handsome fireman didn't soften the blow. The fire didn't spread to my place below, but the water and smoke damage has ruined everything — my clothes, my furniture — I have no home.

'Everything will be covered under your insurance,' the handsome fireman tells me.

But still. I look around, I've lost everything I've created for myself.

'Do you have somewhere to stay?' He asks kindly, 'Friends, family?'

'Yes, I'll be fine, thank you,' I say, waving him off and scanning the options in my mind. I know Dave's got family staying and neither Jill nor Gracie have the room. I could stay at Mish's as she's still in Paris, but I don't have the keys to her new place. I can't live with Mum and Dad, back in my old room; I'm meant to be moving forwards not backwards, plus Dad wouldn't be able to hide his disappointment in me. So, my choice is between the lesser of two evils: goody-two-shoes big sister, Keeley, or loose-cannon younger sister, Nieve. Maybe I do need to loosen up a bit.

When I call Nieve, she's at work — a very loud work. 'I said, where are you this week?' I shout.

'The Three Queens in Brixton, just off the high street,' she barks back over the booming sound system. 'Come down! I finish at nine tonight. We can go back to mine together.'

So here I am, perched on a fuzzy flamingo pink bar stool, humming along to Spandau Ballet's finest, and watching with amusement as my baby sister serves cocktails, the matching colour of my chair, to a group of giggling, well, queens. Tray under her arm she wiggles over to me in a tight-fitting black t-shirt, black skinny jeans and converse. She is so damn skinny; maybe I should consider a lifestyle of morning jogs combined with veganism?

'Melsy!' She gives me a loose one-armed hug before regaining her position behind the bar.

'It's quiet.' I comment at the almost empty room.

'It's early.' She starts pouring various bottles of liquid into one glass and taps on a metal top to shake over her shoulder. 'How long do you need to stay?'

'Not sure yet; they said my flat needs to be given the "all clear" before any kind of repair work can happen.' I sink further into my seat; all the Spanish sun fading out of me.

'Well, not to worry, Melsy,' she pushes a purple liquid in a Martini glass towards me, decorating it with a strawberry, an umbrella, and a smirk before leaning on her elbows.

'Thanks,' I take a sip. 'It's good; what's it called?' She points up towards the stereo now playing Prince's 'Purple Rain.'

She laughs and readjusts the clip in her hair to make her dreads a bit higher. 'I love it here, sis; it's like a big camp hug.' She gasps suddenly and swings an imaginary lasso over her head to the music that's now changed to '5, 6, 7, 8.'

I snarl.

'Oh, come on! How can this not cheer you up? You used to love Steps!'

She jumps over the bar and pulls me off my stool to the middle of the dance floor. She's bouncing now from side to side, remembering all the lyrics and moves. The queens whoop and clap but I'm not so convinced.

'Where's your moves, Melsy? Did they wash away with your flat?'

I cross my arms and plant my feet firmly on the floor. 'I am not dancing to this, Nievo; I'm happy being miserable under my rain cloud.'

'That makes no sense. If you're gonna get wet, you may as well dance in the rain!' She prizes my drink from my hand, places it on the bar but pulls the umbrella off and puts it in my hair. So, throwing all my inhibitions and better judgement to the wind, I pull out an imaginary gun from my imaginary holster.

***

We stumble to Nieve's building hours later; although I have no idea how we made it there. A crowd seemed to burst in whilst we were dancing to Steps, and six or seven purple rains later, my worries seemed to fog over as I led the floor in: 'Saturday Night,' 'The Time Warp,' and an impromptu conga. I'd forgotten how much fun it is to be around my baby sister, and I give her a tight hug close to a strangle.

'It's so nice to see you, Melsy; I was beginning to wonder if you had dropped off the planet. Whoops.' We make for the stairs, arms around each other and she misses the first one.

'What do you mean?' I slur my words slightly as we climb and she stops so abruptly I grab onto the bannister to stay upright. 'We've seen each other every month at least! We...'

'No, no, *noooo*,' she cuts me off. 'I haven't seen *youuu*.' She jabs a finger at me and we start to climb once more. 'The real you. I haven't seen *that* sister in a long, long time. And... now you're not going to like this.' She pulls a face resembling seriousness but her eyebrows are raised and one eye is shut. 'But I think Evan sucked the life out of you. This is the first time since my 18th birthday that we have done something fun and spontaneous just for the hell of it...' She stops for a breath. 'I've missed you, Melanie. You're my only sister—'

'No, I'm not,' I correct her.

'Well, you're the only one I like, then, and what I'm trying to say is, I don't know where you went but it's nice to have you back.' She gives me her best goofy grin. 'Here we are!'

She fumbles in her bag for her keys. 'Now, I should warn you,' her big blue eyes wide, 'it's not pretty, it's not clean, and it may not even smell very good; we've been trying to fumigate Jeff's room since he left, but…' she laughs, 'it's *dry*.' Nieve turns the key and stands back to let me in, 'Welcome to your new home!'

My room smells of feet. Big fat cheesy feet. And peanuts. Which incidentally I keep finding around the room, and in the bed as I lie here completely awake. The sheets have been washed but not with a fabric softener and haven't dried properly so there's a whiff of damp too. I miss my flat; I suddenly want to cry. Throwing back the covers I jump out of bed — instantly regretting it — and I dry-heave into the overflowing bin nearby but don't actually throw up. I fumble for the door handle, tripping over the carpet and a stack of motorbike magazines and find my way into the kitchen.

Stacks of unwashed plates, mountains of cups, recycling and half-eaten leftovers are strewn about with no evidence of a worktop counter. *Ugh, what have I stepped on*? Something sticky. Ketchup? *Blood?* Maybe the housemates killed Jeff for his stinkiness and he's buried in here somewhere; the aroma's about right.

I find a glass, wash it up and fill it with tap water before heading back to my room for a cry.

***

'Can I come in?' Nieve pushes her way through the door moving piles of clothing that are in her way. 'How'd you sleep?' She sits down on the bed next to me. I screw up my face a little, wondering how to phrase this. 'I know it's not like your flat but it's somewhere to live.' She brushes her feet on the carpet and knocks over an old beer can.

'I love you, Nievo and I'm really grateful for you rescuing me, but there's no way I can stay here, even if it's only for a little while.'

'What do you mean? It's great here!' Nieve picks a crusty bit of cereal off of the bed covers, 'OK, you might have a point,' she admits. 'Would you stay if we swapped rooms?'

'I'd stay if you could locate one clean cup in your kitchen.'

She meets my eyes sadly, 'So when are you going to Keeley's?'

***

We wait outside for Keeley as she's on her way to pick up child number two from ballet.

'Did you know she's just got another new car?' Nieve comments from her cross-legged position on the pavement. 'I'm surprised the kids are allowed in it, it's so pristine you won't believe; she may make you take off your shoes before she lets you get in.'

'I don't think you should work at the Three Queens for much longer, you're now quoting songs.'

'Am I? Which one?'

'Shania Twain...what's it called..."That Don't Impress Me Much".'

'Nothing wrong with a bit of Shania, Melsy— *oop,* here we go.'

A pristine, white 4x4 turns into the road, so immaculately positioned she should come with her own entrance music. My big sister has always been annoyingly perfect and I've always felt decidedly sloppy next to her. The shining vehicle slows with a slight screech as she hops out of the car, picks up my two cases and dashes past us.

'I've got exactly thirteen minutes to get from here to Simon's sister's house to pick up Ava before getting Lucy from ballet at 12.30 and Henry from the leisure centre at 1 o'clock,' she opens the boot and throws in my holdall and carry on, shuts it again and resumes her position behind the wheel. 'Nice to see you, Nieve,' she says through the open window.

'Nice to see you, Nieve?' I'm still standing in the same spot, dumbfounded, as Nieve refrains from giggling. 'What about a: "Hi Mel, sorry about your situation, good to see you?"'

Clearly frustrated, she fiddles impatiently with her earring with one hand and waves me towards the car with the other, 'Hi yes, hello, sorry, terrible, good, please get in.' I drag my feet to the front seat and wonder if this really is the lesser of two evils.

Nieve's daring to smirk at my wide eyes, 'I'm off for a run. You two have fun now!' and she stands to wave us off.

'So, how you feeling then?' Keeley asks, staring straight ahead without a hint of any kind of expression on her face.

'A little lost,' I admit.

'I know, I don't know where we are either.' She clears her throat loudly before commanding, '19 West Street,' very clearly, slowly and loudly, leaning towards the built-in satnav.

'Calculating route to 19 West Street,' a mechanical voice responds instantly. She sits back in her seat a little, still remaining bolt upright.

'It's great, isn't it,' she's grinning ear to ear.

Now she shows emotion.

'It was a maternity present from my company!'

'The satnav?'

'No, silly, the car!'

'Your company *gave* you a car?' I ask incredulously. 'Nieve said you bought it.'

'Well, that's what I told her; I didn't want her to feel bad.'

'And you think telling her that you bought it yourself would be a softer blow than saying you were given it as a present?'

'*Yeees*,' she says slowly, looking at me like a small child and then straight back to the road. 'Nieve has never really had a good grasp on money. I suppose it doesn't matter but she's never worked for a company that would be that generous; I didn't want her to feel inferior. Oh, have you spoken to Dad?'

'No, why?'

She goes to open her mouth but the car fills with the sounds of ringing. We glance at the screen on the dashboard that's flashing 'office' at us and Keeley clicks another button angrily to answer 'What is it now?' She barks and a sheepish voice replies.

'I'm so sorry to disturb you again, Mrs Hunt, but it really doesn't seem to be here. I've honestly looked everywhere and still can't find it.'

She slaps the steering wheel. 'What do you mean, you can't find the file? It's clearly labelled, highlighted and categorised in chronological order for the time in which you will need to use each piece of information.'

Cue eye roll at me to indicate her impatience and frustration at her PA's incompetence. Keeley has been working part time from home for the last six months but in truth she hasn't really completely stopped work throughout her entire pregnancy. Going into labour she was ringing the office in between contractions; it wasn't until her midwife prized the phone from her hands that she realised the baby was crowning.

'I really don't care what you think, Danielle. I know it's there; you clearly need to look harder. I will ring you back in half an hour and if you haven't found it by then I think we need to seriously consider if your role at the company is still needed. Goodbye,' and she taps the button again to hang up on the poor girl.

'That was a little harsh, wasn't it?'

'Not really; nothing like a bit of pressure to get you working that little bit harder,' she says brightly. 'Anyway, like I was saying, have you spoken to Dad...would you look at this moron!' She breaks suddenly and beeps her horn loudly as a cyclist appears from nowhere and swerves in front of us.

'What about Dad?' I ask, sweeping my hair back off of my face.

'He and Mum are going on a cruise for two weeks in September.'

'Dad hates boats — why would he go on a cruise?'

'He doesn't hate boats, he hates the idea of being stuck in the middle of the ocean with a bunch of idiots but anyway, they won it.'

'How this time?' My parents are the luckiest people I have ever known and constantly win things, all the time.

'Telegraph travel competition apparently! Dad gave feedback on an article someone had written, something to do with monkeys in Thailand, and they picked him as the winner.'

'Wow. Nice.' Why is my luck completely twisted? The luck of the Irish was certainly not passed down to me.

'Mum wants us to help her shop for it, plus you can start buying your new wardrobe. I told her you're staying with me, so tomorrow after I've dropped the kids off, we'll go then.'

'That'll be nice,' I really don't make the time to see Mum very much.

We pull into a small, newly developed housing estate and Keeley dives out of the car with the engine still running. Simon's sister opens the door looking most perturbed, holding Ava out at arm's length. I give her a wave which she reciprocates half-arsedly and then shuts the door. Keeley opens the back door of the car to put Ava in — she is the most well-behaved eight-month-old I've ever met but Simon's sister seems to hate all children.

'God, I hate her,' Keeley says through gritted teeth, 'She's so rude every time I see her — I swear she thinks I'm a bad mother or something.'

Ava spots me in the front and smiles. 'Hello you!' I say, crinkling my nose affectionately at her. She stretches out her hands towards me, squeezing her fingers open and shut as Keeley secures Ava's seat, muttering to herself rather than me,

'She was only watching Ava for two hours whilst I got my hair done and ran some errands; and she offered for goodness' sake! *Ugh.*' Keeley shuts the door with a thud and makes her way back to the driving seat. Ava sits there beautifully, not making a fuss. She is going to be such a clever little girl; you can see it.

'Right,' Keeley sits heavily back down in the driver's seat, 'Off to ballet!'

'Why has Luce got ballet? It's the summer holidays,' I say, just remembering.

'It's not her normal class, it's a summer school thing. She learns various dance styles and then they put on a little show; want to come?'

'Sounds lovely.' I've really been a bad aunt and haven't

made much effort to go to anything.

'You don't have to come.' Keeley misreads my expression.

'No, no, I want to. I was just thinking that I've missed quite a few things.'

She shrugs, 'Life happens, Melanie. I understand.' Her words are clipped.

'So, what's Henry doing at the leisure centre?' I change the subject.

'All sorts of water sports, can you believe? He's canoeing today!'

***

Back at Keeley's house I'm perching uncomfortably on the edge of the sofa surrounded by a mountain of toys; it feels like I'm sitting in *Toys R Us* rather than in her gorgeous five-bedroom house in Eltham. Little Lucy, now six, still dressed in full ballerina outfit, is piling her collection of books on top of my lap, bringing them over excitedly one by one. Henry, the eldest at eight, is acting like the youngest, having a tantrum on his stomach, screaming at the top of his lungs, banging all fours on the wooden floor and their golden Labrador, Biscuit, is lying down with his head on my feet.

Keeley is in the kitchen; Ava planted firmly on her hip whilst she stirs a pot with one hand and cradles the phone between her cheek and her shoulder, talking to her assistant again, who's managed to find the file, spill something on it and now can't tell what the concluding sentence says. 'Look, this is getting ridiculous now. I'll speak to you tomorrow,' she hangs up and turns to me.

'Do you want me to do something?' I call, 'Oh thank you, that looks exciting!' Lucy beams as she hands me a book about a purple witch before running away to find something else.

'No, no, no, everything's under control— Henry, stop that now,' she says firmly but doesn't raise her voice. He stops immediately.

'Wow…you should be a teacher.'

'Nah, doesn't pay very well.' She winks at me.

'And this is my *favourite* one.' Lucy balances one more book precariously onto the pile but it's one too many and everything topples over into a huge mess on the floor after hitting Biscuit on the way down, and now Lucy starts crying.

'Well, your house isn't boring, I'll give you that,' I say patting Biscuit, who is clearly used to this dynamic and hasn't moved; my ears ring with Lucy's howling.

Keeley raises an eyebrow, 'Oh this is nothing,' she exhales and bends down putting Ava in her bouncy seat and kneels on the floor next to Lucy, 'This is why you can't play with everything at once.' She's so calm. 'Let's clean it up together, come on now.' Lucy wipes her cheeks with the backs of her hands and copies her mum, making a few neat piles back on the bookshelf.

I massage my head before kneeling down and helping. Keeley glances at me, 'A little different from living alone, isn't it?' Does she sound envious? 'But come on, you work with children, this should be a normal soundtrack to you, no?'

'Mainly, the occasional mouthing-off is what I have to deal with rather than crying.'

Lucy stops helping, 'Mummy, what's mouthing-off? Is it a game? Can we play it?'

Her eyes widen at me and then soften for Lucy, 'No darling, it's not a game. It's something that much older children and sometimes grown-ups do when they are unhappy. But beautiful little, well-behaved girls don't act like that.'

Lucy's bright eyes turn to me, 'Do you like mouthing off, Auntie Melanie?'

I stifle a giggle, 'Do you not think I'm a beautiful little well-behaved girl?'

'Well, Mummy used some different words about you earlier.'

'Oh really?!' I fold my arms. 'And what were those words Luce?'

'Well, I can't remember all of them but—'

'Lucy!' Keeley exclaims standing up. She puts her hands on her hips and looks around the room, 'What an amazing job you've just done; thank you for helping so nicely!' She bends over to Lucy, 'Would you like to watch something on Disney Plus now, as a well-done?'

'Yay!' Completely distracted, she settles on the sofa and picks up her Elsa doll to cuddle.

'You are something else,' I whisper to my big sister.

She pokes her tongue out at me briefly, walks over to the remote, and puts on a show I've never heard of. Lucy starts singing along to the theme tune, Henry joins Lucy on the sofa and Ava seems transfixed too. Keeley looks at her small brood with love and then smirks at me. 'I'm too good; I should get a medal, or write a book or something.'

'*Hmm*,' I narrow my eyes at her. 'All about distraction techniques?'

'And control,' she nods. 'I don't even need Simon.'

'What?'

'Oh nothing!' She brushes me away, 'So, spaghetti?'

***

After the kids have been put to bed, Keeley sits on the sofa next to me, 'They're finally down— oh thanks,' she takes the cup of tea I'm holding out for her and sips it gratefully. 'They're good really.'

'Of course they are; they're yours.'

'*Mmm,*' she looks as if she's going to say something but then changes her mind, and I think the subject. 'Do you think you'll ever have children?' She turns to me, her eyes showing signs of strain.

'Well, I always assumed I would but I can't even look after myself at the minute, never mind being responsible for another human being.'

'It just sort of happens…you change. There's no right time or monumental moment where you pass a test. You just make the decision to change and you become the person you're meant to be.'

'How deep for a Monday evening.'

'I know,' she sighs, 'I've been listening to Louise Hay a lot.'

We hear the front door open and a knackered Simon appears. 'Sorry I'm so late; we couldn't agree on something.'

'*Um hmm,*' Keeley sips her tea and doesn't bother getting up to greet him.

Awkward. I decide to stand up and give him a hug; he looks like he needs it.

'Hi, Mel. How are you?' He hugs me tightly with a mixture of gratitude and sadness as his slightly too big for him suit hangs off his small frame.

'Not too bad, actually, for a heartbroken homeless person,' I say brightly.

'You've caught the sun.' He examines my face.

'Yeah, few more freckles — my work colleagues took me

to Spain.'

'Spain? I thought you were in Wales?' He says putting down his briefcase and a stuffed bag full of folders.

'I was...'

Keeley cuts me off, 'Oh yeah, how was the wedding?'

'As wonderfully wacky as you'd imagine,' I smile.

Keeley stands up and walks towards the kitchen. 'Did you see Craig?'

'We may have crossed paths.' I don't want to talk about him. 'Would you mind if I have a bath?' I ask.

'Go ahead,' Keeley says as she gets a plate of food together for Simon, 'Although remember there's no lock on the door.'

'Still haven't put one on?'

'No, we decided to keep it that way after Henry started eating bath bombs,' Simon smirks.

'It was not funny, Simon; we had to rush to A&E!' Keeley breathes.

'I know, I know,' he directs at his wife and then turns to me, 'But it will make for a great story on his wedding day!'

I disappear into the hallway and can hear them arguing in heated whispers. Maybe marriage isn't the way to go.

As I walk up the stairs, I notice the wall is covered in picture after picture of our family at various stages of our lives. My parents have the exact same thing in their house — the house we grew up in. When Keeley decorated last year, she must have done this. Wow, it's been a year since I've been here.

There's a shot of my parents on their wedding day; Henry and Simon in matching outfits each holding up an impressive fish; Ava wrapped up in blankets as a newborn; Lucy with a swimming certificate; Keeley and me on an ice rink as kids; Nieve backpacking in Indonesia; me and my Nana baking. I stop on one of Keeley and Simon from a school trip; I think they were about eight here? I was always jealous that she married her best friend; although, listening to them now, I'm not so sure.

***

The next morning I'm groggy; very groggy. My night's sleep was far from peaceful: Biscuit apparently wants to sleep upstairs now but Keeley won't let him so he started howling, which woke up Ava, who started screaming, waking up the other two, who thought it would be fun to come and play with me. After a rather begrudging game of something on Henry's iPad, I persuaded both of them it was time to go back to bed. Heading to my room after tucking them in, I could hear another hushed argument between Simon and Keeley.

After tossing and turning, trying to read, trying to visualise myself sitting on a deck chair in Spain then on the mountain top in Wales, I finally admit defeat at 6 a.m. and get out of bed. The house is silent as I descend the stairs and pad my way to the kitchen.

'Oh hi. I didn't realise anybody was up yet.'

Simon lifts his head from a mountain of paperwork around his laptop, 'You're up early.'

'Yeah, you know me, I'm a morning person.'

He raises his eyebrows in disbelief but doesn't challenge me. 'I'm sorry about Biscuit.' He rubs one eye. 'It's my fault. When Keeley was away one week on a merger, I let him sleep on our bed. It's been a struggle to settle him downstairs since.' He exhales loudly and returns his attention to his laptop. 'Can't do anything right, it would seem,' he starts tapping angrily. 'Help yourself to coffee, I've made a pot.'

'Oh perfect, thanks.' I make my way over to the mugs and pour what smells like some extra strong coffee, into one with *"Best Mum"* emblazoned on it. 'What time do you leave?' I ask before sipping.

'*Um*, what's the time now,' he looks at his watch. 'About twenty minutes or so.'

'Wow, that's hideous.' I sit down opposite him at the breakfast bar.

'Yeah.' He rubs his eye again then starts flicking through the pile of papers in search for something. 'It'll be better soon, we're just a bit swamped at the moment.'

'When do you finish tonight?' I ask.

'Who knows.' His tired eyes meet mine, 'It's not up to me when I leave.'

He goes to sip his coffee and there's nothing left. 'I'll get it for you.' I stand up and grab the cup before he can argue.

'Thanks Mel. *Ugh*, I don't think I have ever been this knackered. I think I could just start crying if I let myself.'

'Oh, come on, things aren't that bad.' I put the refilled mug in front of him.

'Really?' He looks at me squarely, 'I work in a job I hate to attempt to make a better life for my family, who I never get to see, so tell me, Mel, what is the point?'

I stare at him blankly, 'In what?'

'In existing.'

I pick up an orange and throw it at him. 'Stop being so dramatic. Who truly completely loves what they do anyway? I certainly don't. But you know what? I have amazing friends there who I get to see every day, plus it pays my bills, so I say, suck it up like the rest of us.' If it's possible his face falls even further. 'Although, I'm hardly one to give you advice on family.' I take this opportunity to swallow my singleton sadness, and focus back on them, 'You know Keeley appreciates what you do.'

He raises an eyebrow but doesn't say anything.

'I'm sure somewhere...on some level,' I add. 'I know she'd like to spend more time with you.'

'I don't know, I'm really struggling here.' He looks at me with the saddest eyes I've ever seen, making my problems seem insignificant in comparison and the fact that I've only had about three hours of broken sleep, doesn't seem to matter anymore.

'Look, how about I look after the kids tonight and you take Keeley out for dinner or something?'

'Oh no, that's not fair on you.' We hear Ava starting to cry followed by some movement upstairs. He stands and starts gathering his things, closing our conversation. 'Plus, like I said, I have no idea when I'd be back. So, there's really no point, but thank you.'

'Oh, shut up, I'm not taking no for an answer. Look, maybe my being here is to help you guys rekindle something? I think you need a bit of help.'

Simon admits, 'Well I couldn't tell you the last time we actually went out on our own.'

'Exactly, if you can't remember when, it's been too long.'

I can see his mind wavering, 'And you wouldn't mind? I mean two kids, a baby and a dog? Isn't that a bit much for you?'

'I'm a teacher, remember? Nothing can faze me. Plus, I love Biscuit.' I smile and sit up straight, excited that I've just set my sister up on a surprise date.

'OK, well, I'll tell, *um, ask* Keeley now then.'

'Ask me what?' Keeley appears with a grizzly Ava in her arms.

'Mel's offered to babysit so we can go out for dinner tonight.'

Keeley looks so taken aback with her huge brown eyes. 'You've got the evening off from work?' She says, doubtfully but hopefully.

'*Erm*, no. But I'll speak to them as soon as I get in and hopefully be back around seven.'

'Right.' Her face falls. 'Well, I'll make something too just in case.' She walks off to the kitchen and Simon raises his eyebrows at me with sadness before following her. I move myself further into the living room to give them some privacy but can still hear what they're saying.

'I promise I'll ring you after I've spoken to them this morning, and then make a reservation somewhere. Where would you want to go?'

'You really think you can get away early? I don't want to get all dressed up and excited to just spend another evening in, alone.'

'I don't want that to happen, Keeley; I hate disappointing you, but I'm working hard for us. Do you not realise that?'

She lowers her voice to something that I don't quite catch and then Simon enters the room again.

'Thanks, Mel, I'll let you know what happens,' and he leaves with a dash out of the door.

Chapter 10

'Ta-dah! This one?'

Keeley, Ava and I sit on the comfy seats around the changing rooms in House of Fraser and stare at my mum, who's spun out of the curtains wearing a rather sparkly blue sequined floor-length number.

'A little bright,' Keeley says with a straight face.

'I love it,' I say in contrast and mean it. She looks awesome; not many people could pull that off.

'Keeley, *these* are the comments that are appreciated.' Mum waves her hand in my direction. 'What's wrong with being a little bright?'

'You look like a disco ball.' Keeley furrows her brows.

Mum admires herself in the full-length mirror to our side. 'Oh yes, look at my bottom. I will take this one,' she speaks to the assistant and then to us. 'Right, only six more and then we can move onto Debenhams!'

'Why are you encouraging her?' Keeley frowns at me after Mum's disappeared.

'Encouraging her to what? Be herself? She likes it, I like it, she should take it!'

'I forget. You never were very fashion conscious, were you?'

Ava looks up from her animal book to look at me — does she understand that her mother has just insulted me?

'I think I can pull an outfit together pretty well now,' I say defensively and pull my navy cardigan a bit tighter around myself for protection.

'Of course you can, Melanie,' she says with a smile. 'I'm talking about when we were younger — oh, that's more like it.'

Mum now strides out wearing a knee length wrap-round lavender dress. 'Oh yes, I feel very important.'

I giggle. I forgot how much I love my mum.

'Do you have a pair of six and a half, small heels, that would suit this one?' The small worn-out assistant scurries away once more to hunt the shop floor.

'Oh, it's so nice to see three of my beautiful girls together.' Mum squeezes all of us into a hug and then perches on the side of my chair. 'How long are you staying with Keeley?' She asks me.

'Well, honestly I have no idea; I was told that they would contact me as soon as they had done all of their checks and then they can send people in to gut it and start again.'

'*Hmm*, doesn't sound too speedy, does it? Well, there's nothing like a new start! Let's get you a dress to cheer you up.'

'Oh, I don't need a fancy dress, Mum; I haven't got a reason to wear one.'

'Nonsense darling! Next year your father and I have our wedding anniversary party, I...' We all stop as Keeley's phone starts singing; I see that it's Simon.

'Hi.' She's abrupt but I can hear a hint of hope in her voice. '*Um hmm*. OK. That sounds nice.' The assistant comes back with some strappy sandals and waits patiently with them, outstretched for approval. 'All right, I'll see you then,' Keeley hangs up, 'No, those don't complement the dress; something with a smaller heel and a peep-toe, please,' she barks at the poor lady.

'So?' I prompt. 'Am I babysitting tonight?'

She breaks out into a very small smile as if not to jinx it. 'Yes, you are.'

'Oh, how wonderful!' Mum exclaims. 'Right, I will buy you both a dress — get up and start looking for something snazzy. Ava and I will wait here and find out what colour tigers are.'

We go arm in arm into the store and begin our search.

'So, what colour are you going for?' I ask Keeley as she starts fanning her way through a rail of dresses.

'Well, I look at the style first and then if I like that, I see what colours it comes in.'

'*Huh*. I just see what catches my eye and then if it doesn't look too bad, I buy it.'

'I think that's exactly your problem — you're not in the habit of dressing for your shape.'

'What's my shape then?' I look down at myself.

'Well, you were most certainly an apple when we were younger,' she smiles and I narrow my eyes, '...but you're more of an hourglass now,' she recovers, 'and you don't show it off enough.' She picks up a little black and white number with a red belt. 'Take this, for example.' She holds it up and starts talking like Gok Wan, 'This is a pencil dress: hint of a sleeve to accentuate the shoulders, the pattern travels in a flattering vertical direction and the belt is designed to draw attention to your slim waist. What are you smiling at?'

'You called me slim.'

'Well, you are; you just keep that to yourself. It's a good thing the majority of your clothes got ruined. I'll help you replace everything. Here, try this on and see what I mean.'

She hands me the dress and selects an orange and black

number for herself.

'Wow, I would never have chosen that.'

'Well, I'm a pear, so this makes my top half appear larger to balance me out; my boobs have shrunk since having the kids.'

We unload our bags into a booth two hours later to stop for lunch.

'That was absolutely wonderful, my darlings, thank you for your help,' Mum beams at us both.

'Thank you for the dresses.' She insists on buying us two outfits each because they all look "fabulous".

'So, now you have a new dress, we need to order you a man— oh, hello.' A surprised waiter appears at our side.

'I'm afraid we don't have men on the menu, but would you like to hear our specials?'

I burst out laughing and he tells us there's a prawn salad that he would recommend and we order three, 'We'd also like a bottle of prosecco, please.'

'Would we?' Keeley disapproves, 'I've got to drive, Mum.'

'Yes, you will have a splash and Melanie and I will absolutely partake in at least a glass.'

Our waiter disappears, 'Shame he's not on the menu,' Mum comments as he wanders off.

'Mum!' I exclaim, although I'm more amused than embarrassed.

'Well, he looks just your type Melanie,' Mum says, still watching his bum as he walks off. 'I'm sorry about Evan, my dear.' This is the first time she's mentioned him all day.

'Thanks. Not meant to be, it turns out.'

'Indeed. Well, I hope you don't mind me saying, my darling, but I do think that you are better off without him —

horrible mother; I would have hated having to make small talk with her every Christmas and birthday.

'Yeah, I won't miss her either,' I admit. 'Or his sisters. Or friends for that matter.' *Hmm.*

The waiter comes back with our bubbly. 'Ah, here we are, thank you.' Mum beams at the handsome waiter.

'Would you like me to pop it for you.'

'Well, we've only just met and I'm a happily married woman of thirty-four years, but if you insist!' Mum leans on her hand playfully batting her eyelids at him. I look over at Keeley who's rolling her eyes and looking impatient.

'So,' Mum raises a glass for each for us to take and then holds hers poised in the air. 'Here's to family...' she clinks both of our glasses, '...and to journeys yet to be travelled.'

'To journeys,' I call and we say cheers again. 'Oh, while I remember, Melanie, your father would like you to give him a call.'

The smile wipes off my face.

'He told me to tell you it's been a while and he wants to hear how you are.'

'Really? Why? So, he can tell me just how stupid I've been?'

'Don't be silly, darling. He cares about you and wants to make sure you're OK.'

I don't believe that for a second but I can't bring myself to tell Mum that.

'So, tell me, Keeley.' Mum knows how to move a conversation from one subject to another with ease. 'How's Simon's work going? Any nearer to that promotion yet?'

'No,' she says sharply. 'He's being so severely used there. I keep telling him he needs to start his own practice; that way he can dictate his own time rather than being walked over.'

'It's difficult,' Mum agrees. 'He's far too nice, that's the problem, darling; he doesn't like saying no to people.'

'Exactly,' Keeley downs her small bit of booze.

'It was the same when you were in school; he would follow you about and fetch things for you.' Mum sips her bubbles.

'I don't remember that,' Keeley says, getting a tub of sliced apples out of her bag.

'Oh yes, it was *all* the time, darling. He used to follow you like a puppy. Let's see, I think you were about five when I was a helper on that school trip to the farm? He kept trying to hold your hand and you told him to go and buy you some sweets, and then you would think about it.'

I laugh, 'I didn't know that.'

Keeley faffs with her bag again, 'Well, maybe that sounds vaguely familiar.'

'Oh, come on darling, you bossed him about and he doted on you all through primary and secondary school. Remember when you broke your leg falling off the swing when you were thirteen?'

'Maybe,' she continues to look down at Ava's snack.

'He was the only one of your friends who came to visit every day.'

'That was nice.' Keeley's eyes soften a little. 'But it's not me he's waiting on hand and foot now, it's not even the kids. All he seems to care about, think about and talk about, is his stupid job.'

'He told me this morning he's working so hard *for* you and the kids,' I add.

'You've been in each other's lives forever,' Mum fights Simon's corner too. 'You've grown up together and life is hard, darling, but you two are made of stronger stuff than you think. Of course, you have to compromise to get by sometimes but if life were simple, it wouldn't be worth it. But I know marrying your best friend is harder than it would seem.'

'But you and Dad did it,' I say, enjoying the bubbles and the focus not being on me.

'Well, yes, but there are hurdles in life, like for example when your dad and I found out we were having Nieve; we weren't sure if we would stay together.'

'What?' Both Keeley and I chorus together.

'Oh sure, it was scary. I was working, he was working, you two were happily in school, we had a good routine going and we knew everything would have to change when she came along and for a while neither of us wanted to change; we thought it was up to the other to do that. But, in the end it brought us closer together and I would not have changed any of it for the world.'

'I knew Nieve was an accident,' Keeley says, now feeding Ava.

'Not an accident, darling — a happy little unexpected gift. Like Ava here,' Mum smirks.

'Excuse me! Ava was *not* unexpected!'

'No?' She cocks her head. 'Forgive me, darling, I'm only teasing, of course.'

***

'You look pretty, Mummy, where are you going?' Lucy stops playing with her doll house to stare at her mum.

'I'm going to meet daddy for a nice grown-up dinner, sweetie pie.'

'Can I come?' Lucy asks.

'And leave me here to play with the doll house all by myself?' I say with mock over-excitement, 'Yes, I could maybe move the furniture around...'

'No!' Lucy puts the toy bed back from where I moved it to. 'You're not supposed to touch things. Mummy I better stay here to look after Auntie Melanie,' she says with the utmost seriousness in her voice.

Keeley bends down and gives her a kiss on the forehead, 'Well, if you think that's best sweetie,' and she winks at me.

'All set, then?' I ask, 'You look beautiful.'

'Thanks. Yes, I think so. I've called a cab for half past, so should be any minute now,' she pats down her flat stomach; you wouldn't know she'd had three children.

'*Ooh*, I think I'm a little nervous,' she says with excited eyes.

Her phone goes and the cab tells her he's outside.

'Right, I'm off then. Night, my darlings,' she bends down and kisses Lucy again then Ava who's in my arms, before moving to the sofa to kiss Henry. He looks up from the TV and has just noticed she's standing there.

'Why are you all dressed up?'

'You are as panoramic as your daddy,' she tuts affectionately. 'I'm going out for dinner, sweetie, but I will see you in the morning.' She kisses him. 'Be a good boy for your auntie.' She disappears through the doorway to the corridor and then peeps back again. 'Thank you.' She looks at me with grateful eyes. 'I'm glad you're here,' she says quickly and with that she slips out the door.

The evening goes amazingly without a hitch, as all three kids, Biscuit, and I, enjoy watching *Beauty and the Beast* — one of my absolute favourites as a kid — and I'm thrilled to see that it is just as charming and brilliant as I remember. Finally, with all the kids settled in bed, I curl up in the biggest armchair, pat Biscuit on the head, then open my book to a silent house. Wriggling further into the comfy chair and heaving a big sigh of contentment, I go to read a chapter but hear the sound of keys in the door; they're back early.

A puffy-eyed Keeley walks in.

'Oh my God, what happened?!' I stand up and go over to her.

'He stood me up.' Her eyes are watery but completely furious. 'I'm going to bed. If you're still up when he gets in, you can tell him to sleep on the sofa.' She disappears back into the hallway and makes her way upstairs. What on earth has happened to these two?

Chapter 11

Four weeks of arguments later, and to say that the atmosphere is getting uncomfortable is a huge understatement; even Biscuit knows that barking is not to be tolerated. Thankfully my flat will be ready for me to move back in tomorrow, just in time for the start of term. I'm looking forward to actually starting afresh with everything. I have a whole new wardrobe — thanks to my new fashion adviser, Keeley — and I even did a quick shop in Next Home for some cute accessories to go around the house.

But in the meantime, the tension has become too much, so under the pretence of doing a good deed, I offer to do a family shop. Which, now, is seriously starting to test my patience. I bustle my way through Sainsburys with a list in one hand, phone in the other and a pen in my mouth as my phone rings, again.

'Keeley, I've missed you.' My enthusiasm wavers after five previously panicked calls to add more to my list, making me run from one end of the store and back again, as said items are not next to each other.

'Eggs and toothpaste. Last ones, I promise. Thank you.'

'OK, see you soon.'

Half an hour later, feeling like I've done a circuit workout followed by spin class at the gym, I unload my bags from the cab and shuffle through the double-breasted door of the Hunt residence, to the soundtrack of screaming; not the baby or the

children, but Keeley and Simon. I freeze in the doorway —
should I sneak in? Maybe dump the groceries here and walk
around for a bit? But there's stuff for the fridge and freezer, I
debate with myself. Best to make my presence known, I think.
I lean back and find the doorbell, but it's no match for their
cries. 'Hello!' I try, as loudly as I can muster, but still the
screaming debate continues. As I walk through the offending
room, they both stop as violently as bunnies in headlights.
Putting all of the bags down inside the kitchen, I then turn to
make a quick exit, dashing up to my room. I sit crossed legged
on the floor of Keeley's spare room and decide to finish
folding the last of my things, when there's a tap on the door.

'Come in,' I call.

Lucy pops her little head round the door.

'Hi! Have you come to help me pack?'

She shakes her head and then pushes the door open a little
more to reveal a white outfit with multi-coloured sewn-on
tulips.

'Well, look at you!' I gasp and she gives me a twirl, but her
head is down slightly.

'How are you feeling? Excited?' *Sad that your parents are
screaming blue murder downstairs?* She shrugs her shoulders.
'Maybe a little bit nervous about the show?' She nods her
head but remains silent. 'It's OK to be nervous, everybody
gets nervous sometimes.'

'Are you going to come?' she says in a small voice.

'I am,' I say, nodding my head. 'And I'm going to be in the
front row and probably crying.'

'Crying?' She says confused.

'Yes. I definitely think seeing my eldest niece in her first
dancing show—'

'This isn't my *first* dancing show,' she interrupts me in a dignified manner.

'Oh…well, *er*, seeing my niece in the first show that I've heard about and am coming to…will absolutely warrant a bit of sniffling.'

Her smile is back, 'You're so silly, Auntie Melanie,' and she runs off back to her bedroom, bumping into Keeley's legs on the way.

'Easy tiger! All ready to go?' I watch Keeley smile down at her little girl.

'Yep. Auntie Melanie said she's going to cry at my show. Maybe you need to look after her Mummy.'

She looks down the corridor to me, 'We'll do our best to look after each other.'

***

The show is taking place in a local school's theatre about twenty minutes from their house. After their fight, Keeley and Simon's frostiness is so intense, I'm finding it hard to breathe. Simon heads for the toilets as my sister and I take our seats.

Keeley looks casually at the programme, 'I think I'm going to get a divorce,' she says, just as simply as she were saying she fancied some popcorn.

'Oh no, you can't! Come on, Keeley, Simon is your soulmate…'

'There is no such thing as a soulmate. Anyway, you need a *soul* — Simon seems to have sold his to his company.'

'But you two are made for each other, you can't split up.'

'He is all I've known since school, Melanie; how do you know there isn't anything better for me out there?'

'Are you telling me that you want to be on your own?'

'No, I'm telling you that's what I feel like I am now —

alone. Simon's not around, Simon can't make time for me and the kids; I *am* alone. Why not make that official distinction? Plus, being out there, I might find someone who would want to meet me for dinner and actually have a conversation and see how my day has gone. I'm pretty sure it's over,' she says resolutely and then shrugs at me.

'No, look…' But I can't say anything more; Simon has taken his seat just as the house lights dim, the stage illuminates and music fills the auditorium. Keeley shrugs again and joins in the clapping with everyone else. 'Tiptoe Through the Tulips' comes on and Lucy's in a group with about seven others; she's the tallest and looks like the eldest. Her face is full of concentration and I swear I can see her lips mouthing the steps. 'You used to do that when we were skating,' I say to Keeley.

'Do what?' she whispers, leaning over to me with her eyes not leaving the stage.

'Say the moves before you did them.'

The little girls skip in a circle then stretch out into a long line and kneel to finish as the music ends. We cheer loudly and Lucy gives us a little wave as she runs off stage.

Lucy performs in two other songs in the first half: a tap number, and a street dance. When the interval comes, Simon heads outside to take a phone call, I join the queue for refreshments, and Keeley finds the loos. I look around at the busybody mums and hear a gaggle of them behind me discussing the show.

'Not a patch on last year's performance; she's clearly losing her flair…'

'Oh, I don't know; the costumes are absolutely a step up, I'd say…'

'At least she had the decency to hire a theatre this time,

even if it is in a school...'

'Cressida simply hated the draughty church hall last year...'

Facing away, I raise my eyebrows at no one and silently vow to myself that if I ever become a mother, I will not make friends with mums like that.

'I'll have a coke, please, sis...' I feel an arm around my shoulders and look up to a tall, buttery blonde man, looking over everyone's heads. 'And some M&M's, or maybe some crisps, what do you think?' He retreats slightly in confusion as he realises, I'm not who he thought I was; his cheeks blush with pink as he removes his arm. 'I'm very sorry, you are identical to my sister from behind, and...' he regards me, 'actually, you're familiar from the front; have we met before?'

'I'm not sure.' I smile up at his handsome face. 'But it's not a problem.' He breaks into a smile too. 'I'd go for the M&M's myself; less noisy to munch during the show.'

'Good point.' He raises his eyebrows. 'And what are you going for?'

'I was thinking of some Fruit Pastilles but I might go for some M&M's now.'

'Chocolate or peanut?' he quizzes.

'Chocolate. The peanut would have you making unnecessary noise again,' I nod.

'You've done this before,' he folds his arms, but not in a threatening way.

'No, I'm terrible normally,' I confess. 'A loud popcorn muncher in the cinema.' *This is fun.*

'Even in quiet bits?' he asks with all seriousness.

'Especially in quiet bits.'

'Julian!' A woman's voice comes from behind us in the queue and we turn around.

'Ah. *That* would be my sister.' He waves. 'Well, I completely apologise once again, *er...*' he stretches out his hand and pauses.

'Melanie.' I accept his hand — it's warm and slightly callused. 'It was nice meeting you, Julian.'

He pauses, meeting my eyes. 'Are you here watching your daughter?'

'No.' He's still holding my hand. 'My niece,' I say softly.

'Me too,' his smile returns, 'well, *nieces*.'

The queue moves forward and one of the busybody mums coughs behind us to try to move us along. I laugh, enjoying this unexpected moment of flirtation. He goes to say something but then decides against it, marginally shaking his head before opening his mouth again.

'It was nice meeting you, too.' He finally lets go of my hand, smiles and walks to join his confused sister about ten people behind.

'Wish I had that much sexual tension still with my husband,' one of the mums says behind me and I look at the group of them, taking in their envious expressions.

'I know what you mean,' another chips in, 'I'd give him your number if I were you.'

I look back and meet Julian's eye. 'You know, I just might do that.'

I get my M&M's, some Fruit Pastilles for Keeley, three waters and grab a napkin from the centre of a table. I pull out a pen from my bag and write down my number. I've never done anything like this — giving a complete stranger my number. But what the heck do I have to lose? He's at the front of the queue now with his sister — who, to be fair — is wearing a similar dress to me and has the same chestnut hair colour. How embarrassing, I'm going to have to go over and meet her too? Luckily, she starts talking to another mum and walks back towards the auditorium. Julian scans the crowd and spots me. *This is it. I'm going for it.* I walk in his direction.

'So, I was thinking, you clearly need some coaching on suitable foods for performances.'

'Is that so,' he's holding a pack of M&M's and a coke.

'Yes. See here,' I point to the coke. 'Fizzy drinks are a no go. They give you either the hiccups or burps.'

He chortles heartily. 'And what if I enjoy a good hiccup or burp?'

'See? You need my help. Very inappropriate behaviour for this kind of scenario.'

'It seems I do need some sense of moral direction.' He nods gravely.

'Exactly. Don't worry, there's still hope for you. This is my number.' He takes my scribbled napkin and puts it in his jeans pocket.

'We'd have to sample some food, of course, to make sure I know exactly what I'm doing,' he teases innocently.

'I suppose we would. What's the noisiest food, do you think?' I cock my head, very pleased that I can remember how to flirt.

'Mexican?' He suggests. 'All those crispy tacos and nachos…'

'Sounds like a good place to start.' I smile at myself in triumph. *Look at me.*

People are starting to head back in so we join them and enter the auditorium together.

'Well, I look forward to my first lesson, Melanie.'

'Me too,' I sway my hips ever so slightly as I walk away from him and make my way to the front row. I'm still smiling when I reach my seat.

Simon's not back yet but Keeley looks at me with curiosity. 'Make a friend? He was cute.'

'Yes, I think I did.' *And yes, he was.*

Chapter 12

Today is 'moving back in day' and oh my goodness, it couldn't have come at a better time. Simon missed the entire second half of the performance and needless to say, Keeley hit the roof. I call a cab to whisk me back home and when it arrives, Keeley walks me to it, to give me a send-off.

'I'm sorry you had to witness all of this.'

I give her a big hug, 'No problem at all; I'm glad to see that you're just as unhinged as I am.'

'Now, now,' she lets go of me. 'I wouldn't quite draw that comparison.' She smiles at me and then adds, 'Thanks for being here.'

'Thanks for letting me stay.' I give her one last squeeze before hopping into the cab. Winding down the window, I look up to my big sister as I always have done. 'Love you.'

'Love you too, Melsy. Get home safe.'

'You haven't called me Melsy since we were about seven.'

'Since *you* were seven.' She corrects. 'I was the grand age of ten.'

Keeley stands on the pavement and watches me until I disappear around the corner. I collapse back into the seat and sigh. When we pull up in front of my building, thankfully there are no fire engines or concerned looking neighbours, just my home ready to welcome me back; I pay the driver and practically skip through the front door.

Everything looks and smells clean, fresh and beautiful. I

didn't think my flat could get any more perfect but now, it's a fresh canvas for me to paint on. I walk from room to empty room and fall just a little bit more in love with it as I go.

The insurance company were extremely gracious, and I'm going to be compensated with completely new décor — from a bed, to cupboards, and all sorts in between. But this won't arrive until tomorrow, so in the meantime, I'm sleeping on a blow-up mattress and in a sleeping bag of Keeley's. I do, however, have a few things for the kitchen and bathroom in a nice cardboard box. I fish out the kettle, a mug and spoon, a teabag and some milk that Keeley also gave me.

Kicking off my shoes, I blow on my freshly brewed tea, and sit crossed-legged on the new carpet of my bedroom. I start to draw out a floor plan, deciding that I'm going to move absolutely everything around; it's definitely time for a complete change. From now on, my life is going to be straightforward, everything is going to have a place and a purpose, and my surroundings and head will have order. Yes. I smile at my new plan; *I am brilliant.*

My doorbell goes, so I pad barefoot through the new wooden hallway to open it.

'Hi! How were the family?' I throw my arms around Dave.

'Ghastly but now gone!' He grins. 'You look really good; what happened?!'

'Oh, shut up. Do you want to come in or not?' I raise my eyebrows playfully, taking hold of the door ready to either open it wide or shut it, playfully, in his face.

'Shall I take my shoes off?'

'Absolutely. New rule.'

'Is that so?'

'Yup, just made it up now.' I put my hands on my hips.

'Right then.' He bends down and unties his trainers. 'Show

me the way, madam!'

I lead him in, 'Wow, you really have nothing. It's like a brand new flat,' he says, glancing around.

'I thought I'd be really sad to come back to nothing, but look, I've got new everything.' I attempt to jiggle my overloaded box of goodies on the floor and then wave at my new shiny red kettle standing proudly.

'Well, at least your glass is finally half-full!'

He digs around for another mug and makes himself a cup without asking. 'So, when does your stuff arrive?'

'At 10 o'clock tomorrow.'

'Need a hand?'

'Yeah, that would be awesome, thanks. Mish is back from Paris, so she's coming round for dinner, but I'd love help in the morning. *Ooh*, I'll show you my plan!'

He smirks as I rush out of the room to fetch it. 'I love these worktops,' he yells down the corridor at me.

'I know, right?' I say beaming as I enter the room again. 'How lucky am I to have my flat reincarnated from the ashes?! It's like a phoenix.' I stop and nod, 'No, I am like a phoenix.'

'You've started to find your sparkle again, I'd say.' He sips his tea but his eyes remain on me. 'So, all ready for the new term?'

'By ready, you mean completely under-prepared and haven't really given it a second thought since July, then yes, I'm completely ready!'

'That's my girl.' He puts his arm around me. 'Now, for the rest for the tour if you will!'

***

'Is this the front or the back?' I'm kneeling on the floor with two bits of wood in my hands, screws all over the place and a crumpled-up chest of drawers instruction manual in front of me.

'Beats me. Give that a rest and come and help me here.' Dave is carrying a headboard into my bedroom, 'And I need a hand with the mattress.'

'No wait, that's the side!' I say, consulting the paper. 'Oh crap.' I throw the paper. 'I'm exhausted,' I whine. 'Shall we have a tea break?'

'We've just had a tea break, get off your butt and help me, Butler.'

'Fine! Fine.' I stomp over, enthusiasm wearing off.

'Now. Before we get the rest of the bed in here, we need to know which way it's facing. So before, it was this way.' He holds up his arms. 'But you said you want it this way.' He rotates his body 90 degrees and holds his arms up again. 'Let me look at your plan again; I don't think you've thought about the size of things.' He points at the pathetically incorrectly put together chest of drawers, 'I mean, what size will that be?'

I laugh, 'I have absolutely no idea!'

'Right then,' he rubs his left eye. 'We'll improvise. Let's put this where you say you want it and then after, see if the rest of the furniture fits in, yeah?'

'OK!' I say with complete confidence.

'So, this is the frame.' He points to a pile of wood neatly stacked up against a wall. 'Let's lay it out on the floor and go from there.'

I take to my hands and knees and start shimmying the boards together, like a jigsaw. 'You've still got your tan,' I comment.

'And you've still got a few freckles,' he encourages.

I smirk at him, 'I will have you know that for me, this is

tanned.'

'I am well aware of that, Butler; you're not deathly pale now. Ow!'

I swat him with a pillow. 'Well, I will take half of that as a compliment.'

'It was meant to be,' he says playfully, rubbing his arm. 'You are truly terrible at this.' He laughs as I furrow my brow, wondering which piece goes where.

'I know. I'd've been here until Christmas if you hadn't come to help me. Which part is this, do you think?' I hold out a long thin section with holes all along it.

'It's the spine of the bed, the boards feed into it like this.' He shows me but my face still conveys my confusion. 'Are you this clueless in all bed-related issues?'

'I'll have you know that I know my way around a bedroom very well, thank you very much.'

'Shame you have no plans in the near future to use them, then.'

'That may not be true.'

'Oh?' he enquires. 'Pray tell!'

'I met someone at Lucy's dancing show.'

'Probably married,' he says flatly.

'No!'

'Divorced then, maybe, or perhaps separated?'

'Why would you jump to those conclusions?'

'Why would he be at a kid's dancing show?'

'He was there to see his nieces; I would have you know.'

'Right. Are you meeting up with him, then?'

I frown, 'I don't know, he hasn't got in contact with me yet.'

'Well until then, darling, you can hang out with me.'

Dave manages to assemble everything in the bedroom in

forty-five minutes and I resign myself to standing there and looking pretty whilst trying not to get in the way. After he's helped erect a few bathroom and living room items we collapse on the new sofa. I look around happily; all I need to do is fill it with my Next Home accessories.

'You are incredibly awesome, you know that?' I look over at my hero of the day, who nods.

'You would have been screwed without me.'

'Absolutely.' I wiggle over and rest my head on his chest. 'Your heart is beating really fast,' I say with my ear buried in his slightly damp t-shirt.

'Well, what do you expect, I did the last of the bathroom cabinet and the drawers on my own! You were about as much use as a decaf coffee.'

'Well, on the bright side, you can't say I don't give you a good workout!'

We fall comfortably silent for a moment and I'm thinking I could quite happily lie here all day when the doorbell goes.

'That must be Mish,' I reluctantly peel myself off and flounce towards the door.

'You look brilliant, but awful at the same time.'

'I've missed you too,' I give Mish a sweaty hug.

'*Ugh!* Go and get in the shower now.'

'Dave's in the living room,' I say to prevent her saying anything embarrassing.

'Wonderful. Now,' she gives me a kiss on the cheek, 'I love you, but please go and get clean; you're completely gross. David! How are we? Haven't seen you since Mel's birthday last year.'

Dave stands up; I know Mish intimidates him. 'Michelle, how are you?' he gives her a kiss on the cheek. 'You look lovely; clearly Paris suits you.'

Gosh, he's a charmer.

Mish turns to see me still standing there observing their exchange. 'Go! Go! I'm taking you out for an early birthday meal and you're nowhere near ready.'

'We're going out? Where?' I ask excitedly. I love it when Mish takes me out; she always finds these eclectic, unheard-of places.

'I will only tell you once you've had a shower.' She grins at me then turns back to Dave and I pootle off to enjoy my new bathroom.

When I emerge in my dressing gown, I see Dave has waited for me before leaving.

'I'd better be off. Nice to see you again, Michelle.' He gives her a kiss on the cheek, heaves himself off of the sofa and strides over to me.

'See you later, Butler,' and gives me a huge bear hug. I'm acutely aware that I'm practically naked and that my boobs should be poised a little higher, but I hug him back with gusto; he smells musty but it's not unpleasant.

'I can't thank you enough for today.'

He kisses me on the cheek then let's go. 'Don't worry, I'll think of something for you to make it up to me. See you Monday! Have a good night, ladies.' And with a smile, he's gone.

'So how fancy do I need to dress?'

***

We find our booth and I gaze at the table. We're sitting in a Japanese restaurant near Piccadilly Circus that projects its menus onto the table and you have a touch screen to control it.

'This is awesome,' I say, browsing the wine menu. 'How do you find these places?'

'I had a meeting with a client here once,' she says offhandedly before ordering a bottle of the chardonnay for us. 'So, tell me all; how was the wedding?'

'Wedding? Oh, Poppie's!'

'Memorable, then?' She smirks.

'It seems like forever ago. It was good. Mental, but good. Oh,' I say, frowning as I remember.

'What?'

'Craig may have said a few things to me — just reaffirming how much I hate him.'

'No, you hate that he says it as it is.'

'*Hmm.*' My frown deepens.

'How was Spain?' Mish taps the table to look at the starters.

'Beautiful.' I rearrange my face into a happy expression. 'Just perfect.'

'Did you go to the rooftop bar above the Alcazaba Hostel?'

'Yes! So beautiful with everything illuminated! When did you go to Malaga?' I say, surprised

'Briefly, about nine years ago when I worked for Calco's PR; they had a Spanish branch. There was this delicious man I had to liaise with every day...' she grins like a Cheshire cat.

'I've missed you.' I say beaming.

'Of course you have, I'm awesome.'

The waiter comes back with our wine and we order our food.

'So can you keep a secret?'

'No,' I answer with all seriousness.

'Well,' she continues regardless, 'do you remember about two months ago I had that event in Bath and I told you I'd made a few exciting connections, but couldn't tell you who?'

'*Ah huh*,' I nurse my wine — definitely a good choice. 'This is delicious.'

'You're welcome. So, the real reason I went to Paris was to brainstorm with them on a few details about an event that's in the planning stages for New Year's Eve, somewhere in London.'

'You're being very cryptic.'

'Yes, I am. I need to build up the suspense.' Her face is straight but her eyes are sparkling.

'Sorry, carry on!' I play along.

'So, when I was in Bath, I was talking to a very good friend of the person in question's manager and it turned out that he had been to five of my events without realising. He said he loves my work, my style, my flair and would like to bring me on board as a senior consultant for this New Year's Eve and potentially more after, if they like what they see, which he assured me he would, based on my previous work.'

'That's amazing! Well done you!' I hold out my glass and she clinks it.

'Thank you! This is probably the most exciting proposition that I've ever had.'

'Are you going to tell me who this is?'

She sits there pausing for effect. 'Only the hottest new talent in the UK right now: Luke Braydon!'

'NO!' I catch the attention of half the restaurant.

'And I haven't even told you the best part yet.'

'What's better than that?' I lean forward a little.

'You are going to be there with me.'

'NO!' I yell even louder and bang the table in excitement, frightening a Chinese family next to us. 'Sorry,' I aim at them and then lower my voice to a stage whisper. 'No!'

'It's going to be a relatively intimate, black-tie charity gig where people apply for tickets the week before. They offered me a plus-one and I couldn't think of anyone else I'd rather have there with me.' She holds out her wine glass to mine and I beam.

'What did I ever do to deserve such great friends?'

'Beats me.'

'I'm lost for words, Mish; you're amazing.'

'True,' she nods. 'Speaking of friends,' she pauses to consider her words — something she rarely does — so I know it's serious. 'I like Dave.'

'So do I.'

'How much so?' She cocks her head and her dark locks catch the low light.

'What do you mean?'

'Well, he's been there for you since you started at that crappy school and he opened his holiday hide-away to you, you get along really well, he helped you move back in today...'

'Yeah,' I shrug, '...he's a really good friend.'

'And that's all?'

'*Um hmm,*' I say.

She looks at me in silence for a moment then taking her glass again, she gestures with it, 'I think there should be more there.'

'He's Dave! He's like my big brother.'

'Well, I'm just saying, definitely something to consider. You'd make a cute couple. And I like him, which is the most important thing.'

'You think we'd make a cute couple?' I scrunch my nose.

'Yes. And to top it off, he's good looking.'

'Maybe you should go out with him then?' I laugh.

'Oh no!' She says horrified. 'No, I'd eat him for breakfast. He's charming but I can tell he's slightly afraid of me; an attractive quality admittedly, but no. I think I now want someone to put me in my place. All the men who tend to like me bow down too easily…again, not a particularly bad trait…'

Chapter 13

My weekend of putting finishing touches to my new home was beautifully topped off by a phone call from a school Governor informing me that there will be no teacher training, and my presence is only required from the first day of school, giving me an unexpected extra week off. Strange? Absolutely; but I'm not questioning it as it's given me the opportunity to actually plan my year ahead. However, the real cherry on the cake was a text from Julian, arranging our first date.

When the following Monday arrives, I feel ready for anything. I've mentally fluffed myself up for a confrontation with Creepy Crawley, but, weirdly, she's nowhere to be seen. Seated around the staffroom table waiting for morning briefing, Shirley looks like seven weeks' holiday wasn't enough, but the rest of us start to speculate; my favourite theory so far is alien abduction back to her home planet.

'Who are these from?' Jill asks, picking up a mini muffin and stuffing it in her mouth. '*Ooomf mmy gawwd* they're *soo* good!' she splatters the table with her mouthful.

I grab a few to eat in my classroom as the door to the staffroom opens and a striking immaculately-dressed man walks in; he can't be much over forty with a light dusting of grey over his slightly wavy black hair.

'Good morning, everyone!' He says in a sprightly Scottish accent. 'I suppose you're beginning to wonder where Ms Crawley is.'

Few nods but we remain silent, not wanting to miss anything. He walks over to us and sits down like an equal — something Creepy has never done. He claps his big strong hands together.

'She will not be returning for the foreseeable future. I'm not at liberty at the moment to tell you any more, I'm afraid, but I have been asked to step in for the time being. My name is Dermott McCladden.' We remain in silence so he continues. 'Just to give you a little info about myself: I'm originally from Dunbar in Scotland; I have been teaching for twenty years, twelve of which were working in Edinburgh and then I moved to London, where I took up a post of Deputy Head and then Headmaster; I like bike rides and, sadly, a bit of country music.' There's a faint giggle from the women in the room and the mood lifts. 'So, did everybody have a good summer?' Stunned silence once more hits the room, as we have never been asked. He smiles. 'Any news or exciting events coming up? Yes.'

I look round and Gracie has her hand up. I note she's sitting even straighter than normal.

'It's Melanie's birthday on Friday.'

'Ah yes, I read that, Gracie.' She looks taken aback. 'I studied all of your files; remembering names and faces is my speciality and I made a document of birthdays — something I like to do with the schools I work in.' I'm not sure if I'm freaked out or impressed. 'So, Melanie,' he looks at me, 'I read in your outside interests and hobbies that you love to bake; would you have time to prepare a cake for the staffroom?' I nod dumbfoundedly. 'Perhaps it's something we could all do to celebrate everybody's birthdays? However, I'm afraid this is the best I can do,' he gestures to the store-bought muffins.

I briefly look at Gracie and her eyes are as wide as I'm sure mine are. Dermott's grin lights up the room as we continue to sit there in silence. 'Wonderful! OK, so I'd like to say welcome to Silvia.' His palm points towards a frightened young girl who I've just noticed for the first time, 'let's all help her feel at home. Apart from that, are there any concerns in regards to this week?' Dermott looks around the table and nods at Violet. 'The new reception class: I note that one child has a severe nut allergy so I've spoken to the kitchen. We're fine for this week but we are reworking the lunch menu — I will forward a copy to you all each week before it goes ahead, just in case I've missed something obvious.'

Asking for our opinion? Oh my God, who is this guy?

'So, this morning, I propose we start with an assembly where I'll introduce myself to the entire school. As a follow-up, I've had letters printed out to go home with every student, to inform the parents of my presence. Any questions or queries, can you please ask the parents to contact me directly and I will set up a meeting with them.' We sit, dumbfounded, as Creepy has never allowed a parent to contact her directly. 'And that goes for all of you as well; if you have a problem, please don't hesitate to come and see me.' He smiles warmly and I'm thinking that this could be the best year so far. 'So, please enjoy these; they're my token "welcome back" gesture for you all and...' he reaches forward to grab a muffin and stands up, '...here's to a great year! Oh Shirley, might I have a word please before we begin the day?' And with that, he exits the room with Shirley hanging her head behind him. As soon as the door clicks closed, pandemonium breaks out.

'Can you believe this?!' I almost shriek at Dave. 'This is the most amazing news. What's wrong?'

Dave is sitting there rigid and emotionless. '*Hmm*?' He

shakes his head and then looks normal again. 'Can't believe our luck; maybe she's ill.'

'Well, this is bloody fantastic.' Jill comes round to join us. 'Do you reckon she got the sack? What for?' She furrows her brow and then gasps, 'Maybe it's something to do with Shirley? What d'you think?'

'No idea, but it's nice to see her completely silent for once,' I add.

'My gosh, he's dreamy,' Gracie floats over. 'Like a slightly silver fox.'

I settle back in my chair with a muffin and my phone bleeps. It's Julian.

'Who's making you smile?' Dave leans over to look.

'It's the dancing show man,' I beam.

'You have a dancing show man?' Jill asks.

'Yes, I do. I met him at my niece's dancing show — he was watching his nieces,' I add as Jill goes to open her mouth. I look down at the message. 'We're meeting up on Wednesday and he's just confirming the time,' I tell them all.

'A midweek date,' Dave comments. 'Means he doesn't want to stay up too late.'

I'm sure that's not true.

***

The Mexican place I'm meeting Julian at is in Greenwich. Butterflies fill my stomach as I walk through the fake barn style doors to the crowded, noisy restaurant. I scan the room but think I'm the first to arrive. Suddenly the room goes dark as something has been placed on my head and falls over my eyes.

'*Ole*!!' I hear a voice say as I fumble and feel the edges of what can only be: a sombrero. I lift it up and see Julian's smiling face. 'Suits you!'

'And you!' I say regarding the hat that I assume matches mine.

'Why thank you! There's nothing like getting into the spirit of a restaurant.'

'Nobody else is wearing one of these,' I say to him as I look around the room and see some people giggle our way.

'Well, clearly they have no sense of style,' he says nonchalantly and puts his hand on the small of my back. 'Shall we find our table?'

I feel embarrassed but decide to go with it. 'Sure. *Vamos*!'

He raises an eyebrow, '*Si*, let's go.'

After some nachos, tacos, quesadillas, several complimentary tequilas (as Julian knows the manager), and a jug of sangria later, I learn that Julian is a fireman, lives in Peckham, loves to travel, his parents moved to Greece when they retired, he has one sister, two nieces and another niece or nephew on the way, and he'd love to get a dog just like the one he had as a kid. 'He was a labradoodle.' I think I've had too much to drink, I've no idea what that is. He reads my expression and explains. 'It's a cross between a Labrador and a poodle.'

'My eldest sister has a Labrador. He's gorgeous, I'd take him home if I didn't live in a flat.'

'So, you're a dog person?' he says grinning and I think that's a point towards me.

'Well, I'm allergic to cats, plus we grew up with a border collie called Trigger.'

'Trigger?' he laughs.

I shrug. 'My dad liked *Only Fools and Horses*.'

'Are you close to your family?' He takes a bite of a churro, anticipating a long response.

'*Umm*, sort of. My mum and sisters are all a little mental but I love them; my dad, although he's done a good job of hiding it, favours my big sister so it's hard to be close to someone like that. We're all quite different but we're always there for each other when we need to be. What about you?'

'I go out to Greece as much as I can and I try to see my sister and her family every other week — I never know when I'm working, you see—'

Ah, there's the reason for the mid-week date.

'But I want to see my nieces grow up and I want to be a strong role model in their lives.'

Nodding I dunk a churro in chocolate before eating as much as is deemed polite, to give myself a moment; *what a rubbish aunt I've been in comparison*. I swallow, vow to be better, and decide to change the subject.

'What do you do for fun?'

'Well, let's see. I like running. Helps clear my head and keeps me fit.'

'Sounds like my baby sister. I've done the occasional bit of jogging but nothing further. One of my lifelong goals is to run a marathon, but I'm not really fit enough to classify myself as a runner.'

'Well, you look pretty fit to me,' he says kindly.

My mouth twitches into a smile; I'm pretty sure I'm going to kiss him at some point this evening.

'What?' he asks self-consciously.

I shake my head and smile innocently, 'Nothing at all. I'm just having a lovely time.'

He nods and leans in slightly, 'I'm glad I mistook you for my sister.'

I raise my glass, 'To mistaken identities.' I clink his glass.

'Oh my God, I know who you are!' I say suddenly, surprising him and myself. 'You're the handsome fireman who told me my flat was ruined!'

'Handsome?' he smirks whilst taking a moment to remember, 'Blackheath.' I nod. 'Small world.'

We both take in this moment and I hear Poppie in my head telling me that everything happens for a reason. His mouth now twitches into a playful smile. 'What?' I say, thinking I've got chocolate around my mouth or something.

'I'm just pleased you haven't taken the sombrero off,' he says, laughing, as I put my hand to my head, only now remembering that it's still on there.

'Well, I am partial to a good hat.'

'That's good to know,' he smiles and sips his drink.

Julian takes my bus with me to make sure I get home safely and we don't stop talking the entire time.

'I had a really lovely time, thank you, Julian,' I look up at him as we turn into my road and await his next move.

'Are you doing anything this Friday?' he asks me in response.

'*Um.*' My head's foggy as he throws me with a question. 'I think so, but I can't remember right now,' I shrug, 'It'll come to me.'

'Well, I've got a spare ticket to see Jools Holland if you're interested. Are you a fan?'

'I'm not really sure who that is, sorry,' I admit. One too many tequilas to be coy.

'Boogie Woogie piano?' he tries, but my face remains vacant. 'Has a show called *Later… with Jools Holland* where various acts come and play?' I shake my head, '*The Hootenanny*?'

'Oh yeah, the New Year's Eve thing. Oh, I remember what

I'm doing on Friday!' I almost shout, and then laugh at my own ridiculousness, 'It's my birthday.'

Julian tilts his head at me in what I hope is an adoring way, 'Happy Birthday! What are you doing to celebrate?'

'A little party with a few friends; I'm sort of mixing it into a house-warming too. You could come.' *Too soon? Too keen?*

'I would love to.' His eyes are softly focused on mine. 'But I can't let my friends down.'

'Oh, of course not!' *Too soon.*

He senses my embarrassment, 'Perhaps we could have our own celebration, though? I'd like to see you again.'

I smile. 'I'd like that too.' We reach my door. 'This is me,' I say and fumble in my bag for my keys even though I know exactly where they are.

'Well, thank you for teaching me what foods to avoid in quiet situations.'

'You are very welcome.' We stand there and I wonder if he's going to kiss me properly. Now the moment's presented itself, I'm not sure I'm quite brave enough to make the first move.

He leans in and kisses my cheek softly. I breathe in his aftershave; it's more manly than anything Evan used to wear. Julian straightens up, smiles broadly and promises to message me to arrange another date, before wishing me goodnight.

When I'm back inside my flat, I feel like I'm walking on air. That was the best first date I've ever been on, including when I was twelve and Eric Perkins took me to the funfair and won me the largest teddy bear there. I kick off my shoes in the hallway and skip to my bedroom before doing a running jump onto my new bed, landing in a huge star shape. *There is life out there.*

Chapter 14

As promised, I made a cake for my birthday — well, two actually — a salted caramel cream crumble and a gluten-free chocolate sponge, that both went down a storm in the staffroom.

'We could sell these, Melanie; they really are phenomenal,' Dermott flattered me during first break as he helped himself to another slice of both.

'Have you ever hosted a bake sale or something here?' he goes on to ask.

'*Um*, no. I've never been given the go ahead,' I say cautiously. Crawley laughed in my face when I suggested it and told me to grow up.

'Well, let me have a think about how it would most benefit everybody and let me know if you have any ideas.' He sips his coffee and nods, as if taking a mental note.

'Can you believe how nice he is?' I ask Dave as he helps take out bowls of nibbles from my kitchen to the living room. 'He just seems to be so on it.'

'I know!' Jill twists around from her seat on the sofa to talk to everybody, 'He came into my class just after last break and started talking to me about the sports budget. Let's just say if he is as good as his word, things are seriously going to change here.'

'And he's thoughtful. Have you opened the card he gave you yet?' Shaking my head at Gracie, who's organising glasses, I locate my bag and whip out an envelope.

'It's a voucher for John Lewis!'

'How much?' Dave leans over to try and see.

'£30!'

'I don't know, is he trying to buy our respect?' Dave frowns.

'You don't like him, do you?' We lock eyes.

'It's not that I don't like him — I just don't know if we can trust him or believe all the promises he's making, that's all.' Dave says before taking a handful of popcorn.

'Well, I like him.' Gracie tucks her blonde curls behind her ears and continues the debate while I head to my room to get changed. I take out a slightly above the knee, maroon cocktail dress and hold it up to my body in front of the mirror.

My phone bleeps and I see it's another message from Julian,

"Hi! Hope you enjoy your weekend. Heading into town now for Jools. Looking forward to making another date with you. J x"

My stomach does a backflip and I type back a quick message,

"Hi! Thanks. Hope you have a good time too. Looking forward to seeing you again. M x"

With that I throw the mobile on the bed, touch up my make-up, wriggle out of my casual clothes and then into my new outfit. I whoosh my auburn hair into a quick twisted 'up do' and wait for my other guests to arrive.

My party is small, fun, and full of prosecco — much like myself. I'm leaning on my windowsill, admiring the merriment and feeling blessed for all of these people in my life; Poppie even came down to celebrate. I watch as she tries to guide a small group in some *qigong* exercises — Dave and a few of my university friends being among them.

'I've been dying to tell you,' Gracie wobbles over and leans next to me, '...but I didn't want to take the focus away from you.'

'What is it?' I laugh as Gracie is one of the least selfish people on the planet.

'We've been Facetiming.'

'Who has?'

'Me and Pablo! And he sent me this.' Gracie threads her fingers lovingly around the necklace she's wearing.

'Oh wow; that's amazing! The situation and the necklace.' I clarify.

'I mean, who knows if it can turn into anything serious but...I'm so happy.'

'You deserve so much happiness.' I give her a squeeze.

The party is a huge success and soon the only people left are Poppie, Jill, Gracie and Dave. I leave the girls chatting on the sofa, and Dave inflating some blow up mattresses, as I suddenly feel the need to check my phone. Weaving happily down the corridor and to my room, I hop onto the bed. There are three messages: one from my mum which tells me they have arrived at the airport, ready to fly off to Majorca to catch the cruise; a reminder message from Poppie about a new class she was telling me about earlier, on personal healing, which she thinks I would benefit from, and a message that I think is slightly drunken, from Julian, as most of the words are stuck together.

"Hey!Hopeyouare having a goodtime. Heard some amazingmusicians tonight...maybesomedaywe'll get tosee some together...I'd reallylike that. J x"

Thumbs poised and ready to reply, there's a knock on the door; I tell them to come in.

'All done with the mattresses.' Dave enters and climbs under the covers.

'Make yourself comfy, why don't you?' I laugh as he settles himself in.

'Don't mind if I do; it's far too nippy to be out of the covers.' I rub my arms in agreement and climb in next to him. 'I wanted to run something by you, Mels,' he says now tucking himself in in his seated position. 'What?'

I'm smiling at him. 'I'm sorry, I can't take you seriously when you're tucking yourself in like a five-year-old.'

'Hey. There is nothing wrong with being tucked in,' he says with a straight face. 'It keeps the cold air out.'

'OK.' Putting down my phone, I follow his lead and tuck myself in, not wanting to admit that it is much warmer like this. 'So, you were starting to say…?'

'Yeah, do you remember the apartment I showed you from the top of Alcazaba when we were in Spain?'

'*Um hmm,*' I nod.

'I want to put an offer in,' he blurts quickly, as if afraid he'll change his mind.

'Wow! So, we'd have somewhere to stay whenever we'd like?'

'Definitely, I'd want people to visit me.'

Looking at him, I feel my stomach fall; I know what's coming next.

'I want to live there,' he says, confirming my thoughts.

His eyes wait eagerly for my response; selfishly I know deep down I don't want him to go anywhere, so I remain silent.

'The thing is,' he continues, 'I'm just not 100% sure it's what I should do.'

Good.

'Why aren't you saying anything?'

'I'm not saying anything because I don't want you to go anywhere,' I respond honestly, moving my eyes from his as I start to play with the duvet cover. 'I wouldn't see you every day and who else will put my furniture together for me?' Sadness engulfs me.

'Yup, you would be in a bit of a pickle,' he agrees. 'But, hey, maybe this Julian guy is the one for you, no?'

'Maybe.' It's *far* too soon to be thinking like that.

'So,' he prompts, 'if you were me, what would you do?'

'Well.' I consider this. 'If I were you, I wouldn't be brave enough to do something like that. But then again, you do speak Spanish so that'll help,' I unwillingly justify my own argument. 'I'd be too scared to move somewhere where I didn't know anybody. But you do know a few people there, don't you?' I look at him and he nods. 'Would you teach?'

'I've looked at a few possibilities; there are several openings in schools dotted around the area and Pablo says they would lap up a male teacher — particularly an English one.'

'Gosh.' I take this all in, 'You're really considering this, aren't you?'

He nods his head. 'But I wanted to see what you thought before I did anything.' He shrugs, 'You're my best friend, Butler.'

My eyes fill with tears. 'You can't go anywhere; I'd miss you too much.' I say with a slight wobble in my voice. 'I've seen you basically every day for the last five years.'

'I know, it's been hard for me too.' He scoops me up into a big cuddle. We lie there for a moment before he breaks the silence. 'Why do you think I haven't done this before?' A single tear falls down my cheek but I don't reply. Shutting my eyes, I take in the warmth of his arms. I can't bear the thought of him going; I need him in my life. We stay in the same position, both comfortable to stay exactly as we are and somewhere between teaching me how to ask for a glass of white wine in Spanish (*vino blanco por favor*), and discussing the new headmaster, we fall asleep.

***

Slowly coming to, my left leg, arm, and right cheek acknowledge that I'm snuggling something; it's warm and smells like fabric softener. Blinking, I manoeuvre my head and take in Dave's messy morning hair; we look at each other for a moment of confusion.

'We must have fallen asleep; you're a good snuggler!' he says sleepily to me.

I unwrap myself swiftly from his body, embarrassed, and sit up. 'I'm so sorry.'

'Nonsense; I feel honoured to be snuggled by you, Butler.' I laugh at him as I pull the covers back and head for the kitchen.

'I'm ready for some coffee.' I walk to the door and after opening it, see Gracie outside and Jill just down the corridor.

'How are we on this fine morning?' Gracie asks, looking far more chipper than Jill, who has an eye mask on her forehead and a disgruntled expression on her face.

'I need coffee!' Jill cries as she joins Gracie's side. What's the time anyway?'

'About half eight,' Dave answers as he appears behind me as if it were completely normal to pop out of your friend's bedroom at that time.

'What were you doing in there?' Jill says, waking up

quicker than perhaps deemed possible.

'We thought you'd gone home. Did you sleep in there?' Gracie asks with her eyebrows raised.

'We were talking and must've fallen asleep,' I say, sounding rather guilty, even though I know nothing happened. My work friends look at each other but don't say any more as Dave takes the lead to the kitchen, in a semi-dressed parade. Jill grabs my arm as he's out of his earshot.

'Are you serious? Getting it together with Dave? Have you thought about how this will affect your friendship?'

'We didn't sleep together!' I say in a hushed but firm tone. 'I mean, we slept *next* to each other but nothing happened. He wanted to ask me a question, that's all.'

'*Um hmm*, what question?'

I hesitate.

'See, you definitely slept with him.'

'No! He just might not want me telling everybody.'

'Fine.' She seems to have dropped it but after a moment adds, 'I always knew you'd get together.'

'Look, I love Dave...'

'*Aha*, there we are! I knew it!'

'No, let me finish. Like I said to Mish the other day, Dave is like a brother to me. He's one of my best friends. I'd sooner have a relationship with you than I would with him.'

'You know I like you a lot,' she says reasonably, 'But I'm afraid it's men and men only for me, darling.'

***

Poppie is staying another night before driving back to Wales tomorrow. After we've finished dinner and I'm making tea, she announces, 'I have something to tell you.'

I pause with the kettle aloft and she laughs, obviously reading my mind, 'I'm not pregnant yet. The news isn't to do with me.'

'Oh. OK, who's it about then?'

'You.'

'I'm confused. What news do you have about me that I don't know about?' I sit back down with two mugs of peppermint.

'Well, did you know that there's going to be a new sports unit built in your school?'

'No! Oh, Jill will go mental. Wait, how do you know that?'

'Because my brother told me.'

'Your brother?' I say, dumbfounded.

'Yup. He's just signed on as the architect and site manager!'

I nearly spill my mug in shock.

'How on earth is Craig involved in a project like this? It's far too small for him.'

'His boss went to university with your new headmaster and he owes him a favour.'

'Oh, the world is so small.' I feel like my head might explode.

'Amazing isn't it!?' she enthusiastically cries.

'Yeah,' I sigh.

'So, you'll have to give him a big hug from me each time you see him.'

I pause; I'd sooner give him a slap than a hug, 'I'll certainly say hello,' I muster.

'Oh, come on now. From Monday, you'll be seeing him every day for the next six months at least! Be nice to him.'

Later, when I've run myself a bath, I sit on the cold porcelain for a moment and stare into space. *I don't want to see him at my school.* I frown at myself in the mirror. Well, I don't have to talk to him, do I? There probably won't be much of an opportunity to, anyway. If I see him, I'll be polite and smile and that will be that. I nod at my reflection. I take my clothes off and get in; the water's just perfect. I lie back, close my eyes and try to get all thoughts of Craig out of my head but his face keeps surfacing. *Go away!* I shout in my head, but all I can see is his smug little face gazing back at me. *Think of Julian,* I will myself, but then I have the image of Craig and Julian in the pub laughing as Craig tells horrible stories about me. I snap my eyes open. Why am I so self-destructive? They'll probably never meet anyway. And with that thought I finally start to relax.

Chapter 15

Autumn is drawing in sooner than expected and I'm a little chilly from not bringing a coat or scarf on my walk to school. There's no sign of any workmen yet so I breathe a little sigh of relief as I walk down the corridor to the staffroom.

When I open the door, I'm completely shocked; the uninspiring colour scheme of cream and tawny brown has been spruced up with a bright white, and splashes of colour as far as the eye can see, from wall art to furniture. The central conference table with its uncomfortable chairs have all been whisked away and replaced with brightly coloured tub chairs, huge beanbags and small coffee tables, positioned neatly in sociable circles. I spot Dave and Gracie in the far corner.

'What is this?' I cry as I sit down in the red tub chair next to Dave's purple and Gracie's orange one.

'It's like a fairy came in over the weekend and waved a magic wand, isn't it?' Gracie replies.

'I still think he's trying to buy our respect,' Dave says with his legs comfortably propped up on the coffee table.

'And you really look like you're complaining,' Gracie says to him.

'Well, it's not bad, is it?' he says back.

'Not bad?' I question, sitting down, 'Oh, I am so comfortable right now; I could absolutely sleep here,' I say, settling in. 'Where's Jill?' I notice for the first time.

'Not sure.' Gracie sits up and frowns but our question is

answered as the door opens and she walks in with Dermott, grinning from ear to ear.

'Good morning, everybody!' he calls and commands the attention of the whole room. 'I hope you are enjoying my little surprise?' he gestures to the room and smiles at our approval. 'It turns out there has been a fund for this kind of refurbishment that was stacking up so I thought, why not!?'

Still grinning, Jill sits next to me on a chair the shade of Kermit the Frog. 'You're not going to believe what he's about to say,' she whispers to me. I haven't got the heart to tell her I already know.

'There has also been a budget to expand certain areas of the school,' Dermott says as he sits down in a sunshine-yellow chair. 'So, I hope you don't mind, that I've already gone ahead and made arrangements for this before consulting you all, but it was something that I feel quite passionate about and I'm sure you'll agree that this will be a great addition to our school.' He pauses for someone to step in with a comment but the room remains silent, so he continues, 'I signed a contract at the end of last week for a team to design and construct a sports building.'

Jill turns to me again, mouth wide open in a silent excited scream before turning back to Dermott, her new hero.

'The plans are nearly finalised, after meetings throughout the weekend, and there will be a team coming in later on today to check out the site before building starts. So, if you see any strange men you don't recognise, don't worry, they're coming to see me.'

Strange men indeed, I think to myself as Craig's smug face appears in my head. Dermott leaves the room and leaves us with the information to "digest".

Jill turns excitedly to us all, 'We're getting not only a new building, but new equipment! Equipment!' She wiggles in her seat in a small happy dance. 'Can you imagine, I actually get to teach them in a proper sports hall fit for basketball, netball, gymnastics, dance, you name it! He said he's not only come across a whole library of sports team pictures since the school opened, but boxes of trophies and awards too that have been hidden, so we're going to have a gallery in the corridor as you walk in and a glass display cabinet with everything — which I can add to with everything that I've had to take home with me. Plus, he wants me to sit in on the meetings and share my thoughts and ideas and I haven't even told you the best bit…' She pauses for breath more than for dramatic effect. 'I get my own office in the building! An office, people!' She sits back and slaps the sides of the chairs. 'This is a great day.' Her eyes are sparkling away and I couldn't be happier for her.

'Yeah, I agree it's amazing, but dare I ask again, where is all this money coming from?' Dave says with frustration. 'This room too.' He gestures around. 'Something like this doesn't design itself; where has this budget that he keeps talking about, been hiding?'

'Who cares!' Jill practically shouts. 'I've been on about this for years and it's finally happening! I've been either outside in the rain or inside the dining hall, having to finish my lessons early for break times and lunch and this is what the school has been screaming for since I got here seven years ago. And this room is insane,' she adds looking around and noticing for the first time that it's changed.

'It makes you wonder what could possibly happen next, doesn't it?' Gracie says excitedly.

My morning of maths equations and art projects zoom by and before I know it, it's lunch time. I dismiss my class and start organising the pile of artwork that's sitting on my desk.

I try not to laugh as I look at Mia's attempt of a painting and I'm trying to decide whether it's a boat or a banana, when I feel like I'm being watched. Sure enough, I look up and see Craig leaning on the doorframe, arms folded, one leg crossed effortlessly in front of the other.

'It's really rather rude to laugh at children's work, you know,' he says to me with a straight face.

'I was not laughing,' I defend.

'Not out loud,' he continues.

I put down the banana boat and sit back in my chair. 'Nice to see you,' I say, proud of my politeness, despite my natural urge to throw something at him.

'I asked where your classroom was,' he says, as if I'd asked him why he's here.

'OK,' I say, matching his folded arms.

'Poppie wanted me to say hello.'

'Well, you haven't said hello; you've pointed out that I was laughing at Mia's work.'

'Well…hello then.'

'Hi,' I force a smile.

'It's weird seeing you in a professional environment,' he says now, walking in and looking round.

'Thank you?' I furrow my brow.

'Your classroom is very tidy,' he says, examining the wall displays.

'Why do you sound surprised?' I ask, still seated and tighten my folded arms.

He turns to me and sits on a desk near the back. 'I thought it might reflect your mind more…' My eyes narrow, daring him to insult me. 'A little scattered,' he continues with a crooked smile.

Standing up, I feel my hand subconsciously move to the

stapler. 'I said to Poppie that I would be nice to you but you make it so impossibly hard. I—'

'Oh, come on,' he cuts me off from his seat, 'you know you like our banter really,' he's now swinging his legs gleefully.

Taking a deep breath, I move my hand away from the stapler. 'I do, do I?'

His slightly stubbled face forms into a full smile now, 'Yes, you do.'

'So,' I decide to change the subject. 'You probably won't be here that much will you, as you're just the architect.'

'*Just* the architect?' he repeats. 'Well, I'm assigned to look after the entire project; make sure everything's on track. So, no, I won't be here all day every day but you'll be seeing lots of me, I would imagine.'

'Great,' I say, deadpan. 'Well, I'm going to grab some lunch now so—'

'I'd love to join you, thanks,' he hops off the desk.

That's not what I meant.

'I don't know where the staffroom is,' he says now at my side.

'Haven't you already eaten?' I say as uninvitingly as possible.

'Oh no, Dermott's put on a spread for everyone.'

'He has?' I say.

'That's more the Melanie I know! Confused and slow on the uptake,' he says as we walk out of my class. I frown at him again. 'You want to be careful, Mel — if you keep looking at me like that you're going to age terribly,' his smile widens as my frown increases.

'Hi, Miss!' A small girl with freckles and pigtails walks past us with her lunch box.

'Hello, Mia,' I say.

'Oh, *Mia*, Miss Butler was just telling me how much she loved your artwork,' Craig chips in.

'Oh, you are something else,' I shoot him a fiery look as Mia goes skipping off down the corridor out of earshot.

'Yes, you're going to have to watch me, I feel,' he nods.

We walk into the staffroom and it's already full with happy voices and faces, all mingling with five other men that I don't recognise, who must be with Craig.

Jill leaves her seat and comes over with her plate, 'This spread is fantastic!' she says at me still munching something. 'Hello, I'm Jillian,' she directs at Craig after swallowing and extends her free hand to him. I smile as she never refers to herself by her full name.

'Nice to meet you, Jillian, I'm Craig,' he greets her so warmly I don't recognise him.

'Craig is the head architect on the sports project,' I say and he looks at me, impressed with the introduction.

'Oh!' she says, not letting go of his hand. 'Thank you so much for taking this on; we're so excited about it all!'

'No problem,' he says, trying to prize himself away from her grip but she still hangs on to him.

'I'm the sports specialist here,' she tells him with bright eyes, 'and this project is going to make a huge difference to the school. Dermott said that I could share my thoughts with you in regards to design, and I have *lots* of ideas; I can't wait to share them with you!' She finally lets go of his hand.

'Well, I can't wait to hear them,' he says politely, but I know he's being sarcastic and probably thinks she's just as barmy as me. 'I'm just going to grab some food, but I look forward to hearing everything in our meeting later. Bye, Melanie,' he adds to me before walking away.

'Well, he seems nice!' She guides me back to her seat 'And

141

cute too, I wouldn't say no, and he's learnt your name already.'

'Yup, he's known it for the past twenty odd years,' I say, helping myself to a cucumber stick on her plate.

'You know him? What a small world. How do you know him?' she says, moving her plate to the side to get it away from me — she hates sharing.

'Craig is Poppie's brother.'

'NO!' she looks round to take another glance at him.' But he's so lovely, how could he be *that* Craig?' she says with heavy disappointment. 'You never told me he's so good looking.'

'Well, it's hard to see the looks over the personality,' I say.

'Shame,' she looks back at me with a straight face, 'I have to hate him now.'

'No, you don't, don't be daft,' I cross my arms but am secretly happy at her taking my side.

'Well, I'll keep my eyes open, then.'

***

For the next two weeks, Craig only makes the odd appearance in between meetings in Dermott's office and of the handful of times I see him, he either nods in my direction or completely ignores me; I'm not sure if I'm offended or pleased. But Jill, on the other hand, is finding it increasingly hard to dislike him, as she tells me one morning break time when we're both on duty.

'He's just brilliant, Mel, brilliant! I'm so sorry, I know you don't like him, but my God, is he talented. He understood my terrible drawings and has transformed them into actual plans; it's exactly what I imagined.'

The morning that construction is due to start, Jill turns up in a bright pink helmet and matching fluorescent vest.

'I'm completely ready!' she says to us all over a morning brew.

'You know that you're not actually building it, right?' Dave says, holding back a smirk.

Gracie looks up from her phone, 'I think it looks cute; it shows your support for the project,' and then she gets back to messaging Pablo.

'Are you planning on teaching your lessons like that?' I ask, with no doubt that she would if she wanted to.

'I'd like to, but might get a bit hot doing a beep test.'

'I think you're the only PE teacher in the world who does the beep test *with* the kids,' I say to her.

'Well, why not? Best to get a work out when you can. Right. I'm going to visit the site before my first class!' and she skips out of the staffroom.

'She's insane,' Dave comments while sipping his coffee.

'We all are,' I say, standing up, '...all loonies happily working away in the asylum!'

Dave looks at his watch, 'Where are you going, you've got at least another nine minutes before you have to go anywhere.'

'Want to make sure everything's ready for this afternoon; I won't have time in the lunch break.'

'Why not?' Gracie pauses from writing her message.

'Because I'm meeting Julian for lunch!'

'After weeks of flirting by text, he's finally taken the time to ask you out again,' Dave states.

'He's just been busy at work, that's all.' I defend whilst staring at Dave. He hasn't mentioned Spain at all and neither have I; I'm secretly hoping that he's gone off the idea.

'Where are you meeting him?' Gracie brings me back

whilst swiping her finger quickly across her phone screen.

'That new cafe that's just opened up around the corner? Think we'll have enough time to get something quick before the bell goes.'

'Maybe we'll catch a glimpse of him, *huh*?' Gracie raises her eyebrows.

'Not unless you're in there with us.'

'No need to look so horrified!' Gracie takes in my expression. 'I meant if he's meeting you outside the gates or walking you back to school.'

'Oh,' I relax a little. 'No, we're meeting there; I don't think he'll walk me back.' Although now I secretly hope he will; that'll show Craig I live in the moment.

'Well, have a good time,' Dave says but his disgruntled face says something else.

The bell can't come soon enough for lunch time and I resist the urge to push past the kids to get out the door before them. I check my reflection in the loos and top up my lip gloss and mascara before heading out the gate. It's only a five-minute walk to Marco's, which doesn't give me long to try and calm the butterflies in my stomach. I spot Julian in the window seat before I've walked through the door. He's reading a newspaper and my heart does a little flip as I step over the threshold. 'You're early,' I say as I go over to him.

He stands up, pulls my chair out for me, his intensely blue eyes smiling into mine, 'Well, I haven't got you for long so wanted to make the most of it.'

Wow. No one has ever talked to me like that before. I smile back at him and then sit down.

'I'm glad we've finally managed to meet again,' he says, taking his seat once more.

'Me too.'

144

We spend a moment just looking at each other, like teenagers who clearly want to rip each other's clothes off but haven't quite gotten to that moment yet.

'Are you hungry?' he asks.

Very. 'Yes, I am,' I smile and gaze at the menu, feeling naughty for my last thought. We both order a panini and a coffee. 'Slightly different from the last time we ate together,' I say.

He looks around, 'I don't know, I think these people might appreciate a sombrero.'

'Maybe.' I smile, 'But I meant more the drinking; my head was a little fuzzy at work the next day,' I admit.

'It was your idea to have the last tequila,' he reminds me.

'It was?' I say with no memory of that at all. 'Well, that may be so but I think you were trying to get me drunk,' I say and narrow my eyes playfully.

'Is that so?' he says as our order arrives.

I think I could really like this guy.

'Speaking of sombreros and tequila, I got you a little something as a belated birthday present.' He fishes under the table and retrieves a little light blue gift bag with white handles.

'Oh, you shouldn't have!' I say out loud but reach forwards in excited anticipation.

'It's just something silly.'

Wrapped in tissue paper is a small bottle of tequila with a sombrero hat for a lid, accompanied by a DVD of *Only Fools and Horses.*

Laughing, I reach across the table and take his hand, 'Just what I've always wanted!'

'It's a reminder of our first date. Perhaps next year I'll be able to get you a real present.'

Wow. 'Well, thank you; that's really very sweet of you. You think we'll still be seeing each other then?' I tentatively dare to ask before letting go of his hand and taking a sip of coffee.

'I'd like to think so.' His eyes twinkle at me. 'Don't you?'

I pause for a moment. 'Yeah,' I grin at him like a fifteen-year-old. 'I maybe think so.'

He mirrors me, picking up his coffee cup, and smiling with his eyes, 'You maybe think so.'

'Yes. Maybe.' I nod, leaning back in my chair and feel completely in control.

'Well, I accept the challenge to see if I can turn that maybe into an absolutely. But in the meantime, I was wondering if you have any plans for Bonfire Night?' He takes a bite out of his chicken tikka panini.

'Bonfire Night? That's like a month away.' I haven't ever thought that far ahead.

'Well, I wanted to get in there and ask you before you made any other plans.'

'Oh, I normally go to the Heath with my friends from work. What were you thinking?' I ask him.

'I host a fireworks party at my house every year for friends and family.'

'You want me to meet your friends and family?' I ask, not sure if I'm terrified or excited.

He shrugs and smiles. 'Yeah. It's just close friends and considering you've already met my sister, there's just her husband and children.'

Well, that's not too scary.

The rest of lunch is divine; I can't remember the last time I laughed so much. By the time he's paid, walked me to the school gate and kissed my cheek once more, I'm left floating back to my classroom. Sitting back at my desk, I'm pretty sure I could get completely smitten.

For the rest of the afternoon my kids are confused as to why I'm in such a good mood and their whispering makes me smile even more; I even cut the last lesson short to play a game before letting them go.

After school we all have a meeting to discuss the latest on the sports unit, but first, I rush up the stairs to Dave's room to tell him about my date.

'He seems a bit keen, doesn't he?' Dave doesn't meet my eye as he packs his class's books into a bag to go home.

'Yea. But, maybe that's a good thing?'

'Maybe.' He's short and distracted.

I pick up a white board marker on his desk and play with it, 'Why are you being weird? Did you have a bad day?'

He looks up sharply. 'I'm not being weird. Come on, we're going to be late.' Dave grabs his jacket, shoulder bag, the bag full of books, then leaves his classroom hastily, heading for the stairs.

'Wait!' I yell after him, throwing down the pen and grabbing my bag. 'What the hell's wrong?' I jog to catch up and he pauses at the top of the stairs.

'Will you just stop asking me questions?' Dave shifts the bag full of books angrily from one hand to the other.

'OK, well, let me take something for you; you're carrying too much.' I go to grab the bag and Dave throws his hand back so swiftly, he loses his balance and dives down the stairs. I'm frozen to the spot, hands over my mouth, screaming.

Classroom doors fly open along the Year Six corridor, and soon a crowd of teachers, including Jill, has gathered around the limp body at the bottom of the stairwell. Finding my mobility skills, I run down the stairs, pushing teachers out of the way to get to him.

On my knees I yell, 'Oh my God, Dave, are you OK?!'

'I'm not deaf, Mels, but I'm pretty sure that I've twisted or broken something.' I look at his slightly contorted body and try to ignore the wave of nausea that oscillates through me.

'Excuse me, please.' Dermott's voice can be heard through the commotion and he bends down over Dave, 'What happened?'

'I lost my footing and just took a dive,' Dave says with a bit of strain.

'I'm going to call for an ambulance,' Dermott whips out his phone and stands up to dial.

'*Ah* diddums!' Jill says giving his cheeks a pinch before laughing. 'Didn't have you down as the accident prone one.'

She shoots a look at me and I furrow my brows. 'I told him he should have given me something to carry down the stairs.'

'Maybe I've been hanging around you too long and you've taught me how to be a klutz.' He nods, '*Um*, yeah that's probably what it is.' Dave looks at me sadly then pulls me in to whisper, 'Maybe I should go to Spain before I really hurt myself?'

'Can you move?' Gracie arrives, looking down at him, most frightened.

'I'm not sure—' Dave begins, but Dermott, who's still on the phone, cuts him off,

'Don't move; they've said to leave you just as you are. OK, thank you very much,' he says into the phone before hanging up. 'An ambulance should be here in ten minutes. They said to give him some room—' he looks pointedly at the gaggle of women. 'The meeting will still go ahead, everyone; I'll ask our lead architect to run through everything with you while I accompany Mr Wright to the hospital.'

Dave gets a proper send off with all the members of staff in the playground; thank goodness no children were here to witness this! Apparently, our meeting consists of venturing around the site; most of the staff are wearing hard hats and vests to match Jill's (still fresh from this morning, despite the beep test), all in varying colours. Picking up a purple one I give Dave a kiss on the cheek before he's loaded into the ambulance. Dermott addresses the crowd. 'Thank you all for staying, everyone. Craig,' he gestures to his right, '…is doing a fantastic job at making this become a reality. He will fill you in with the progress and plans thus far. Melanie, while I remember, can I have a quick word please?'

With no idea what it's about, I make a face at Gracie, before going over to him. He takes me to one side as Jill holds Craig in an intense conversation.

'There's nothing particularly wrong,' he says to me with a low voice, clearly clocking my expression. 'It's just that you forgot to sign out when you left the school for lunch today.'

'Oh. Sorry, I wasn't thinking.'

'Understandable; he was very cute,' he says to me, winking, and I find myself blushing furiously. 'Just make a conscious effort next time,' he says to me in the most unthreatening voice (not so much a telling off but a request), before he hops into the ambulance.

Craig shifts his weight ever so slightly and nods at everybody; I know when all attention is on him, it makes him nervous. My eyes then fall onto Jill who's taken her place next to him and is practically gushing; she really needs to get herself together.

'So, what I'd like to do,' Craig clears his throat, 'is to very quickly give you all a tour, show you what is going to go where, and how it's all going to look in the end.'

149

We follow Craig around the site, which currently consists of a frame and piles of materials, and are told (mainly by Jill), to imagine the gym hall, changing rooms, her office and the equipment room.

As everyone is leaving, I feel the need to say well done to Craig so hang back to talk to him.

'She's quite something, your friend,' he says, before I have a chance to say anything.

'Don't be rude. Jill's been wanting this for years — she's just got a lot of ideas.'

'You're telling me. I stupidly gave her my email and I'd safely say I know almost everything about her.'

'Well, serves you right for giving it out.'

'*Umm.*' He narrows his eyes ever so slightly at me, 'So who was that fella you were with earlier?'

So, he saw me. 'Who? Dave?' I play dumb, knowing exactly who he's talking about.

'No, not stretcher, I've seen you with him millions of times. You were at the gate with him.' He looks at me, '...around lunchtime,' he adds as if that would jog my memory.

'Oh. That was just someone I'm seeing at the moment,' I say casually as we start walking back to the school.

'Can't remember his name, *huh*; were you daydreaming at the time he mentioned it?'

'Oh, shut up,' I snap at him. 'Why do you care anyway?'

He considers this before bluntly saying, 'I don't particularly.'

Ouch.

'Just curious, I guess,' he adds with a shrug. Neither of us say anything until we reach the main building and he opens the door for me. 'But I would say he's too tall for you.' I look at him blankly. 'Or you're too short for him,' he continues; I walk past, hitting him in the stomach.

Chapter 16

October passes by in a literal and figurative blustery fashion, but that day seems to mark a change in dynamic between Dave and me. His confirmed strained knee and ankle mean he has to hobble about on crutches for a few months, and I honestly think he might blame me for what happened. I try to ignore this by focusing on my relationship with Julian and also by discussing with Gracie how Jill seems to be spending every break and lunch time at the sports unit with Craig and his team. But nothing can deny the fact that Dave is becoming increasingly more withdrawn from me; I miss my friend.

Julian came to the pub to meet everybody after work — just after Halloween — and Dave seemed snappy the entire time. Thankfully Julian had to leave to get an early night, so, after kissing him goodbye, I offer to get drinks for everyone and take the opportunity to corner Dave at the bar.

'What is your problem?' I bark at him slightly louder than intended, so the new guy behind the bar looks up to have a listen.

'What d'you mean?' he says to me, sipping his merlot.

'You were vile to him the whole time he was here,' I say, paying the now frightened looking barman.

He shrugs. 'I wouldn't say I was vile; *unfriendly* maybe, but not vile.'

'But why? Don't you like him? Don't you think he's good for me?' I ask with sad eyes and sink into the empty bar stool.

He cocks his head at me, 'I'm sorry. He was fine. Nice even. Definitely like him a lot more than Evan,' he sips again.

'Well, why were you rude then? You're meant to be one of my best friends.' I take my wine and glug a little.

'I'm *um*, I don't know. I've just been a little bit preoccupied. And I'm tired. And a little grumpy. He seemed like an easy target, that's all. Come on, I'm sorry, let's join the others again.'

'No. You've been really weird with me recently. What's going on with you?'

He opens his mouth to say something and then closes it again as if battling with something in his head. 'I told you, I'm tired; my leg hasn't given me the opportunity to sleep very much. That's it.' He stands up, leans his forearm on his left crutch, then holds out his hand for me to accept.

'I don't believe you,' I say, taking his warm hand and he pulls me out of the chair. 'You no longer wince when you move on those crutches now.'

'Well, it's getting better, it wasn't before,' he says, starting to get irritated.

'Fine.' I stand facing him and match his irritation. 'Lead the way then.'

Things don't improve between us after that and I'm pretty sure he's started to avoid me. I want to tell him how nervous I am, not only about going to Julian's place for the first time tonight but about meeting his friends and family. And to add serious insult to injury, Craig has started to be nice to me. He keeps holding doors open for me and today he waved me over when I was walking through the playground.

'Poppie's on the phone — she wants to say hi,' he grins away at me.

After I've caught up with her and found out that Michael

has completed the extension for her yoga studio, I hand the phone back to Craig.

'What's that face for?' He asks me.

'I don't understand you. You've always been horrid to me; why are you suddenly being nice?'

'Like I've said to you before, I am always nice to you; you just miss it behind my teasing. You choose to focus on actual words rather than the context behind them.' He leans back on the now fully-formed front entrance to the sports unit, waiting patiently for me to respond.

I exhale. 'Why do you always feel the need to analyse me.'

'You're easy to analyse.'

'Stop it!' I exhale again. 'I haven't got time for this; I have to get ready to go out.' I turn to walk away.

'Are you going to the fireworks on the Heath?' he asks my back.

I turn around. 'No,' is all I offer.

'All right then,' he straightens up, 'well, have a good time with Julian.'

'Thank you. Wait; how do you know his name?'

'I talk to my sister,' he says simply.

'And discuss me?' I fold my arms; I hate it when people talk about me.

'Sometimes.' He looks at me and seeing my hurt expression continues, 'I said I'd seen you with someone and she told me his name. And she might have mentioned that you're nervous about meeting his family and friends, which by your paler than normal complexion, I'm guessing is tonight.'

Not knowing what to say, I stay silent.

'But people seem to like you regardless, so I don't think you'll have a problem.'

I still don't know what to say — this new Craig has completely thrown me.

'Well, you'd better get going then,' he starts busying himself and tidying tools around him.

'Yes, I'd better,' I say, finally finding my voice. 'Thank you.' I walk off and suddenly feel rude although I've no idea why. 'Have a good weekend,' I say over my shoulder and he looks up.

'You too,' his usual cheeky grin doesn't seem as offensive, for some reason.

***

When I arrive outside Julian's semi-detached Georgian property, I'm so full of nerves I think I'm going to be sick; if they are anything like Evan's friends and family, I'm running the other way. Ringing the doorbell of Flat A, I wait nervously, hugging the bottle of wine I've brought with me. The door opens and Julian greets me with a warm smile.

'Hi! Come in, come in!' He pulls me through the door and into the hallway. 'Are you OK?' his expression changes when he looks at my face properly.

'I'm fine. Just a little nervous,' I admit with a small smile as I unbutton my coat.

'Oh, there's nothing to be nervous about; everyone will love you!' he says kindly.

'Thanks, well, this is for you,' I hand him the wine.

'Australian,' he says, impressed, looking at the bottle. 'Nice, thank you.' He takes my coat, hangs it up on a decorative coat rack, and then takes my hand as he leads me through a long corridor, towards what I'm guessing is the living room.

'You've got a lovely home,' I say as we now walk past a floor to ceiling bookcase and I take in a few thrillers and history books among mainly travel guides.

'Thanks. I've lived here for two years but it's just started to feel like home after my sister insisted I give it a makeover and start to add some of my touches.'

'So where have you felt the most at home?' I ask, looking at some mounted aboriginal masks.

'*Erm*,' he stops to think, then breaks into a smile, 'Probably Perth, Australia.' He lifts the bottle of wine. 'I think the lifestyle suits me more than it does in London — too many grumpy faces — I think people should lighten up; life's too short, you know?' I nod but I think to myself, I'm normally quite content to be one of those grumpy people bustling through London.

We walk through an open doorway to his living area which is full of happiness and laughter. Small groups of people are everywhere talking animatedly, enjoying each other's company; I feel my shoulders relax a little. 'Wow, this is gorgeous.' We move through the open plan room past the living space, a small dining area with a table spread full of snacks and nibbles, and finally alongside a patio door to the garden, right next to the kitchen; I take a seat on one of the bar stools.

'Yeah, it does have something about it now that was missing,' he looks around momentarily to take in his home and then his eyes fix on me for a moment longer than they probably should. I'm not sure if my cheeks heat up visibly but thankfully, at that moment, he turns and puts my bottle in a high cupboard. 'We'll save this one and maybe have it together another time? So, what can I get you to drink? Wine? Beer?'

'A white wine, please.' He swings open the fridge and takes a fresh bottle out, opens it with ease, and pours into an empty glass in front of me with one hand. 'You look like you've done that before,' I say, taking it gladly.

'I did a little bit of bartending when I was in Thailand,' he says with a grin. 'Are you hungry? I made soup and bread if you'd like some.' He turns back to the fridge to put the bottle away and grabs a beer for himself.

'You *made* soup and bread?' I'm slightly sceptical.

'Yes,' he says confidently.

'All from scratch?' I'm rather impressed.

'Yeah. I like experimenting in the kitchen.' He takes a swig.

'So, you're actually a good cook?' I say, taking a sip of the Chenin Blanc.

'Well, you can try some and tell me for yourself. Why?'

'It's just, this is coming from the man who said he needs my help on choosing appropriate food.' I do like flirting with this man.

'Well, you've caught me.' He holds up his hands. 'As much as I love jumping into burning buildings, I'm actually considering a career change by opening up my own restaurant; although I haven't really told many people that yet,' he adds.

'Wow. What kind of restaurant?' This man gets more and more interesting.

'Well, see that's the issue! I like cooking too many things, I can't quite decide what my niche should be; you need an angle really to succeed in that business.'

'You should have him cook his home-made ravioli for you.' A rather radiant pregnant woman with the exact same hair colour and style as mine sits down in the adjacent bar stool and extends her hand. 'I'm Charlotte, Julian's sister.'

She looks a lot more approachable than when I first saw her.

'Hi, nice to meet you,' I say, accepting her hand and shaking it. 'I'm Melanie.'

'I know,' she smiles at me. 'My little brother may have mentioned you a few times. Can you pass the orange juice, please?' she says playfully and raises her eyebrows at him; he narrows his eyes at her. I'm not quite sure how to take that; was that a compliment?

I change the subject, 'So my eldest niece is in the same dancing school as your girls.'

'Oh, Jocasta and Gilly love it there. How old is your niece?'

'Almost seven.'

'*Ah*, she's in Jocasta's class. What's her name? Thanks,' she adds, accepting the carton from Julian and pours it into a nearby empty wine glass.

'Lucy.'

'Oh, Keeley's daughter?'

I nod.

'She's a little sweetheart.'

'Thanks, I think so.'

'I don't know your sister very well, though — we don't see much of her — she's always rushing around.'

'Yeah, that sounds like her.' I sip my wine, not wanting to go into the fact that although she's put aside the idea of divorce, her relationship isn't exactly thriving.

'Well, tell her from me that we'd love her to come to breakfast with us — a few of the mums and I grab something quick and have a gossip while the girls dance,' she explains.

'That sounds nice. I'll tell her. Although with the other two kids, I know it's a challenge sometimes.'

'Oh, she can bring them along if she wants! I bring Gilly

when Jocasta is dancing. So, Julian tells me you're a teacher,' she moves on so quickly all I do is nod. 'I was a teaching assistant for a while but after having Gilly and now with another one soon,' she strokes her bump, 'Joe — my husband — and I decided that I'd stay at home. But I miss it. I'm bored, I think. Not of the kids, but sometimes you need to do something for yourself.' She takes a sip.

'Is your husband here?' I ask, wanting to get introductions out of the way as quickly as possible.

'Yes.' She spins the chair around faster than I think a pregnant lady should and tries to spot him. 'No idea where, but definitely here somewhere. Maybe I should see where he's got to; he has a way of losing himself. Well, nice to meet you properly.' She stands up and refills her glass a little more before she goes. 'Thanks, bro, see you in a bit.'

'Beyond her Saturday breakfast with the dancing mummies, she doesn't get out much, so she's making the most of it,' he says, with a hint of embarrassment but mostly affection.

'I think she's lovely,' I say honestly. 'How far along is she?'

'About twenty weeks now, I think.'

'Did she find out if she's having a boy or girl?' Keeley did each time; she didn't want a surprise like some people do.

'Another girl,' he smiles. 'Another girl to spoil.' He looks at me and smiles even more broadly. 'So,' he leans on his elbows, inching his face closer to mine, lowering his voice. 'Now we've hidden in the kitchen a little, would you like to meet some of my friends?'

'I'd love to,' I say brightly. 'Especially since I'm now feeling less nauseous.'

His friends are so welcoming, I feel right at home and

completely silly for building this up to be such a big deal. Before I know it, I'm chatting easily with his next-door neighbour over soup, (which is absolutely delicious), playing a competitive athletics game on the Wii with some of his university friends, (slightly regretting the soup at that point), and laughing with some school friends about stories from days gone by. It's as if I have always been here and these people have always been my friends.

'Uncle Julian!' Two little girls sing at him, the taller one I'm guessing is Jocasta and the smaller, slightly podgier one, must be Gilly. Jocasta pulls on his sleeve to get his attention, 'Can we please play with the sparklers now?'

'You haven't used them yet? I thought you'd already done that?' He smiles at both of them and you can see the love in his eyes.

They shake their little heads in unison, 'No, we were waiting for you,' Gilly says and her mousy blonde pigtails bounce as she tilts her head to one side. I can see that she might just walk completely over Uncle Julian.

'All right, let's do it! Fancy a sparkler?' he says to me.

'Absolutely! Are there enough for me to play with too?' I ask them both. Gilly nods but Jocasta makes a face at me. 'Although you'll have to remind me what I'm supposed to do, because I haven't played with one of these since I was in Brownies!' I say to them.

'I've just become a Brownie,' Jocasta says, her face now forming into a smile.

'And I will be a Brownie when I'm old enough!' Gilly joins in.

'Well, let's get our coats and go outside!' The girls run off towards the garden and Julian goes to get our coats. 'You really are very good with children,' he says when he returns.

I shrug as I put mine on. 'It's my job.' He doesn't say anything in response to that but he does squeeze my hand as we walk towards the patio door. Outside the temperature has noticeably dropped; I pull my coat even tighter around me and stand near the wood fire burner that's in full swing.

'OK.' Jocasta comes over to me and hands me a sparkler. 'So, what you need to do is hold it here and light it here.'

'Well, that doesn't sound too hard, thanks,' I say.

'Are you ready?' Julian says to us all, holding a lighter.

'Yes!' we all shout with equal enthusiasm. He lights the girls', and then mine and lastly his; they all start sparkling in the black of the garden.

'Now what you need to do is move it from side to side,' Jocasta instructs; Gilly follows her exactly.

'Like this?' I imitate her.

'Yup, very good. Come on, Uncle Julian, you're not doing anything!'

She's right, he's just standing there watching us. 'Sorry, JoBo, carry on,' he smiles at me and she continues like a bossy teacher.

'So, like I was saying, side to side to begin and then you can make a figure of eight like this.' She shows us and we all copy obediently.

'And now you can draw anything you like,' she says, waving hers all over the place.

'How about writing your name?' I ask.

'Yeah!' she giggles and both girls write their names over and over again as fast as they can before they disappear into the night.

'So, you could write sentences?' Julian says to me.

'Yes, I suppose you could,' I say, midway through writing my name.

He stands right next to me and starts waving his sparkler, drawing white letters into the air:

I-'d r-e-a-l-l-y l-i-k-e t-o k-i-s-s y-o-u.

We both lock eyes and then look over to the sisters. They're still giggling away and completely oblivious of us adults, so he leans in towards me slowly. I can feel the warmth of his body as he draws nearer, now inches from my face…

'*Ahhhh*, mine's gone out!' We break away before Gilly turns to us with a sad face.

'There are more inside, pumpkin,' Julian says, giving me a longing sideways glance.

'But we don't know where! Can you go and get them, please, Uncle Julian?' Gilly tilts her head in the same manner she did before and sure enough it turns out she does get what she wants, as Julian heads back to the house. As he goes in, a few smokers come out and I feel that the moment has most definitely sizzled out, like Gilly's sparkler.

After we've played with three more sparklers each, Julian's friend Tylor announces that everyone should go outside for the firework display.

'We've done this every year since we came back from Vietnam,' Julian tells me excitedly before he goes over to Tylor for final preparations. 'This time, everyone here has brought something — don't worry about it,' he adds when he sees my face, 'I didn't tell you and we've bought four mini displays between us as our finale!' He turns to help and then spins back to me, 'You OK on your own for a few minutes?'

'Of course,' I smile at him, touched that he asked. 'I might use your loo, though, quickly, before it starts.' And maybe send a quick update to Mish.

'Through the living room.' He directs with his hands, 'Out to the corridor and it's just on the right.' Back inside, the apartment is still, as everyone is excitedly chatting outside, waiting for the display. I get my phone out to message Mish and walk to the bathroom; I might give her a quick call, I decide as I open the door.

'Oh! I'm so sorry,' I see Charlotte sitting on the closed toilet seat with her head in her hands.

She jumps at the sound of my voice and looks up at me, 'No, no, it's all right, I'm nearly done here.' Her eyes are red and puffy and it's clear that she's been crying quite heavily for some time.

I stand there awkwardly for a moment without knowing what to say. The first thing that comes to mind is, 'The fireworks are about to start if you wanted to go and watch them,' I say softly, quite aware that she clearly has no desire to do that.

'Oh, thanks,' she says politely and reaches over to the toilet roll to blow her nose with, 'I'll make it out in a moment; I just need to get myself together.'

'Can I help?' I ask, although I'm not sure how.

She smiles at me gratefully and then her expression changes into somewhere between torture, anger and sarcasm, 'Can you help the fact that I'm sure my husband is having an affair? Not sure you can,' she shrugs and I feel so uncomfortable that again, I have no idea what to say.

'I'm sorry,' she carries on after a toot of her nose. 'Didn't mean to lash out like that.'

Walking fully into the bathroom, I close the door. 'Why do you think he's having an affair? He's here now, isn't he?' I ask, sitting on the side of the bath.

'He was here, but said there was a—' she pauses either to find the word, or is struggling to believe the next word, '*crisis* at his office that he had to help with.'

Victoria Mae

'At 9:30 at night?' I say without thinking and she nods.

'Exactly. A believable story, right?' she says with more sarcasm than before. 'He is so uninventive — how stupid does he think I am?' she asks me with angry eyes.

'Well, maybe it sounds so far-fetched because it's the truth?' I venture, not quite believing my own reasoning.

'Really? I'm not so sure any more.' She sounds worn-out and stands up to look at herself in the mirror. 'Oh my God, I look so old,' she says at her reflection, pulling the skin over her cheekbones up.

'No, you don't,' I say honestly. 'Anyone who works full time as a mum is a hero in my book.'

'You really don't need to be so nice, but thank you,' she adds and smiles at me from the mirror. 'Right.' She's talking to herself now, not me, and wipes her face with her hands to get rid of any lasting evidence of tears before opening her bag and bringing out some make-up to freshen up.

'Well, I'll leave you to it,' I say, ignoring the fact that I actually need the loo.

'No, no, please stay, I won't be a moment — and didn't you need the toilet?' she adds observing a little dance I'm doing.

'Yes, just remembered, apparently!' I say, realising that I am in fact dancing.

She laughs and gives me a soft, regarding look.

'What?' I can't help but ask.

'I think you're very good for my brother,' she says.

'Thanks.' I'm quite taken aback; no one's ever said that I'm good for someone before.

'And don't tell him I told you this because he would kill me, but he really likes you, like, *quite a lot*,' she says, with emphasis on the last part of her sentence.

'Oh?' is all I can manage. Am I ready for this to turn serious? Do I feel the same?

'I've freaked you out, haven't I?' she says looking at me in the mirror.

'Maybe a little,' I admit.

'Sorry I'm being so forward, I think it's the pregnancy, or maybe that I want two people to be happier than I am and if you've got a shot at that, why beat around the bush? Life is too short.'

'He said that when I arrived.'

'Well, it's true. If you like him then go for it and make the most of it.' She packs her make-up away and you would never know that she had been crying. 'All yours.' She stops in front of me. 'Thank you, Melanie,' and gives me a hug before walking out. When she's gone, I lock the door and freshen up. As I'm washing my hands, I look at my reflection; I do look a lot happier than before. It's OK to be a little nervous; the best things happen out of your comfort zone, Poppie has always told me. I should stop trying to over-analyse everything and just let things happen.

When I'm back in the garden, the fireworks have already started and I can't spot Julian, so I stand happily by myself near the fire burner and gaze up, like I did in Spain, in awe and wonder at these colourful explosions in the sky. I've always thought fireworks were magical; they make you forget everything as you stand still and wait excitedly for the next one. I feel some warm arms around me; turning, I lift my head up, to face Julian.

'Did you get lost?' he asks.

'I was talking to your sister,' I say, deciding not to tell him much more.

'I see.' Being surrounded by little women, I guess he's

learnt not to ask questions.

We stand and watch the dance of light in the night sky and I '*ooh!*' and '*ah!*' with everybody as the display gets increasingly impressive. I snuggle deeper into Julian's arms. Feeling nervous but wonderful, I turn my head and face up to look at him. He bends down and I stand on my tip toes, still wrapped in each other's arms, our faces near and this time I know it's about to happen. His lips gently meet mine and we kiss softly at first and then a little deeper. There's an odd tightness in my stomach, but I try to ignore it as we're so in sync it's like we've done this our whole lives. My lips break into a smile, mid-kiss,

'Something wrong?' he asks, now kissing my bottom lip. I shake my head, still smiling and we kiss once more.

Chapter 17

I'm floating on air for the next couple of weeks. Nothing can bring me down, not even when it's my class's turn to put on an assembly; nor when I'm told all the Year Four teachers (which includes only Dave and me), have to organise a school trip. Both of these things normally send me into a tizzy, but for the first time, I feel extremely relaxed and from nowhere, I'm suddenly a clear-headed, inspired young woman. Dermott commented on how informative and inventive my assembly was and with the school trip due to happen at the end of the month, (and since Dave has wanted even less to do with me), I have taken charge of everything — booking and planning — all by myself. When I try to get Dave's opinion on something, he just nods and says, "Sounds fine" without any input whatsoever. Things with Dave get so frosty that I stop asking him what he thinks and just go with my gut. I keep telling myself that whatever it is that's bothering him, he will tell me in his own time and I just have to let what will be, be.

It's not until the day before the school trip that I finally corner Dave and get him to agree to meet me in the staffroom at 7:30 a.m. the next day to finalise plans for the day.

'Fine,' is all he can muster before he walks off and leaves me standing in the corridor wondering if things will ever go back to the way they were. I don't seem to understand what's happening in my life: Dave is becoming a distant memory and I've been talking more with Craig, who is becoming increasingly nicer as every day passes. As I walk over to the sports unit, I think about the Monday after the firework party at Julian's; Craig raced, yes raced, over to me to ask how things went, and I've even been confiding some of my worries in him. Actually, wanting to go and chat with Craig is still a very bizarre concept to me: maybe I'm trying to replace Dave?

'How's it going?' I ask as Craig finishes yelling at some poor new Polish chap who skulks away when I arrive.

'Good,' he says brightly, 'when you don't focus on stupid little details.' His eyes follow the young man with daggers, then back to me, 'Anyway,' he says, smiling, 'how are plans going for the trip?' He gestures for us to sit down on two plastic chairs nearby. 'Want a coffee?'

'Sure, thanks. Yeah, everything's all set.' I stare out the window to the playground and see Dave hobble back to the main school building.

'Has he started helping yet?' Craig asks, following my line of sight while he pours some steaming dark liquid into disposable cups and walks over to me.

'Not exactly,' I say sulkily. 'But whatever, I'm doing such a good job on my own, it really doesn't matter if he decides to join in or not.'

'Modest as ever,' he sits down, handing me the coffee.

'Thanks.' I accept the cup and blow to cool it down. 'How's your day gone?' I ask.

'It's gone so well!!' A third voice comes from nowhere and Jill then bounces into view.

'Hey! Come and join us for a coffee,' I invite warmly, even though I know she won't; she hasn't in the last two weeks.

'Oh no, no, I couldn't, I'm just helping out Jakub here.'

'Who?' Craig asks, confused.

'Jakub.' She points towards the Polish guy Craig just told

off, who is now hiding in what will be Jill's office.

'He needs all the help he can get,' Craig says bitterly.

'He's lovely!' Jill says, 'Does anything I tell him to,' she adds.

'Well, maybe *I* should give *you* instructions to give *him,* because he can't seem to do anything correctly so far,' Craig blows angrily on his coffee.

'Will do! We're just getting the final floating shelving organised now,' she says to him and then adds to me, 'See you later,' before heading back in and launching into a full-blown conversation with Jakub.

'I thought Jill was a massive pain in the arse when I first met her—'

'Hey!' I defend my friend, but let him continue.

'But…she's been a real asset here; getting things done and almost doing my job for me, keeping everyone under control.' Craig leans back in his chair and rests his right leg across his left. 'Not that I would ever tell her that,' he adds quickly. 'So how are things going with Julian?' he asks and I'm comfortable but still finding this almost ridiculous how we've become nearly, dare I say it, friends?

'He's asked me what my plans are for Christmas,' I say and venture a hot sip, burning my lip. 'I do this every day!' I cry and run my tongue over my lip to try and cool it down.

'I know, I quite enjoy it,' his eyes sparkle at me.

'Me hurting myself?' I say.

'No, you being a bit daft. So, Christmas? Is he aware that it's not Christmas for about another month?'

'He likes to plan,' I say, almost defensive. Even though I'm happy, it does scare me a bit just how quickly our relationship seems to be developing.

'There's no need to freak out,' he says, obviously reading

my face.

'What are you doing for Christmas?' I say, wanting to direct the conversation away from me.

'No, don't divert the focus to me. So, what did you say?'

'I said I would think about what my plans were. He wants me to go to his sister's.'

'Right.' He contemplates this silently and I wait for a clever comment but instead he says, 'Do you want to go?'

I look at my lap, 'Yes.' I pause. 'I think so.' My head lifts slightly, 'I'm not sure. I'm confused…it feels a bit fast, really,' I decide to be honest.

'You need to be comfortable with where this is going,' he says to me. 'You need to decide what exactly you're doing with this chap because it's quite clear where he wants this to lead.'

My stomach does a flip. 'Really?' I add weakly, although I do know where he wants this to go. He keeps dropping hints about the future together and although I'm really enjoying being part of a couple again, quite honestly, I don't think I'm ready for that sort of commitment; but I'm hoping to sweep that under the rug for a while and ride on with blissful and naïve denial.

'You were telling me how he wants to go around the world with you — men don't just say that offhandedly — most men rarely say anything at all, even when they want to.' He takes a sip from his coffee. 'So, moving on from dream-boy, I should probably get back; better make sure Jill isn't planning an extension again without me.' He stands up and regards me sitting there for a moment.

'What?' I say to him.

'I don't know; there's something different about you.'

I put my hand up to my head, 'My hair's up today?' I venture and he grins at me again,
'Well, that must be it.'

***

'So, the coach arrives at 8:30 and we'll arrive at the Natural History Museum at 9:30...' I've been blabbing away for about five minutes non-stop with Dave vaguely nodding and looking at the printout for today that I did for him. I carry on with just as much enthusiasm, 'We've got six mums coming to help now—'

'Why six?' He continues to stare at his clipboard. 'I've got seven written down here,' he says shortly.

I ignore the tone and answer, 'Mrs Thompson left a voice message on the school phone this morning saying she's ever so sorry but she'll have to drop out.'

'She really needs to seek some help,' Dave says looking at me for the first time in what feels like months and my heart starts beating a little faster. 'I think she was drunk yesterday, picking up poor Casey.'

I shrug my shoulders gently and try not to look like I'm ecstatic that he's finally making eye contact again, 'Maybe. All her message said was she's not feeling very well. But she didn't sound too clever,' I add, wanting to agree with him so furiously so we can continue to talk like we used to, but then Dave stands up.

'Right,' he goes back to looking at his sheet, 'Anything else changed on this printout?'

'Nope, that's it,' I say, trying to lace my words with enthusiasm rather than disappointment that he's cutting this so short.

'All right, well.' He stops his own sentence and then says quickly, 'Thanks for putting this together,' his eyes still on his clipboard.

'Dave,' I say.

'What?'

'Please look at me.' His eyes slowly lower to mine and stay steadily there. 'We can't carry on like this; at least I don't want to, do you?'

He stays silent but shifts on his still plastered leg.

'We can't have a trip together and not talk to each other — the kids pick up on the littlest things; you're the one who's always told me that.' He still remains silent, so I decide to go for it. Screw him, taking his time to talk to me. My tone continues in a rather forceful manner, 'We need to be together on this. Plus, I don't want to sit next to you in uncomfortable silence for an hour. You know me, I'll probably start going into some external commentary that should most likely never be said out loud, never mind on a coach full of children, and with a poor driver, who, when you aren't talking to me, I'll most likely turn my attention to. But I want to know how you are, for God's sake; there are too many questions that I have. I have no idea how your stupid leg is or if anything has happened with Spain yet; I miss knowing what's going on in your life. Also, things are going on in *my* life that I want you to know about, be involved in, and I want to ask you things and tell you what's been happening. There was a funny story on the way here that I was dying to tell you about but after seeing your face, I remembered that there was no point. What's happened to you or what have I done to make you act this way towards me? Tell me and I can apologise, because this,' I pause for a breath and draw out the invisible line between us, 'cannot continue and I will not let it continue.

Behind the Clouds

You are one of my best friends Mr Wright and quite frankly, I think you're being a moron for absolutely no reason. But until you tell me the reason, I will just continue to think that you are in fact a big fat moron.'

He laughs a deep, hearty, warm laugh which again, feels like the first time in forever.

'And I've missed that laugh,' I say, standing up.

'So have I,' he admits, tilting his head at me and his eyes soften. 'I'm sorry I've been pushing you away,' he sighs. 'My stupid leg is better; I should be out of plaster by Christmas and I did put in an offer for the apartment in Malaga but everything fell through.'

'Oh no,' I say and find that I mean it. 'Why didn't you tell me?'

'You've been a little preoccupied lately, but hey, not meant to be, I guess. Plus, there's something else that—' he pauses, 'I want to tell you but I'm not ready yet and, *erm*,' he perches on the side of a red tub chair, 'I just need to sort some things out; that's all.'

'Can I help?' I offer, so desperate for things to go back to normality.

'I'll let you know if you can.' He smiles at me and for a moment we just look at each other until the silence is broken by the staffroom door. We look over to see Jill, hugging her clipboard.

'Morning!' she bounces over. 'They're starting on my office today! You're here early,' she adds, just realising that it's quite unusual for either Dave or me to be the first in the staffroom and she glances at Dave's paper. 'Oh yeah, it's your trip! Well, have a good time, I've got to dash.' She goes over to the coffee machine and refills her flask. 'Craig and I have a meeting now,' and with that she's gone.

'God, he must be sick of her,' Dave says, now getting to his feet.

'Nah, he thinks she's amusing. We've been talking,' I explain when he looks at me in surprise. 'I know,' I add when he raises his eyebrow. 'It's one of the things I wanted to tell you about.'

His face comes over all embarrassed and he puts his arm around my shoulders, 'Well, we've got a whole coach journey to catch up.'

'Yes, we have,' I say and my heart feels a little fuller.

The morning seems to go without a hitch: all kids have remembered a packed lunch and any medications or inhalers, and all adults are on time and raring to go. When we board the coach and I've read out the rules and expectations of the day, we settle in our seats. I'm just about to tell Dave about Julian and Christmas when we hit the biggest traffic jam I have ever seen. We're completely stationary for the best part of an hour and it takes a further hour to get to the Natural History Museum, so by the time we arrive we've got forty-eight kids (and eight adults) all busting for the toilet.

I have purposely put the nicest kids in my group so I'll have a great day with minimal fuss. Unfortunately, at the time of my organising this trip, I was still pretty mad at Dave so he, on the other hand, has all, and I mean all, of the difficult ones.

'Why would you give me all of them?' he whispers at me, after I've read out who's with who and instructed all the kids to line up to the right of the steps in their groups.

'Well, let's just say it's my way of showing how much you'd got to me over the past month.' I grin at him and feel a little guilty, but mostly justified.

All the kids are ogling over the ice rink as they assemble into their groups.

'Oh, I love the ice rink!' I cry with glee, allowing myself a moment to just stare at it and become just as excitable as the children.

'We're not going on it, are we?' Dave says, flicking through his activities for the day.

'Yes, I've got you a special sledge and your group are going to pull you along.' For a moment he looks at me, not sure if I'm kidding. 'Well, actually, I have spoken to someone about us using it after we've finished inside, but I thought I'd see how the day goes, see if they behave themselves, and then let it be a surprise treat if they've all been good. You can hold the bags,' I add, nodding at his leg. 'Unless you do like my original idea?' I love this. It's almost like normal.

After everyone has relieved themselves, we all reconvene under the hanging blue whale skeleton, in the main entrance.

'There used to be a Diplodocus here,' I hear one of my lovely girls in my group tell the others, 'nicknamed Dippy.'

'How did you know that, Lara?' I ask, impressed.

'I read an article,' she says, very Hermione-like.

Of course, you read an article, I think to myself and feel that I may be learning more than the kids today.

'No, we cannot go in the gift shop now,' I hear Dave telling Dylan — a particularly horrible child in my class — who is now stamping his feet. Dave catches my eye and I mouth, 'I'm so sorry,' at him and he narrows his eyes, but they're sparkling at least.

The sheer size of this building has always amazed me. I remember coming here on a school trip when I was about five. Poppie and I got in trouble for stroking 'Dippy.' Who would have thought that I'd be here as a teacher telling kids like me to behave themselves. I look at Dave who is hobbling around the gift shop after a delirious Dylan; impressive speed considering he's still in plaster. I shouldn't laugh, really.

We're met moments later by our guide for the day, Justin. He extends his hand to meet mine, 'Glad you've made it safely!' His dark hair frames his youthful oval face.

'I'm so sorry for our tardiness.' His hand is warm and rough and he waves my comment away with a shake of his head.

'Not at all. The travel news on my way here mentioned the accident, so I had a feeling it would hold you up. So, as we're a little tight for time now, I'd say let's move straight on to examining skulls...' I nod and adjust my list as we walk. '...gets them interacting and involved straight away rather than just a tour and I think we'll have to forgo the ice skating?'

'I agree, sounds great.' I finish scribbling and my group start shushing everyone; I nod at them gratefully as the noise settles.

'Everyone, this is Mr Brown.'

A whiny chorus combining, 'Good morning/good afternoon, Mr Brown,' followed by some giggly sounds and I raise my hand to silence them before continuing, 'Mr Brown is going to be our guide for the day.'

'Hi, kids! Now, hands up, who's fed up of sitting down?' Most of the kids and adults put their hands up. 'Me too, I've been sitting down all morning so far, so, who thinks they can help me organise some skulls?' A few squeamish girls leave their hands by their sides but the majority, again, all raise their hands to the ceiling. 'That is fantastic news!' he beams, 'So if you'd all like to follow me this way, we can get started.'

***

When we have a bite to eat, we sit in view of some art students sketching away. Eating my mozzarella, pine nut and pesto pasta salad, I wonder what it's like to be that creative. Just to sit there, not quite knowing where to begin but just being patient enough to let a blank page develop into something beautiful.

'Penny for your thoughts?' Dave comes to sit with me. 'Look at them over there. They're so into what they're doing; I wish I was that creative.'

'Well, you are.' Dave says matter-of-factly.

'I am?'

'Sure. You make the best creations in the kitchen. You can teach someone the basics but you can't teach them flair.' He bites into his plain white ham sandwich.

'That looks horrible,' I say at his dry, uninspiring lunch.

'I know,' he agrees. 'If I had you to sort me out, I'd be eating something a little more exciting.'

'Miss, Dylan is eating my chocolate bar!' Rosie cries at me. Kids know just when to interrupt you.

***

By the time we've had a tour of the insects and played in the interactive zone, it's time to head back on the coach. I'm ticking everyone off as they board and Dave's group is the last to get on.

'Not a bad trip, eh, Butler?' Dave says to me as they all file on.

'Where's Dylan?' I say, with my pen poised over his name.

'He's already on, isn't he? He was chatting with Bruce.'

'No. He didn't pass me,' I dash onto the coach and scan the seats then run off again. 'No, he's definitely not here.' I start to worry.

'Little bugger,' Dave says, turning around and looking around to no avail. 'And here I was thinking he'd turned a corner.'

'Oh, my God.' I look just to the right of Dave.

'What?' Dave follows my line of sight.

'He's on the sodding ice rink,' I say and march over with Dave hobbling to keep up.

'Dylan Michaels, get off of there right now!!!' I yell at him.

'Sorry miss, I can't hear you,' he cheekily retorts and glides off.

'Where did he get skates from?' Dave says, as we make our way to the main booth to access the rink.

'He must have manipulated someone into getting them. Excuse me please,' I say as we push through the queue. 'Excuse me, we've got a child on the ice rink—' I say to a tall muscular man who doesn't let me finish my sentence.

'So have lots of other parents, miss, may I suggest you and your husband observe from outside?'

'We're not his parents!' I say with outrage.

'He's on a school trip and snuck on somehow; please let us through,' Dave says and we push our way onto the entrance area.

'You can't go on in shoes…' the muscly man says. 'You have to put on some skates.' He points to a rack of shoes.

I throw my clipboard at Dave, whip off my pumps, and tie up skates faster than I thought was possible.

'Dylan!!' I say, from the mouth of the ice rink, 'You have no idea how much trouble you're in.'

He floats past with flair. 'Miss! You've come to join me! Now, tell me, can you skate backwards?'

He weaves past a hand-holding couple and I apologise as I

whisk after him. As I near Dylan, he picks up speed and I'm starting to realise how ridiculous I must look.

'You will come here this instant!' Dave says, looking on from the inside of the tent.

'Are you going to come and catch me, sir?' he laughs and spins around before coming to a stop to try and contain himself. Snorting back a laugh, then taking advantage of him being stationary, I pick up speed as he's now doubled-over laughing, and gracefully skid sideways to a halt right next to him, taking hold of his coat. 'All right, you've had your fun. Let's go.' Dylan admits defeat and comes peacefully.

'You're a good skater, Miss,' Dylan says, impressed as we walk towards the coach.

'As are you, Dylan,' I say, trying not to blush with the compliment.

As we approach, I see all faces pressed up against the windows, cheering. Dylan goes to raise his arms to greet his crowd and I stop him with a quiet, but meaningful, 'Don't you dare.' The coach erupts with whooping as soon as we set foot on and I silence it with a lift of my hand,

'OK, that's enough.' Adrenaline is still pulsing through my veins with each word. 'Dylan, you will sit here next to Mrs Collins for the journey home and I will spend my journey thinking of a suitable punishment for you.' He hangs his head but knows better not to say any more.

We set off and Dave is looking at me incredulously. 'What?' I ask.

'Since when do you skate — like *that*?'

I shrug, 'My dad used to take me and Keeley when we were little—'

'I know, you've told me before. That was more than a few classes worth of skating. We've been skating and you didn't do *that*.'

'Well, I may have won a few medals, but that was ages ago,' I say, playing it down.

'A few medals.' He considers me with his eyes somewhere between impressed and disbelieving.

'Why are you looking at me like that?' I feel quite uncomfortable.

'You're scatty and quite unbalanced at the best of times; that poised person performing on the ice wasn't the Mels I know.'

'Thanks.' I take the compliment and then a deep breath. 'My dad pushed us into competitions. I wanted so badly to please him, so I worked really hard and became quite good. But when I came up against kids who were better than me, my confidence started to wobble. And I think I realised it was his dream, not mine.'

'So, what was your dream back then?' he asks, waiting patiently.

'Oh, I don't know; I guess I wanted to bake. Or bake with my Nana; I liked learning from her. But I liked eating everything and then I gained so much weight, I wasn't exactly a dainty ice skater so I stopped.'

'Well, it all seemed to flood back to you,' he says. 'The skating, not the weight,' he adds quickly.

'Yeah, it did,' I smile.

We sit in comfortable silence before he breaks it. 'Thank you for handling him,' he lowers his voice. 'I'm glad you're here.'

'I'm glad you're talking to me again,' I say, honestly.

The journey back to school takes no time at all but it gives Dave and me a chance to talk about Julian and Craig.

'I've missed quite a bit, haven't I?' Dave says

apologetically.

'You have,' I agree. 'I actually look forward to seeing Craig...how ridiculous is that?'

'Considering that you were contemplating moving schools so you wouldn't have to see him every day, I'd say it's quite ridiculous.' He pauses. 'Are you happy with Julian?'

I fold my arms and shift a little in my seat. 'Yes.'

'But...?' he prompts.

'But, *erm.*' I scratch my nose while choosing my next words. 'I think he wants to move things on too fast. Maybe he likes me more than I like him — at the moment,' I add, feeling bad.

'He hasn't asked you to move in or marry him; he just wants to spend Christmas with you,' he says reasonably. 'There's nothing wrong with that.'

'For the first two years with Evan, he spent Christmas with his family and I spent it with mine,' I shrug. 'It just feels different.'

'Who said that's a bad thing?'

I don't answer as we pull up outside the school.

Chapter 18

Things with Dave return to just about normal. We're talking and laughing like we always have done, but there's still something that I know he's not telling me.

'I know he's struggling with something but for some reason he won't share it with me,' I tell Poppie when she rings me one particularly blustery Saturday at the beginning of December.

'Men don't like to talk about things that make them feel uncomfortable,' she says knowingly. 'Sounds like he is trying to come to terms with what it is. When he's ready, he'll let you know.'

'Maybe. Julian said something similar to that the other day,' I tell her.

'Well, he seems very wise. Are you seeing him this weekend?'

'No, he's on a stag do in Prague so I've got the weekend to myself. What are you doing?' There's an awful lot of clattering.

'I'm just helping Michael put up the new bannister,' she says, as if this were a normal everyday occurrence.

'Shall I call you back?' I ask, staring out my window, watching the last of the falling red and amber leaves dancing in the wind.

'No, no, I can hold this and the phone at the same time; I'm not doing the hard work, Michael is.'

'You're insane, you know that?' I smile down the phone and realise how much I miss her.

'If we were all not a little insane, life would be very dull.'

'I miss you. When can I see you next? Are you coming to London for Christmas?'

'We're going on a spiritual retreat over the Christmas period but I might come and see Craig before the New Year.'

'Any time to squeeze in one of your oldest friends?' I ask excitedly.

'Of course — we could all have dinner together or something?' she says.

'Awesome! When might you come?' I pull out a notepad and pen from the coffee table but there's silence on the other end. 'You still there?' I ask, clicking my pen.

'Yes,' she says slowly. 'I think I'm in shock. You've never been happy with the idea of seeing both me and my brother.'

'Well, I see him every day at school and we've been getting on...' I pause to find the right words, '...surprisingly well.'

'Well, who would have guessed it.' Poppie sounds quite delirious. 'I told you he's always liked you.'

'You did.' I start doodling a cupcake on the paper in front of me and then I jump as there's a big bang on the end of the phone. 'You OK?'

'Michael's just dropped something,' she says ever so casually.

'Is he OK?'

'Oh yes, but I think I'll call you back later,' she says dreamily.

We hang up and I continue to look out the window; it really is a beautiful day. Maybe I'll go for a walk? I grab my bag and wrap up warm, deciding to stroll to Greenwich Park. It's only about a half hour walk from my house, but shamefully I rarely go there; it's so easy to take things for granted.

I enjoy the scrunch of the leaves as I enter the gates and marvel at the odd runner having a workout. The sun is shining down, illuminating everything and even though the cool breeze is brushing my cheeks, I'm nice and cosy. I grab a hot chocolate from the kiosk near the Observatory and walk over to a bench to take in the view. *Gosh, this is a beautiful place. I love London.* I don't think I could ever consider leaving it, like Dave wanted to. Sure, the weather here is nothing like Spain and we don't have the mountains like they do, but it would take a lot to replace the grandeur of this view, in my opinion.

'*Mi scusi.*' An attractive young woman approaches me with a camera. 'I, *a, er, you take picture*?'

'Sure!' I put my chocolate down under the bench and standing, tell the family of five to huddle together and say cheese — which they don't as they clearly don't speak English — but they smile beautifully at me.

'*Grazie.*' She takes back her camera and I nod at her, smiling, as the family walk off arm in arm. I take my seat again and blow on my hot chocolate, starting to feel quite Christmassy — *ooh I could walk to the market maybe?* My phone beeps and it's a WhatsApp message from Julian.

"Hello you…"

I can hear his voice through the message:

"Just arrived at hotel. Journey interesting with half the stags already merry before we boarded…nearly didn't let us on! It's stunning here. Maybe we could talk about getting away at some point? What are you up to beautiful?x"

I smile at my phone; I like being called beautiful. But then I pause over the screen and hesitate before replying. Is a holiday a good idea? Again, it really all feels a bit too rushed for me.

"Hi. Let's talk when you get back...glad you've arrived safely and hope it doesn't get too rowdy! I'm in Greenwich with a hot chocolate. Have a great time."

I press send, realising as it goes that I've left off a kiss, and put my phone in my bag before making my way towards the market. As soon as I've zipped up my bag, my phone beeps again. Wow, Julian replies quickly. I scramble to get my phone out again. But it's a message from Nieve.

"Dude! Hope the new man is exciting you, mine still is..."

My little sister has such a way with words.

"...thought you'd like to know, saw Keeley and she was...wait for it...nice! I'd even go so far as to say...happy! The world is not the same. Maybe Simon finally got that promotion? Who knows. Anywho, love you and looking forward to seeing you at xmas :)"

I'm really looking forward to Christmas, it will be the first time in a long time that the three Butler sisters will all be in one place at the same time. And I'm also a little terrified, as it will be the first time in a long time that we're each bringing someone to dinner. Julian and I decided that we'd have lunch at his sister's and dinner at my parent's. Nieve is bringing her latest flame, who she met at her most recent job in a new bar in Shoreditch. The only thing I know about him is that he has a lot of tattoos and his name is Marcus.

I type a quick message back to Nieve as I continue my way down the hill and into the market. There's definitely a Christmas vibe already here; oversized baubles are hanging from the ceiling and the scent of cinnamon floats past me as someone is selling mulled wine.

It's very crowded in each aisle between the stalls and I happily move at a snail's pace with everyone else, allowing myself time to take in the hand-crafted gifts. I stop at a stall that sells vintage teacups that have been turned into candles. Keeley would love these. I'm pondering over a yellow or light blue flower pattern when I'm sure I hear Keeley's laugh. I look around and can't see her so continue, deciding that I must have imagined it, and go for the yellow. Maybe I can hear her laugh because I'm thinking about her. I thank the lady and wonder if there's anything in here I can buy for Nieve when I see Keeley being kissed on the cheek, and her smile drops as she sees me. Nieve was right, she is happy; ecstatic, in fact. Who wouldn't be when they're holding hands with and being adored by a handsome man. Unfortunately, that handsome man isn't her husband.

Keeley untangles herself from this stranger, he looks directly at me and his smile drops as well. I'm frozen to the spot and for a beat we all just stare at each other. Eventually she makes her way over to me and he, sensibly, stays where he is.

'Hi, Melsy,' she says weakly and gives me a hug that I don't return, 'What are you doing here?' I stare at her, lost for words. 'That's, *um*, a friend of mine.' She looks at me desperately, not wanting me to make a scene. I am still numb and look past her to him. Of course I can see the attraction, what girl wouldn't; his curly brown hair is as playful as his expression. 'He's helping me shop for...' she trails off as I look at her with a mixture of disappointment and disbelief. 'Please don't look at me like that. Please say something,' she adds.

'Oh, Keeley how could you?' I say with such sadness as I think of Simon and the kids. I look at this stranger, pretending to busy himself with some colourful handmade woolly hats.

'You don't understand. You've no idea how it's been.

Look, can I come to your house later and we'll talk?'

I manage a nod and she grabs me again, giving me the tightest squeeze. 'Thank you,' she says, almost tearful. She lets go of me and walks towards him without a backwards glance and they disappear out of my sight, leaving me standing quite speechless.

***

When Julian rings me later that day before having dinner with the stags, he knows something is wrong, but I can't tell him. Keeley has always been my role model and it's devastating to find out that she's not only flawed but she's committed the same crime that turned my world upside down.

'I'm fine, honestly, just think I might be coming down with something,' I lie to him.

'Well, if you're sure. I feel bad having a good time when you're feeling rubbish,' he says to me sweetly and ever so tipsy.

'Don't be daft, I'll get an early night and I'll probably feel just fine in the morning. You go and have a good time, OK?' I say to him, half thinking how sweet he is and half thinking he should grow a pair.

'All right, well, if you take a turn for the worse you ring me, it doesn't matter what time it is, OK?'

'OK,' I promise.

'I love you,' he says quickly. I'm speechless for the second time today. 'You still there?' he asks.

I don't want to answer. 'Yes,' I say in a very small voice.

'I'm sorry, I felt it so I wanted to say it. Don't worry, you don't have to say anything. I just wanted to say it,' he says quickly.

'Oh. Well, thanks.' I say, scrunching my nose and hope that doesn't sound too harsh.

'You're welcome,' he says warmly. 'Well, now that I've made us both feel uncomfortable, I will go.'

'You haven't made me feel uncomfortable,' I lie again.

'OK, good. Rest up and I'll message you tomorrow. Goodnight, you.'

'Goodnight,' I say and we hang up. I throw my phone away from me like it's a big spider. My God, Evan wouldn't move anywhere and now Julian wants to move too fast. I throw my hands over my head; this is ridiculous.

Before Keeley arrives, I decide to make my key lime pie as it's her favourite. I'm just putting it on a plate when the doorbell goes. When I answer it, her face is like one of my students who knows they're about to get told off.

'Hey,' she says weakly. 'I thought we might need this,' she holds up a bottle of wine.

'Come in,' I say and stand back to let her in.

'Thank you for not making a scene,' she says as she perches on my sofa.

'Who would I have been making a scene to?' I fill up the glasses that I had waiting on my coffee table. 'You don't know anyone in Greenwich.'

'That's why we went there,' she says and then grabs one of the wine glasses as if to shut herself up.

Taking a deep breath, I promise myself to reserve judgement until I've heard her side of the story. 'So?' I say. 'Go for it.' I grab my wine and sit down.

Keeley talks for about an hour without stopping. Telling me that Simon has finally got the promotion that they were hoping for, but instead of the hours letting up, they've got even worse. He now leaves before she wakes up and arrives back home after she and the kids have gone to sleep. All they've been doing is arguing for the last year and neither of them have been happy. Even the kids are starting to be affected by it.

'Who's looking after the kids today?'

'Nieve,' she says, with a voice as shocked as my face.

'Nieve?' I say disbelieving.

'I know.'

'She messaged me earlier and didn't tell me.'

She shrugs. 'She's been a Godsend, helping me out with the kids recently. And she's modest and thoughtful but still her quirky self. I think this new guy of hers might actually be a good influence.'

'Wow. Maybe our little sister is actually growing up?'

'Maybe,' she says, refilling her wine.

'So, you haven't exactly told me how this all happened. When it started...' I say, reminding myself that I will not judge until the end.

'I'm so sorry that you found out. I was just horrified to see you in the market,' she says.

'You know I live near there!'

'You've been spending so much time with Julian; I thought it was quite unlikely to see you there.'

Well, that's fair enough.

'So, Sebastian's someone I've known for a while. I was really upset one day, about a month ago and I bumped into him and he took me for a coffee and then, well, one thing led to another and...he makes me smile, Melsy. I can't remember the last time I smiled before him.'

'And he doesn't mind that you're married and have three children?'

'He's in the same position,' she says quickly and then picks up a pillow to hide behind.

'You're cheating on your husband with someone else's husband?' She stays silent. 'Has he got kids too?' Her eyes poke over the pillow and the pillow nods. 'What are you doing?' I grab the cushion away from her. 'You're trying to destroy two families!'

'I know. It's a mess,' she admits. 'It was only meant to be a one-time thing and I know it's gone too far now; I've been trying to break it off for ages.'

'Yeah, it really looked like you were trying in the market.'

'But that's the thing, he'll then surprise me or buy me something pretty and it's a lot harder to stay focused when you're holding something shiny.'

I thought she was the smart one. 'I can't believe that you're capable of being the other woman,' I say, disheartened.

'Neither can I,' she says sadly. 'But I had a chance to have a fleeting moment of blissful happiness and I selfishly took it; I'm human, it happens.'

'I know it happens, it happened to me!'

'Oh yeah, I'd forgotten that, sorry.' She puts her hand onto mine. 'I promise I'm going to break it off. I know I considered a divorce but I don't seriously want to leave Simon; he's my childhood sweetheart. I do want to try to make it work and I certainly don't want to hurt the kids or tear apart another family, either. I just selfishly wanted a bit of fun; I was starting to forget what fun was. I wanted to forget for a moment that I'm a mum, a wife, whatever, and just be carefree and reckless.'

'Why didn't you tell Simon you were so unhappy?'

'You don't think I tried?' She stands up and starts pacing the room. 'He just hasn't been there and Sebastian was. I'm not saying I did the right thing but it felt like it was at the time.' She stops pacing. 'Oh God, I need help,' she turns to me and her eyes are filled with tears. 'What if Simon leaves me?'

I go over and give her a hug but I'm not quite sure what to say. What if he does leave her? There's always a chance of that. 'You just need to be honest with him, I think. Hopefully he'll understand and you can all move on.'

Chapter 19

Promising Keeley I wouldn't tell anyone, gets harder and harder. Julian keeps suggesting what might be wrong and asking how he can help; Dave is now annoyed as he knows I'm keeping something from him (I told him we're now even), and Craig even notices something's different. 'What's up?' he asks when we arrive at school at the same time.

I exhale. 'There's just something that I've recently found out and it's, well, a bit crap and I can't tell anyone.'

'Right.' He opens his folder to a page and then looks back at me. 'What do you think of this for the girls' changing rooms.'

I furrow my brow at him. 'Don't you want to ask me more about what's bothering me?'

'No. You said you can't talk about it,' he says simply, 'so why would I continue to ask you more about it?'

I wish everyone would adopt that attitude, 'That's a *very* good question.'

But when I go over to Mish's for dinner that evening, I crack.

'Well, holy balls,' she declares whilst unpacking a take-away Chinese. 'And she hasn't told Simon yet?'

I shake my head. 'She's terrified to. But I know she's just going to let it fester until the shit really does hit the fan.'

***

Behind the Clouds

The following week is the final week of the term, which holds many little gems, the brightest being the annual Christmas concert. Scarlet, our poor music teacher, as hard as she tries, cannot get the little blighters to sing or play in tune or together. She spends the entire show flapping and perspiring with a look of sheer disbelief at the children's inaccuracies, but to every other member of staff, it's a real highlight of the year; the time to play: "who can keep a straight face for the longest". I glance at the programme and see we have the orchestra first, delighting us with their rendition of 'Jingle Bell Rock'.

'So, who d'you reckon? I've actually got a fiver on Silvia, it being her first concert.' Dave swoops down and examines the programme. 'Oh Christ, Dylan's doing a trumpet solo?'

'I reckon it'll be you,' I smirk at Dave's shocked face.

'Me?!' He shakes his head in disbelief, 'Oh, Miss Butler, I may still have an injury but you don't know who you're dealing with.'

Gracie and Jill file in with the last few members of staff and sit next to us.

'I think it will be Dave,' I say to them.

'I think she's finally lost it,' he retorts.

'I think it'll be Dermott,' Jill confesses, looking around. 'He's never played witness to this sort of carnage.'

'Oh no, he's far too together—' Gracie starts, but at that moment all the performers start filing in, followed by an exhausted looking music teacher.

'Here we go!' Dave says with glee.

The orchestra take their seats and as the opening bars offend the hall, we look around to see who's the first to crack. Everyone's doing well so far; I'm particularly impressed with Dermott, who raises his eyebrows only a fraction but his expression doesn't change. Just when we think it's over, half the orchestra puts down their instruments and then picks them back up quickly, as the other half of the group go back to the beginning of the song. Scarlet starts to wave her arms frantically and Silvia stands up and leaves the room quietly.

'Yes!' Dave whispers. 'I knew it!'

The rest of the concert takes out several of the lower year teachers and also Gracie whose shoulders shake so violently during the choir's rendition of 'Step into Christmas' she nearly falls off her seat.

'I think that was the best yet,' Dave says as we all leave the school still with tears in our eyes from the "pick any key you fancy" finale of 'White Christmas,' that came to its climax as Dylan fell back into the drum kit and a governor basically wet himself laughing.

'Oh, that was exactly what I needed,' I say, wiping a tear from my eye.

'I agree,' Gracie is blowing her nose, with her eyes still streaming with hysterical tears. 'My favourite part was the wind group.' We all burst out laughing as true to its name, three of them decided to fart simultaneously.

Jill contains herself, 'Right, I'm off now, everybody, see you in the morning.'

'You're not coming for a drink?' I say, rubbing my sides that are now hurting from laughing.

'I am, but with — now don't be mad —' she says quickly to me.

'Why would I be mad?' I ask, still giggling slightly.

'Because I'm going for a drink with Craig.'

'He asked you to have a drink with him?' My giggles stop. I knew that he was growing to like her, but not in *that* way.

'*I* asked him to go for a drink with *me* as a thank you. You don't mind, do you? Would you rather I didn't?' she asks, although her face says it doesn't matter what I say.

'Why would I mind?'

She brightens up, 'Great. Well see you all tomorrow then,' and she bounces off in the other direction.

'Interesting turn of events,' Dave says when she's out of earshot, 'I thought he'd end up punching her before asking her out.'

'Well, *she* asked *him* out, not the other way around,' I say defensively.

'*Are* you mad?' Gracie asks me.

'I don't think so,' I say honestly.

'Jealous?' Dave adds and I think about this for a moment.

'Not particularly. I just didn't think that they would even like each other that much, but it goes to show how observant I am, I guess.'

***

The first day of my Christmas break, I have a lovely long lie-in and get up at 11 a.m.. So far since we've been together, Julian hasn't stayed over here and I haven't stayed over at his; it's been my way of trying to slow things down. But today, I think I might ask him to, I decide over my bowl of porridge; maybe that will throw me out of this scaredy-cat phase I've got going on. I pick up my phone and ring him; he answers after two and a half rings,

'Hello, you! Did you get a good lie in?'

'I did, thank you,' I say warmly. 'What are you doing today?'

'Well, I finish my shift at six and then I'm free. What were you thinking?'

'Oh, I forgot you're working, I'm sorry.'

'That's OK,' he says softly. 'Did you want to do something tonight?'

'I was thinking of taking you out for dinner.'

'Sounds tempting.'

'Or…maybe I could make you something at mine?'

There's a slight beat of hesitation as he clocks on to what I'm saying. 'Sounds even more tempting. Maybe I could cook for you, though, and you make dessert?'

'Sounds even more tempting than that,' I say.

'See you at, let's say, seven or so?'

'Perfect.'

When we hang up, I trot over to my cookbooks, pull out a few, sit back down at my breakfast bar and start flicking through. What dessert would best suit sleeping together for the first time? I giggle to myself and start taping a shortlist into my iPad when Mish FaceTimes me. I swipe the screen and hold it at arm's length, waiting for the picture to come into effect.

'*Buongiorno*!' she says as soon as her face appears. 'How the devil are you, gorgeous?' She's sitting at her desk at home.

'I'm deciding what dessert would best suit a bit of sex.'

The comment doesn't faze her and she contemplates this, 'Well, the obvious answer is anything with whipped cream or chocolate; however,' she wiggles her finger at me, 'this can cause more scenarios than romantic ones if the person in question is lactose intolerant — had that once — not the best evening of my life.'

'He's not lactose intolerant,' I confirm.

'Ah.' She thinks for a moment, 'How about those chocolate rum balls you made at my Christmas party last year?'

'That is down here on my short-list.'

'Good girl. Now, have you done your Christmas shopping and if not, can you get ready in ten minutes?'

'Sort of and yes,' I say to her twinkling eyes.

'Grand. I have two-and-a-half hours free before I have to be at an event. That should give you more than enough time to get back and bake something.' The end of that was a statement rather than a question.

When I arrive back three hours later, my arms are full and my purse is empty. I put everything away in my bedroom closet and then take my Sainsburys bag into the kitchen with my ingredients, to start prepping. There's something very therapeutic about being in the kitchen, I've always thought. I do decide to go for the rum balls which I assemble swiftly and throw into the freezer to set.

Amazingly, I have enough time to sit and write out my Christmas cards after both myself and the house are looking beautiful. When 7 p.m. arrives, the bell promptly rings and a very handsome Julian, carrying several paper bags, greets me as I open the door.

'So, I wasn't sure what you would be in the mood for, so I've just gone for it and decided to cook Thai food.'

'I love Thai food,' I say, holding the door open a little more.

He visibly breathes a sigh of relief. 'Phew!'

'Come in,' I say as he makes no attempt to move — is he waiting for my permission?

He steps in and kisses me gently, 'How was your day?'

'I bought half of Blackheath with Mish,' I say as we reach the kitchen.

He laughs. 'Sounds expensive.'

'So, what can I do?' I say, taking some lemongrass out of a bag.

He hands me a bottle of red wine. 'Pour yourself a glass of this and maybe show me where your pots and pans are.'

'Can I at least chop something?' I say, opening the cupboard where all my cooking utensils are and then get out two glasses.

'Thank you but no. Sit down,' he says firmly. That's more like it.

I pop the cork and think I could get used to this as within moments all hobs are on and he moves effortlessly around my kitchen, getting out a board, taking a knife from the magnetic strip on the wall and chopping with such speed and accuracy all I can do is watch the action with awe.

'I love watching a chef chop vegetables,' I say, pouring the Beaujolais. 'I've tried to imitate that movement but just can't seem to get it.'

He smiles but doesn't take his eyes off the asparagus. 'It's all about the wrist action. You've got to be loose but firm. See, watch my wrist.' He moves in slow motion and I do as instructed, miming the movement with my right hand.

'Nearly,' he says gently. 'But you actually need to practise with a knife, come here and try.'

I get up and he gives me the knife then puts his hand on top of mine and moves so I'm standing in his arms. I will myself to concentrate as I feel his firm chest against my back and my mind wonders what it looks like.

'Feel the movement,' he says, as I bring my mind back to the now. Slowly and rhythmically, we move the knife up and down; I can feel my heart beating faster.

'Can you feel that?' he says seriously, his eyes still on the veg and I nod mutely, hypnotised. 'And after you've got that motion, it's about getting your speed up, like this.' He gradually moves the knife faster and faster and I giggle as we go. He stops moving suddenly and I turn my head, gazing up at him, still giggling. 'You're amazing, you know that?'

'Well, I try.'

He leans down and says softly, 'No, you don't,' and kisses me. We drop the knife on the chopping board and I turn my whole body to face him, stand on my tip toes, wrap my arms around his neck and he slides his hands around my waist, pulling me closer. He then lifts me up with one arm, moving the chopping board with the other and puts me on the counter top. Slowly and seductively, he takes my hand in his and kisses it gently, gazing deep into my eyes; the anticipation of what's about to happen building up in my stomach. He places little whispers of kisses on my neck, shoulder, collarbone, back to my neck; then cupping my face in his hands, he draws me closer for the deepest kiss yet. Standing it no longer, I move my hands from his back to find the buttons on his shirt as he continues to drive me wild with kisses. I fumble but finally his shirt becomes free, revealing, as expected, an impressive fireman's six pack. He helps me pull my top over my head, revealing my purple bra then draws me in to kiss my naked shoulder whilst lifting me off of the counter. I wrap my legs around him and he walks in the direction of the bedroom. Kissing his neck, I feel his warm skin on my lips. Then my foot feels a vibration.

'Oh no,' he says, as a piercing alarm sounds.

'What?' I'm still kissing his neck.

'I'm on call tonight.'

NOOO! I stop and face him. 'Why didn't you tell me?'

'There are enough people in, I thought the chances of anything happening were pretty small. I'm so sorry.' He lets me down and grabs the 'alerter' from his jeans pocket. After a moment he looks at me with so much longing but musters words I don't want to hear, 'I have to go.'

We walk back into the kitchen to get dressed, every part of me still tingling.

'Oh God, I didn't even cook for you,' he says, buttoning up his shirt again and looking at the still fired-up stove.

I pull on my top with disappointment. 'Don't worry. You can make it up to me.' I raise an eyebrow and he comes over and scoops me up in his arms again for one more longing kiss.

'Oh, you have no idea how much I don't want to leave. I'm so sorry. I'll give you a call after, just in case I'm not too long.'

'See you later,' is all I can muster and with a flash he's gone and I'm left standing in the kitchen, so frustrated I can barely stand up.

After practically downing the rest of my glass of wine, I finish cooking the meal and then turn everything off — my appetite for food, completely gone. Heading to the bathroom to start running a bath, my phone goes. I skip back to the kitchen, expecting to see Julian's number but it's a number I don't recognise.

'Hello?' I answer, all geared up to let someone trying to sell me something have it.

'Mel?' It's a bad line.

'Yes, who's this?' I say impatiently.

'It's Craig.' I think he's driving.

'Oh.' I'm not in the mood to talk to him. 'How did you get my number?' I snap at him.

'Jill gave it to me,' he says, taken aback. 'Look, something's happened.'

'Is Jill OK?' My heart skips a beat.

'What? I don't know, how should I know how Jill is? Would you stop talking for once!' He raises his voice. 'It's Poppie, you moron.'

'What? What's happened?' I brush over the moron comment.

'She was coming to surprise me; I'm guessing, as she was on the A12 but, *um,* there was an accident.' His voice remains strong but I detect a wobble.

'Is she OK?' There's too long a pause. 'Hello?' I notice my voice has a wobble too.

'She's...*um*...alive but not in great shape.'

'Oh my God, was Michael with her? Is he OK?'

'No, it was just her. They can't get hold of Michael, that's why they called me,' he says, hurried.

'Where are you?' I walk to the living room, grab my bag from the sofa, and move towards the door.

'I'm driving to the hospital but I'm practically passing you, so I thought you would want to come.' Tears fill my eyes and I realise I've dropped my bag. 'You still there? Is that a, yes? I have to know in the next five seconds, Mel, or I'm turning the other way,' he snaps at me now.

I swallow, 'Yes, yes, please come and get me.'

'OK,' he hangs up and I'm left stunned in my hallway. Picking up my bag and putting on my coat, I decide to wait outside my door for him.

***

'It seems the van driver fell asleep behind the wheel and took out four other cars as well as Poppie's,' a round-faced nurse tells us as we're seated in the waiting room outside head casualties. She scribbles something on her clipboard and continues shaking her head. 'I'm amazed he's only got minor cuts and bruises when everyone else...' Her voice drifts off and she bites her lip.

'When can we see her?' Craig asks, his eyes a little glossed over.

'Not for a little while, I'm afraid.' She doesn't look up and doesn't look apologetic enough for me.

'Any idea how long?' I say.

She does meet my eyes this time. 'The doctors are just settling her and want to do a few more checks, but I promise I'll come and get you as soon as you're allowed in,' she smiles. 'But I'd advise maybe using this time to prepare yourselves; it's hard to see a coma patient for the first time.'

She leaves and we're left alone, sitting in complete silence. You hear about terrible things happening to other people but you can never imagine that it's possible for anything to happen to somebody you love, somebody in your life, someone who means so much to you. You always assume that your friends are always going to be there throughout your whole life.

'When we were kids,' Craig starts talking to the floor, 'Mum and Dad took us to Yellowstone Park.'

'I remember that,' I smile sadly, knowing which story he's going to tell.

'And we went rock climbing,' he continues, still avoiding my eyes, 'and Poppie slipped. It took her about two minutes to come round.' His eyes look up at me, 'It was the longest two minutes of my life. I can't lose my big sister.'

'You're not going to lose her,' I say, with far more conviction than I feel.

'I never thought I'd lose my parents either, but it happened.'

I put my hand on his and he doesn't shrug it off, so I leave it there. 'History is not going to repeat itself, OK?' I say to him and tears start to fill my eyes.

Behind the Clouds

Craig and Poppie's parents were eccentric. Their dad loved bungee jumping and parachuting and their mum was fascinated by climbing, especially the extreme kind, where you have no equipment and complete confidence in your own ability; something I have always been envious of. With all the extreme sports they did, you wouldn't think that a car crash would have taken their lives. Poppie was seventeen and Craig was fifteen. A lorry driver lost control and hit them head-on. Both Poppie and Craig were in the car and watched their parents die. After the funeral, Poppie went completely off the rails: went missing for days on end; experimented with drugs; drank excessive amounts; and went through a very extreme case of bulimia. For Craig, though, it had the opposite effect. He grew up fast and basically became the older sibling, looking out for Poppie at every moment, and as soon as he turned seventeen and got a driver's licence, he was constantly getting her out of sticky situations.

He was Poppie's guardian angel for the following five years. Despite help from Nora, he worked three jobs to support them and when she truly hit rock bottom, he sent her to a rehab clinic. During her stint there she had a lot of counselling, discovered various anger management techniques and outlets, but really found her niche during meditation and yoga sessions.

'After Mum and Dad died, I thought I had lost her.'

'I never told you how grateful I was for you being there for Poppie; you really were her guardian angel.'

He shrugs and stares at the floor, 'She was all I had left.'

The door opens and the nurse reappears, 'OK, you can come through if you're ready.' I move my hand off Craig's and we follow the nurse in silence. As we approach another door, the nurse turns to us. 'Her outer wounds look worse than they actually are, but it can be a shock to see for the first time,' she warns and opens the door for us to walk through. Poppie is lying looking quite peaceful, despite a huge, nasty graze that's running from her forehead down past her left eye and onto her cheek. I inhale sharply, freezing to the spot.

'Remember she may be able to hear you so it's important to keep talking; it's often what brings them round.'

I grab Craig's hand without thinking about it and again he doesn't shrug me off, so we walk, hand in hand, further towards the bed.

'I'll give you a moment alone,' the nurse leaves and we're left in deathly silence. We both take her and the room in. The private room is colder than I think it should be and moodily lit, making it funereal; I have to remind myself that she is still alive. We move right to her bedside and Craig sinks into the chair next to the bed, letting go of my hand.

'It looks as though she's asleep, doesn't it?' My eyes can't tear themselves away from her face but I nod mutely at him. 'We're meant to talk to you, Pops,' Craig shifts forward in his seat and looks up at her, pausing before his next words. 'It's me and Melanie's here too.'

'Hi, Poppie,' my voice cracks and I wish I'd kept my mouth shut.

'Apparently it helps if we talk to you so we're, *um*,' he takes her limp hand, 'we're going to talk to you and hopefully you can hear us. If you can hear us, you've got to let us know, OK?'

Silence.

'OK,' he nods and blinks away some tears.

Chapter 20

I go to see Poppie every day at the hospital and talk to her about everything and anything that comes into my head. Craig and I cross each other in the corridor most days rather than see Poppie together, which I'm grateful for; I'd hate him to know that Julian and I still haven't slept together and how frustrated I am, but in all honesty, I haven't been in the mood when I see him. But it's not just that I'd be embarrassed for him to learn about Keeley's affair and I'd be horrified for him to find out about my new found interest in puzzles.

'I need you to stay in my life, you see, I need you to tell me it's OK that I'm enjoying the puzzle so much,' I tell Poppie on Christmas Eve. 'I've brought you something.' I fish out a present from my bag. 'Now, you can't open it yet, obviously, as it's not Christmas,' I jabber on. 'It's a little piece of me, well, us, so you're not alone tomorrow. I know Craig will probably be here at some point but I can't be, I'm afraid, hon, so, here.' I put it on the side of her bedside table; it's a framed photo of us wearing matching friendship bracelets when we were nine. 'I'm not going to tell you what it is, you'll have to open it and find out.' I look at her motionless body, so far removed from my friend who couldn't wait to rip into a present; my eyes fill with tears.

'She won't be alone on Christmas, Mel,' a soft voice comes from behind me and I turn to see Craig leaning against the door.

'How long have you been standing there?' I say to him, blinking away my tears.

'A little while.' He walks in casually and is also holding a present.

'What did you get for her?' I motion at the neatly wrapped gift that he's holding.

'*Hmm*? Oh, no, this is for you,' he holds it out for me to take.

'Me?' I accept it but continue to stare at him blankly. 'You got a present for me?'

'It's only something small; I wouldn't put on a whole parade about it.' He sits on the side of Poppie's bed.

I'm stunned. 'Thank you.'

'You haven't opened it yet; you might not thank me when you do.'

I crinkle my nose, 'All right, I take back my thank you.' I don't care what's in it; I'm touched he got me something.

'So, what's your plan for tomorrow?' he asks me, adjusting his position and trying to get comfortable.

'Julian and I are going to his sister's for lunch and then my parents' for dinner.'

'Sounds busy.' He moves his eyes to Poppie's face and I suddenly feel overwhelmingly guilty. 'I finally managed to get hold of Michael…'

'Oh my God, is he OK? How did he take it? Is he coming straight here? Where's he been?' I add almost angrily.

'You really do have far too many thoughts in that head of yours, don't you?' I fold my arms and frown at him but stay quiet, trying to prove him wrong. 'He was on a spiritual retreat which included a meditation solitude break; he sounded calm. He'll be here tonight, so Poppie will have the two of us here tomorrow.'

'How was your grandma when you spoke to her?' He finally brought himself to ring her yesterday. 'In denial.' He shrugs. 'She's convinced that it's not as serious as I was saying and refused to come visit.'

'Well, maybe it's too much for her to comprehend? Might be easier this way for her to pretend everything's fine?' That's always been my way of dealing with things I don't want to face up to.

'Maybe.' He exhales exhaustedly.

I look at my watch. 'Oh shit, is that the time?' I stand up abruptly, nearly dropping his present but grab it just before it hits the floor, 'I'm meant to be at Keeley's for a family dinner now.'

He looks at me patiently and amused. 'Have a good Christmas, Mel.'

'You too.' I smile weakly at him and then look at Poppie again.

'Stop feeling guilty for not coming tomorrow. You've been here every day. She'll be fine.'

'OK,' I nod at him even though I feel terrible for not coming tomorrow. 'Thank you. And thank you for this, whatever it is.'

'You're welcome.' We look at each other in silence once more but it's not uncomfortable. I go over to him, bend down and give him a kiss on the cheek.

'Merry Christmas, Craig,' I straighten up and smile at him.

'Merry Christmas, Melanie,' his eyes are sad but I can recognise gratitude too.

I leave the hospital and jump into a cab. As we speed towards Eltham, I feel so guilty that my tears can't help but spill onto my cheeks. Poppie's accident puts into sharp focus just how ungrateful I have been for all the people in my life. I take absolutely everybody for granted and I rarely tell them I love them or how much they mean to me: something needs to change in my life.

'So how is she?' Mum asks about Poppie as we're pouring drinks.

'The same,' I shrug. She comes over and gives me a huge hug; her hugs always make me feel better.

'Keep the faith, my darling. Maybe she's simply enjoying a long meditation of sorts,' she says now, holding me at arm's length.

'Maybe,' I say weakly back to her.

'Come on, you're missing it!' Nieve shouts with excitement; we're watching *It's a Wonderful Life*. I almost didn't recognise my little sister when she answered the door as I arrived. She's taken out her dreads and is now sporting a neat brown bob. Not only that, instead of her typical all-black ensemble, she's dressed in brightly coloured clothing from head to toe; not the Nieve I've known and loved for twenty-one years, but I've never seen her happier.

We rejoin everybody just as George is about to stand on the bridge to contemplate jumping off. 'I hope if things were to get that bad for me, I would think of a better solution!' Mum says to the TV, like she does every year.

'So how are you doing?' I whisper to Keeley who's to my right.

'*Shhh*!' Dad frowns at us.

'It's not as if you don't know what's going on, Dad!' I say.

'That's not the point,' he says, shuffling huffily back into Simon's armchair. I turn my attention back to Keeley and raise an eyebrow.

'Everything's...' she pauses in her almost audible whisper '...better.'

'Better?' I repeat, even quieter, as Dad is clearing his throat and trying not to get angry.

She nods at me and then focuses back on the TV. I'll speak to her properly tomorrow.

**

Christmas morning comes in crisply and I take advantage of being alone before the madness of the day. After a leisurely shower, I get ready and then pour myself a coffee and contemplate my breakfast, when the doorbell goes. *Oh God, what time does Julian call this?* I check out my reflection in the toaster and give my cheeks a little slap before rushing to the door.

'Merry Christmas!!!' To my huge relief Mish is standing on my doorstep, and with a huge present too.

'Merry Christmas!' I smile back at my friend, who's wearing a fantastic papakha.

'Love the hat!'

'My Christmas present to myself.' She poses momentarily on the doorstep, 'Now I'm not stopping.' She barges in and puts the surprisingly heavy gift in my arms, 'But thought I'd drop this off before heading to my dad's.'

I kick the door to close it and follow her through to the kitchen.

'Do help yourself,' I laugh at her with the coffee pot.

She raises it to me before filling a mug and sitting down at the table, 'So, feeling festive?'

'Not especially,' I say, putting the box down in between us.

'Well, open that, maybe it will make you feel better.' She nods at the present she brought. I open it to reveal a whole box of naughty goodies including several manuals and pleasure aids; I shut the lid of the box with a puce face. 'Are you serious?'

'I thought some of these may help light a spark when Julian comes over.' She grins from ear to ear. 'Or you could get yourself started before he arrives.' She laughs at my horrified face.

'Come on, lighten up — it's Christmas after all — and nothing says Christmas like...' she fishes around the box to pick something out at random, 'edible underwear.'

'Am I interrupting?' A male voice makes us both jump; Dave is standing there. 'The door was open.' He smirks at the scene.

Mish, completely nonplussed, swings the pants around her finger, 'Yes, we were just about to get going, care to join us, David?' I snatch them from her, throw them in the box and shut the lid. Mish stands up and comes over to me. 'I guess there's no use trying to help loosen up the only woman in London who didn't read or watch *Fifty Shades of Grey*.' She laughs and gives me a kiss on the cheek. 'Love you.' She then strides over to Dave and kisses him on the cheek too.

'Have a great day everybody!' and with that, she turns, and leaves.

'She's completely nuts,' Dave confirms, after we hear the front door click.

'Yup. That's why I love her. Hi. Happy Christmas.' I give him a hug.

'Hi,' he says into my hair. 'Thought I'd surprise you with some Christmas muffins and Asti to get the day started.'

'Amazing,' I say, grabbing some glasses.

'So have you joined some weird kinky group since I've last seen you?' Dave asks, examining the rude box.

'That's Mish's idea of a present,' I say, turning red again.

'Of course it is,' he winks at me.

I smile at him, 'You're out of your plaster,' I gesture to his now free leg.

'Came off yesterday!' He gives it a wiggle. 'Feels completely normal.'

We sit chatting and finish the bottle of Asti, completely losing track of time until Dave looks at his watch.

'Oh crap, it's nearly 12 o'clock.' He stands up abruptly and I see him to the door. 'My mum will kill me.'

'What time are you meant to be there?' I ask as we reach the corridor.

'12 o'clock.' He makes a face at me.

'You can blame it on me, say I'm having a meltdown or something and you needed to be here.'

'I'll try it.' He opens the door and comes face to fist with Julian's hand that's up and ready to knock.

'Oh. Hello,' he says uncertainly to Dave.

'Hi!' I say to his concerned face, 'Merry Christmas,' I greet him happily, to detract from how suspicious this must look.

'Happy Christmas,' he says, forcing his face into a smile.

'Well, I'll see you later.' Dave turns to me and makes a 'whoops!' face and I try to keep a straight expression, before he squeezes past Julian and hurries down the road.

'I thought you wanted a quiet morning to yourself,' Julian says cautiously as he steps over my threshold and shuts the door behind him.

'I did.' I tip toe and give him a kiss on the cheek in an attempt to unfreeze his frozen face. 'But then Mish turned up and so did Dave.' I know I've offended him. 'Anyway,' I try to move on, 'what does that matter?' I give him a kiss on the lips this time. 'I'm very happy to see you.'

His face falls into a natural but slightly tight smile. 'You

211

too. And I'm glad you have such kind friends who pop round and give you alcohol first thing in the morning.'

'A little festive morning booze is completely acceptable, I will have you know,' I add with minor irritation.

'All right then,' he nods. 'We're expected in half an hour; you ready to go?' he asks me, noting my slippers.

'Almost, did you want to have a drink or something and I'll grab my shoes and the presents?'

When I return, he's looking through the box Mish gave me. 'Your friend has an interesting sense of humour; what exactly is a love egg?' he asks, holding up a packet with mild interest.

'I have no idea.' My face returns to a festive crimson and I hurry to put on my boots before rushing over to throw it back in the box. '*Mish*,' I emphasise, 'thought some things in here…' I stumble but decide to be honest with him, '…might be useful for us.' I stand with my arms folded.

His right eyebrow raises. 'Well, I've got to say, I'm not particularly into the things in here.' His eyes smoulder into mine. 'But I'm game if you are?'

I burst out laughing in embarrassment but decide, what the hell, 'Well, let's have a look after dinner, shall we?'

He strides over and gives me a very passionate kiss. 'We haven't really got enough time now, have we?' he asks, his breath unsteady.

'I'd hope not,' I say and we both laugh.

***

'I'm surprised that she's hosting lunch, she's nearly seven months, right?' I say as we walk to Charlotte's front door and ring the bell.

'Well, Joe isn't the best cook and I think she'd rather the

kids were distracted with their own toys rather than pack everything up and come to mine. Mate!' The door opens and Julian greets Joe with a firm handshake, 'Happy Christmas! Something wrong? You look like you've seen a ghost.'

Joe shakes his head, 'No, no, just feeling a bit squiffy; might have been the salmon I had this morning. Hello, I'm Joe,' he says quickly, extending his hand to me and swallowing hard, afraid that I'll say something. The last thing I want to do is shake this man's hand but I accept it anyway.

'Hi there,' I say to the curly-headed man I saw in Greenwich market, kissing my sister.

'Now, you look weird.' Julian says to me. 'Are you feeling alright?'

'Oh yes, I'm fine,' I say after a beat and smile. 'Joe just looks very familiar, that's all.' I cock my head and narrow my eyes ever so slightly at him. 'I'm just trying to place him,' I say a little spitefully, but Julian misses it as the girls come running to the door.

'UNCLE JULIAN!!' Jocasta and Gilly hug his legs and he scoops them up together.

'Did Santa come?' he asks them both, with all seriousness.

'YES!' they chorus with more volume than I'd like after my Asti.

'Come see, come see!' They wriggle out of his arms and he follows them, running down the corridor, smiling back at me then disappearing around a corner.

'You're Julian's girlfriend?' he says disbelievingly and I nod. 'I knew he was seeing someone who Charlotte knew from the girls' dancing class but, oh shit.'

'Shit indeed,' I agree. 'I thought your name was Sebastian.' I say as I step over the threshold.

'It's my middle name,' he says simply, 'I use it at work'.

'Oh. Right.' I take off my coat, trying to comprehend what has just happened. He puts out his hand to take my jacket, looking at me with frightened eyes.

'Are you going to say anything?'

I hush my voice and say with so much sarcasm it's dripping off every word, 'Am I going to tell my boyfriend and his two adorable nieces that my sister is having an affair with his rather pregnant sister's husband? Yes, I think that's perfect small talk for Christmas Day lunch, don't you?' He looks so sheepish with all the colour drained from his face that I almost feel sorry for him. 'No. I won't say anything.'

'Oh, thank you,' he breathes a sigh of relief. 'We're absolutely going to call this whole thing off after the holidays; there just hasn't been the right time, you know?' I feel like I could punch him.

'Hi!' Charlotte waddles her way into the corridor to greet us. 'Honestly, Joe, how long does it take to hang up a coat?' Both Joe and I realise he's still holding my jacket and he hurriedly and clumsily hangs it up.

'Nice to see you again.' She gives me an awkward hug as her bump has gotten so large; I have to sort of bend at the waist to make it happen.

'You too.' I can't believe my sister is having an affair with your husband. 'You look lovely.'

'Oh shush, I'm fricking huge; I swear we're having twins here.' She rubs her stomach affectionately. 'Well, come on in!' She links my arm and we walk into her living room. 'Everything is almost ready. Can I get you a drink?'

'I'll get it for her.' Joe appears again, 'You sit down for a second.'

'I told you I'm fine, Joe,' she says with a strained smile.

'Well, let me get *you* a drink then, sweetheart,' he says,

with just as much strain.

'You know,' I interrupt as politely as I can manage, 'I'm OK for a drink at the moment, thank you. I think I'll just go and say hello to the girls.' I turn quickly and the two continue to bicker.

'Do you like *Frozen*?' Jocasta says to me, frowning, indicating that my answer will dictate the tone of the whole day.

'I do,' I say very seriously. Although if I have to sing *'Let it Go'* one more time with Lucy, I think I may shoot myself. 'Best film in the world!' I say out loud, keeping my real thoughts to myself with a smile on my face. That seems to have done the trick as she jumps into my arms and I think I've just secured the position of her best friend for the afternoon.

'Everything OK?' Julian says to me quietly whilst Gilly is waving an Elsa doll in his face. I nod, and then take a look at Joe and Charlotte, who are now gritting their teeth. 'I'm sorry,' he mouths at me, seeing what I see but not knowing the half of it. 'I'm not sure what's going on.'

'Right!' Charlotte moves from the kitchen with such speed I feel she may go over in her slippers. 'Are we hungry?' The girls scream with joy and fly towards the table. 'Not so fast, young ladies,' she stops them in their tracks, 'You need to wash your hands, girls, please; I can still see some of that glue.' They disappear obediently down the corridor and she explains to me, 'They were making antlers earlier. Now, do you want to sit here, Melanie?' She gestures to a chair next to where Joe is already sitting. I'd like to tell her I'd rather chew on the antlers the girls have made but settle with a, 'Sounds lovely,' and smile as I sit down.

Julian is already in the kitchen, 'This looks amazing, sis.'

She joins him and brushes his comment off quickly, 'Well,

I'm no Julian Morgan but thank you.'

They banter in the kitchen and Joe whispers to me, 'If it's any consolation I'm absolutely horrified that you're here.'

'Do you charm my sister with those lines?' I whisper heatedly to him.

'I mean,' he struggles with a red face, 'I never meant for anyone to find out, especially not a family member.'

'Well, you shouldn't have gone walking around in public; what were you thinking?'

He shrugs. 'I'd seen these lovely teacup candles that I thought she would like and I wanted her to pick one.' *Oh my God, he knows her. Is this more than an affair?* 'We knew it was a bit risky but that somehow adds to the danger, doesn't it? I'm sorry,' he adds after seeing my face. 'And if it counts for anything at all, I didn't mean to fall in love with your sister.'

'You *love* Keeley?' I say, looking at him horrified.

'What are we talking about?' Julian places a full plate with all the trimmings in front of me and then does the same for Joe, before leaning on the back of my chair. Charlotte comes over with the kids' plates and moves her eyes from Joe to me, suspiciously,

'Just…' I rearrange my face into what I hope is a pleasant expression and search my brain for anything to say. 'How much I love your house and how I could never keep it this tidy, especially if I had two kids and one on the way. You're just like my older sister: a real super-mum.' I smile and Joe looks as though he might pass out.

Charlotte blushes. 'Well, thank you. It's nice to have someone say such nice things.' She briefly looks pointedly at Joe but it's long enough for both Julian and I to notice.

'Mate, you really don't look very well at all,' Julian says

looking at Joe who's positively green now.

'No, I'm fine, really,' Joe says hurriedly and takes a sip of water.

The girls clamber onto the dining room chairs as Julian returns with the remaining plates.

'So how is your sister, Melanie?' Charlotte asks, placing down a bottle of wine and taking her seat whilst Joe starts choking. 'What's wrong now?' she directs heatedly at him.

'Wine went down the wrong way,' he says with some strain.

'You mean water,' Charlotte looks at him with distaste.

'Yes, yes, water.' Joe looks at me.

'She's fine, thanks.' Julian also looks at me but with concentration, hanging onto my every word, which I still find odd. 'I saw her yesterday and we'll see her later at my parents.' I put a forkful of turkey into my mouth to stop myself from talking, just in case I come out with something inappropriate.

'Well, wish her a Happy Christmas from all of us,' she says, and I feel a combination of guilt and helplessness.

'I will,' I say and reach for the wine.

As we get back into Julian's car to head to my parents' several hours later, I breathe a sigh of relief.

'You were really nervous, weren't you?' he says to me, smiling with affection as I enter the address into his satnav.

Oh, if only you knew the real reason. 'Maybe a little,' I say aloud and then feel bad for lying. Should I tell him?

'Charlotte really likes you and so do the girls. There was something weird going on with Joe, though — he's normally the life and soul of the party — very strange,' he says as we join the dual carriageway.

'Well, how are you feeling about meeting my family?' I

ask, to turn the conversation away from me.

'Rather bricking it,' he says honestly to me with a sideways smile. 'I've just about remembered everyone's names, I think.'

'You'll be fine. My mum?'

'Patty,' he confirms.

'Yes, Patty. She's like me: insane but fabulous.' He reaches over and squeezes my hand.

'And your dad is called Nigel and if I talk to him about travel, he'll be on my side.'

'And also, Nieve—'

'The youngest sibling?'

'*Um hmm*, particularly anywhere in Indonesia. Oh God, what's her boyfriend called?'

'Marcus.'

'What a team!' I say to him.

'And that leaves your big sister, Keeley, the sensible one,' he adds. 'And her husband Simon and their kids: Henry, Lucy and Ava.'

'Full points. You'll get along with Simon, he's easily one of the nicest guys I've ever met and Keeley *was* the sensible one,' I correct him.

'What do you mean?'

Whoops. I think quickly. 'She's made some interesting decisions as of late — most of which I don't particularly agree with — but anyway,' I reach over and put my hand on his, 'it's just one evening; I'm sure it will all go swimmingly.'

Lucy answers the door looking disgruntled.

'Merry Christmas, sweetie,' I say to her. 'What's wrong?'

'Henry is eating all of the chocolates,' she says in exactly the same disapproving tone that Keeley would use.

'Well, I'm sure he will share if you ask nicely?' She shakes her head. 'Can we come in?' I ask, as she is very much blocking the way.

'Who's that?' Lucy asks, pointing at Julian.

'This is my friend Julian,' I say.

'Is he your *best* friend?' she asks.

I look at him and open my mouth to answer as Keeley appears. 'Didn't hear the door go.' She sweeps Lucy up effortlessly in her arms, and onto her left hip, steps back to let us in and gives me a huge out of character hug with her free right arm. Letting go of me, she turns, 'Nice to finally meet you, Julian,' and taking his hand, she gives it a firm business shake.

'You too. Would it be possible to use the bathroom?' Julian asks politely, taking off his coat and I see that he is visibly rather nervous.

'Of course. Upstairs and to the right,' Keeley directs and we watch him go. When we hear the sound of the door click, she whispers to me. 'He seems nice; what's up with you?' She takes in my angry expression. 'Lucy,' she looks at her eldest daughter, 'can you see if Nanny needs any help setting the table, please?' Lucy hops down obediently and walks off with purpose.

'Any idea how I met Julian?' I whisper as soon as she's gone.

'It was at Lucy's dancing show, wasn't it?'

'*Um hmm,*' I stare at her with my arms folded, waiting for her to comprehend.

'So?' She says with impatience.

'So! His last name is Morgan.'

'I'm sorry, I'm not following.'

'He has a sister called Charlotte.' She takes that in and then her face falls as her brain clicks in gear. 'And you're bloody having an affair with her sodding husband and,' I lower my voice even more, 'I just had to sit next to him during Christmas Day lunch!' Her eyes widen but she remains silent. 'You've ruined Christmas for me and possibly also cost me my relationship.'

'Oh, come on now, don't be so dramatic!' Her expression changes to the patronising big sister that I grew up with.

'Is that all you have to say?' I ask incredulously.

She thinks for a moment. 'I'm sorry you were put in that position. But we've basically broken up so I don't really see what all the fuss is about.'

'He told me he loves you.'

She starts glowing like a teenager, 'He did?'

I hit her on the arm. 'What the hell are you doing? What about Simon? What about the kids? What about Joe's wife and kids?'

'Joe? Who's Joe?' she says confused.

'Sebastian. His first name is Joe.'

'Oh yes, sorry. He's Sebastian to me. Sorry,' she adds when my frown deepens.

'So, what are you playing at?' I ask.

'Look, you're not in my position,' she exhales. 'It's complicated and I get that you can't understand, but I am going to end everything, OK.' Her face falls again. 'You haven't told Julian, have you? I'm guessing not, based on the way he greeted me.'

'No, of course I haven't said anything to Julian. How am I supposed to...'

'What are we whispering about?' We both turn to see Mum and Lucy hand in hand, creeping down the corridor.

'Nothing important,' Keeley says in a normal voice and then scoops Lucy up in her arms once more.

'Mummy. Henry is still eating all the chocolates!' Lucy

says.

Mum opens her arms to me. 'I know, sisters like to have their secrets. Nice to see you my darling,' and she gives me a big kiss on the cheek. 'Now where's your new man?'

'You didn't have to wait for me.' Julian appears at the top of stairs and I notice his face redden slightly as he takes in three generations of Butlers staring up at him.

'You must be Julian,' Mum says warmly, walking to the bottom of the stairs, opening her arms and giving him a huge hug when he reaches the bottom.

'Very nice to meet you, Mrs Butler.'

She pushes him away, 'My name is Patty. Mrs Butler was my mother-in-law and I have no intention to be anything like that old rat bag.'

'Mum!' Keeley says as Lucy giggles.

'Anywho,' she now links arms with him, 'Let me introduce you to the family, Julian,' and walks him through to the lounge.

Keeley goes to follow them and I tap her arm. 'We're not done talking,' I breathe at her.

'Yes, we are,' she mouths back at me.

'What are you whispering about?' Lucy asks.

'Nothing, sweetie. Nothing at all.'

***

'You look weird,' Nieve says to me in the kitchen as we do the washing up together. Keeley has managed to not be alone with me the entire time so I haven't had a chance to corner her again.

'Thank you.' I automatically put my hand to my hair to smooth it down.

'No not your hair. In the nicest way possible…it's your face.' She grins at me in the way only a little sister can. I bat her with the tea towel. 'Oh, come on! I know something's up. Everything all right with Julian? I really like him, by the way.' She pokes her head round the kitchen door to peek in the living room. 'He and Dad haven't stopped talking since you got here.'

'I know. They really seem to like each other.' I come and join her at the door and watch as Dad shows Julian and Nieve's boyfriend pictures from the cruise. 'Dad likes Marcus too, despite those tattoos, and everything's fine with Julian,' I say walking back to focus my attention on some glasses. 'Are you with me?' I say to the back of her head.

'I really like him, Melsy,' her face beams at me.

'I could have told you that; you've completely changed your look, you're laughing at Dad's jokes, you're helping Keeley with babysitting…'

'Well, a few things seem to have just fallen into place and it makes me realise that I might want to be a little more…grounded.' Her huge eyes stare vulnerably but happily into mine.

'That's amazing,' I beam.

She shrugs. 'It had to happen one day, right? And, I'm here for you if you decide you want to share anything; I know something's up,' she adds.

'Thanks.' I smile at my baby sister and think she may be turning into the most sensible one of us all. Julian comes into the kitchen and I know exactly what he's going to say from the look on his face. 'You have to go.'

'I have to go.' We say at the same time.

'Oh no, why?' Nieve says, walking casually back over to start putting things away.

'I'm on call,' he directs at her and then looks back at me. 'I'm so sorry.'

'Any idea what time you'll finish?' I ask, knowing he's sorrier about the fact that we're not going to go back to mine than the idea of leaving my family early.

'Have to play it by ear, I think.' He kisses me on the cheek. 'I'll give you a text later.' He makes his apologies to my family and is gone before I can put down the glass I'm holding.

Chapter 21

Julian doesn't text me until about four in the morning on Boxing Day. 'He has to work long hours all this week too so I'm not going to see him; maybe I will dive into that box that Mish gave me,' I take the opportunity to tell Poppie as we're alone. 'But if I'm honest, I'm kind of glad.' I confess. 'I need some time to decide if I can keep Keeley's affair from him; I don't want a relationship based on lies.' I look at my friend waiting to see if she will respond. After a silent moment I carry on. 'I was going to spend the day with Dave but he cancelled on me again. But hey, that just means we can hang out, right?'

'Knock, knock.' Craig enters the room. 'One Americano as ordered.'

'Thanks.' I accept the takeaway cup he offers me.

'Pops, let me know if do you want a green tea.' He looks hopefully at his sister. Unintentionally, I've seen more of Craig than anyone else this week, as we seem to keep arriving at the hospital at the same time. We sit together, sometimes in understanding silence and sometimes in constant conversation. Today is particularly drizzly and we both stare out of the window.

'So, what were you going to do with crutches?'

'He's off his crutches now,' I inform Craig and then emphasise his name. '*Dave* and I hadn't set anything specific. I thought maybe something active to burn off some of

Christmas.'

'Have you ever been climbing?'

'Climbing what?'

'A climbing wall. There's one about twenty minutes from here; we could go, change the scenery a bit; I know Poppie would want that.'

I face him. 'You want to go climbing with me?'

He regards my face. 'Yes.'

'Why? So you can enjoy me struggling and falling on my arse?'

'An added bonus, perhaps, but I think it might be something that you might enjoy; you were always fascinated talking to my mum about it.'

I take my time to answer. *How does he remember that?* 'I don't know, climbing just seems way too out of my comfort zone.'

'Well, Poppie would say that's exactly why you should do it.' He stands up and holds his hand out to me.

I hesitate then extend my hand to his, 'What does one wear to go climbing?'

***

'Oh my God, it's like *The Wall* in *Gladiators*.'

All harnessed in with crotch and arse unflatteringly squished into full display, I grip tightly onto my rope and stare incredulously up at the eighteen-metre-tall wall.

'Just grab on and start climbing, Melanie,' Craig assesses his first move then jumps and crawls up the wall like Spiderman. 'It's easy!' He looks down at me, hanging with one hand and one foot free. 'Come on! I see you as a bit of a 'Jet' myself,' he smiles encouragingly.

'She was my favourite,' I admit as I look up to him.

'I know she was. Now start climbing.'

I find my footing slowly and reach up. Oh holy Jesus, this is how I'm going to die. Unsure and unsteady I pull myself completely off of the ground — spread-eagled and terrified.

'Perfect. Now all you have to do is look slightly less like a squashed bug on a windscreen and we're good to go,' he laughs as he leans back, fiddles with the clip in front of him and abseils down again to meet me. I face him hoping that my fear doesn't show completely across my features. 'All you have to do is shift your weight like this.' He climbs a little and then comes down to meet me again, swinging from side to side.

'I don't think I can do this.'

'Of course you can; I'm here to guide you.' His eyes are steady and focused, I suddenly feel I can trust him for the first time in my life. 'Now follow my lead and you can't go wrong.'

'What if I slip?'

'Then you will die,' he says with all seriousness and my eyes pop out of my head. 'Come on, look, this rope isn't going anywhere.' He gives it a tug. 'Maybe just concentrate on working your way up rather than falling down…a mantra for life, perhaps?'

***

'Nearly there, Mel, two more moves and you're at the top,' Craig says from above me.

I find I'm actually not bad at this. Although I wish I'd stretched beforehand, as my arms feel like they're falling off. Reaching up just a little higher, I feel the top with my right fingertips. 'Oh my God,' I pant and pull myself completely up and turn to face Craig. 'I didn't die!'

'It's more of a mental challenge than a physical one,' he says, grinning, again only hanging on with one hand.

'Well, I don't know about that.' My heart's beating so hard I feel like it's in my mouth. 'But I'd very much like to be back on the ground.'

An hour later we're driving back to mine in Craig's BMW and I find myself shaking my head and smiling.

'What are you smiling at?' Craig gives me a sideways glance after overtaking a learner.

'I can't quite believe that we're basically friends now.'

'I've always liked you, Melanie,' he says simply. 'I thought you knew that.'

'Of course you have,' I say darkly.

He continues to look straight ahead. 'All brothers tease their sister's friends; it's natural.'

'Craig, it was so bad that I often put off meeting up with Poppie just in case you might be there.'

'Well, that's just sad.' He turns the radio on and Nat King Cole's, 'When I fall in love,' swoons through his speakers. '*Ugh*.' He goes to change it and I stop him.

'No, I love his voice; keep it on.'

'Load of nonsense drivel,' he mutters.

I turn to him. 'Have *you* ever been in love?'

'We've travelled back to the vacant dreamer in you, haven't we?'

'Shut up,' I say but I'm not angry. 'Have you?' I press.

He huffs and shifts in his leather seat, 'Love is just a word; how can you be *in* a word?'

'It's not just a word,' I say with conviction. 'It's a…a state of being…a feeling…'

'Feelings change,' he says flatly. 'So many people throw comments like that around without any meaning or consequence. Saying 'I love you' to someone is simply just that, saying it; it has no worth if your actions show the opposite. Did…' He stops himself and then decides to continue. 'Did Evan tell you he loved you?'

All the time. 'He may have done once or twice,' I say, slightly put out as he's flattened my argument.

'Well, there we are then. See how much meaning he had behind that?'

'Excuse me, you weren't in my relationship, you don't know what went on,' I say roughly and turn the radio off. 'OK, so things might not have been perfect, but I'd still like to believe that *real* love exists somewhere. And that one day I'll find it.'

'So Julian isn't *the one,* then?' he says, turning into my road.

Oh. I bite my lip. 'I don't know,' I say quietly. We ride in silence until we're outside my door. 'Thank you for driving me home,' I say and shut the door before he has a chance to say anything.

***

There's something about New Year's Eve. I don't know what it is; maybe the possibility of change. Everyone has good intentions and resolutions; there's the promise of a new chapter and I'm going to embrace it with both hands. My phone beeps and it's Julian.

"Have an amazing time beautiful…looking forward to hearing all about it xx"

It's a good thing he's working, really, as I couldn't have

got him another ticket; Mish has completely sold out.

I start typing to reply and another message comes through, this time from Mish.

"You've got ten minutes to get your sexy arse together! Just getting in the cab now."

I type back a quick message to them both, then grab my mascara and add another coat before applying some pencil eyeliner on my lower eyelids. I've gone for a smoky eye effect with a hint of gold, as it's a black and gold themed event.

Padding over to my wardrobe I stroke my floor length black gown, my real Christmas present from Mish, that was in the bottom of the box of pleasure. It reminds me of Jessica Rabbit's dress and wriggling out of my dressing gown, I step in; the material caresses my every curve and I've never felt so confident. Taking in my reflection, I am striking if I say so myself. I step into my four and a half inch heels which instantaneously elongates my body and if it's possible, my confidence. I touch my hair that I've swept up into a chignon, exposing my dangling gold earrings and pendant necklace. Grabbing my gold clutch, I throw my long black coat over my arm just as a car horn toots outside.

'*Ooh* sexy lady! Give me a spin!' I twirl in the doorway, careful not to fall out of it and land on my face. Mish hangs out of the cab window to wolf whistle. 'Now get that tiny heinie in here; we've got twenty minutes before I have to make an appearance!' We're driving to Kingham Hall in Greenwich.

'Thank you, Mish,' I say as we make our way.

'For what?' She pauses from touching up her perfectly flawless face.

'For the dress, for this evening…' I shrug, feeling suddenly overcome with gratitude and love. 'For putting up with me; I feel very blessed to have you in my life.'

She smiles at me and then opens her red lips, 'Well, thank goodness for Billy Burns I say.' She returns to her compact and moves her head side to side, sucking in her cheeks to highlight her cheek bones. 'I feel blessed to have you in my life too; you were definitely worth the detention.'

Kingham Hall is warmly floodlit as we pull up. The gardens are glittered with lanterns and candles. Like I said, New Year's Eve is magical.

Mish's assistant Clive rushes towards the still moving vehicle with a clipboard and a worried expression; Mish opens the window.

'*OhmyGodsogladyou'rehere* — small explosion in the fricking kitchen; guests have started arriving and the canapés aren't ready; the warm up band isn't here—' she cuts him off.

'I left you alone for two hours! How could things go so drastically wrong in that time?'

She steps out of the car and continues barking at him. I love it when she puts her work head on; she really is scary. I pay the driver then get out slowly.

'Mel,' she pauses and turns her back on Clive, 'Would you mind going into the Darlington Room by yourself? I'll just sort this mess out and come and find you after.'

'No problem, go, go. I'll see you in there.'

Mish snatches the clipboard, headset and dashes off towards the entrance, despite her six-inch heels, leaving Clive lagging behind like an apologetic puppy. I watch the cab driver go and then hear the screeching of tyres and a loud honking, followed by swearing. A dark blue van weaves dangerously down the gravel and stops directly opposite the entrance. The side door flies open and a succession of well-dressed men burst out carrying instruments and run past me, all smiling and paying me compliments. The driver reverses and parks a little more safely than when he arrived and gets out; he's not carrying an instrument.

'Have you forgotten something?' I venture, looking at his empty hands quite amused.

He runs his fingers through his blonde hair and it falls effortlessly into place. 'Only the singer could get lost, apparently,' he says casually, lighting a cigarette as the sound of brass and wind instruments warming up floats out of the open door.

'I see. Well, don't you need to do a scale or two?'

'I'm all right for a minute.' He takes me in. 'You're musical?'

'No, I just remember the song about scales and arpeggios from *The Aristocats*.' He lets out a deep laugh and then cocks his head.

'You waiting for someone?'

'No,' I say, comfortably.

'With someone then?' he prompts.

'Yes. Sort of,' I correct myself.

'Complicated. I get that. Well,' he stubs out his half-finished cigarette on the ground, 'can I at least accompany you in?' He offers me an arm.

'Sure.' I check-in my coat before approaching the Darlington Room where we are greeted by two footmen dressed in black and gold tails. This is most surreal — I wouldn't be surprised if they started dancing and singing — but sadly they merely nod, open the ridiculously tall double doors and welcome us in. The big band are on a stage at the far end of the room and have started playing some instrumental Cole Porter. Two more footmen offer us some champagne from a shiny gold tray, which we both accept;

Mish has done an amazing job. The "room" is nearer a banqueting hall with beautifully dressed round tables lining the edges, revealing a huge dancing space below chandeliers that are glistening in the soft lighting. Floor to ceiling curtains drape gracefully down, framing the windows and exposing the starry night outside. Couples parade arm in arm laughing and discussing the décor, while groups mingle among numerous smartly dressed waiters, who are prancing to and fro with canapés — I see Mish has got everything sorted now.

'Well, Red, I must take my leave.' He downs the contents and then puts his empty champagne glass on the tray of a passing prancer.

'Thank you for your arm.'

He contemplates my face. 'You're cute, Red. I look forward to seeing you later.' And with a gentle kiss of my hand, he walks in the direction of the stage. What a presumptuous sleaze-ball.

'Who's your friend?' I turn with surprise to see Craig's grinning face.

'What are you doing here?' I ask, wavering slightly in my heels, not sure if I should give him a hug.

'The Fletchers are clients of mine,' his steady eyes glance briefly up and down my body and then back into my eyes.

'Who are the Fletchers?'

'The hosts,' he says slowly. 'Are you in the right place?'

'Yes,' I say defensively then looking around add, 'I think so. My friend Mish is the organiser.'

He thinks for a moment. 'Michelle from school?'

'The one and only,' I say proudly then sip my champagne.

'Well I never. Haven't seen her since…since the day you crashed your dad's Volvo in front of our house, what, ten years ago?'

I blush. 'Well, I misjudged the position of that tree. So,' I change the subject, 'are you here alone?'

He pauses. 'No. Are you?'

'Mish is my date. Julian had to work so…'

'From the way you came in arm and arm, anyone would think you were with *him*.' He looks up to the stage, 'Or at least from the way he's looking at you now.'

I follow his line of sight to the stage where the singer has started crooning the room with Nat King Cole's 'Unforgettable,' intensely looking straight at me. I stand there awkwardly as Craig looks from the stage to me and back again; all I can do is smile at the ridiculousness of the situation.

'I don't even know his name,' I say laughing, 'We met outside and he offered to walk me in. This is most bizarre,' I confess.

'What is?'

'That some complete stranger appears to be singing a song for me; that we're here having this conversation; that we've been having conversations at all and that, like I said before, I actually consider you a friend now.' I shake my head. 'My world has changed. As has my view of you: it's like you're a different person.'

'You're different too,' he says calmly.

'No, I'm not, I'm exactly the same,' I say defensively.

'You're more confident,' he confirms. 'But I'd say I haven't changed either.'

'Well, whatever it is,' I decide to leave it, 'I like it — just don't go back to insulting me,' I say almost playfully.

'I couldn't if I tried this evening; you look stunning.'

I stare at him speechless.

'Why are you looking at me like that?'

I point at him. 'That, there — you've never given me a compliment before. Ever.'

'Well, any man in here would be mad not to give you a compliment this evening.'

'Stop it.' I hit him on the arm.

'You need to control that arm of yours: it's been hitting me since we were kids.'

'Well, you've always deserved it,' I say firmly.

'So just so we're clear,' he rubs his arm. 'A compliment also warrants a whack on the arm?'

'Sometimes it does,' I say to him. 'So…where's your date?'

Who's your date? I want to say but change my mind at the last moment.

He looks around. 'She went to the loos to freshen up — we'd just arrived — how can a woman need to freshen up when all they've done is walk from a car into a building? It's beyond me. Oh, here she comes.'

I turn to the door and wish I hadn't. If I looked stunning, how would Craig describe her? A twelve-foot blonde sashays in and the whole room watches as she glides over to us; she looks like she's just stepped out of a *Victoria's Secret* catalogue.

'There you are. I thought you said you'd wait outside the ladies for me.'

'That's what *you* said I should do; I said I was going to go in. Cassie, this is Melanie.'

'Oh, hello,' she says, clearly just noticing my existence for the first time. Her face transforms into a mildly patronising smile as she extends out her long slender fingers for me to shake stiffly.

'Melanie is a school friend of my sister's.'

'You have a sister?' she says with surprise.

That's it, I hate her; I let go of her hand sharply.

'Remember, I told you…' Craig starts to say but she cuts him off and looks over his shoulder.

'Oh right, yes, vaguely. Oh look, there's Tanya over there,' and she walks off again.

When she's out of earshot I fold my arms, 'She's a real treat.'

'I know, she takes a little getting used to.'

We watch her air kiss Tanya and then they both take a canapé each.

'Why are you with her, then?'

'It's nothing serious but she's alright really. Maybe I need to get her drunk; she's lovely when she's drunk.' He stops talking as she marches back over to us.

'This food is horrible; whoever organised this needs to be sacked.'

'Right. Craig, I'll see you later.' I widen my eyes at him, 'Lovely to meet you,' I say to her with as fake a smile as I can manage.

'You too, Molly,' she says carelessly.

'Her name is Melanie…' I hear Craig say as I'm walking off, not sure where to, but I spot Mish and weave towards her. She looks more relaxed now.

'All problems now averted. What have I missed?'

'Since I last saw you, the singer has flirted with me…'

Mish looks up at the stage, 'Nice,'

'I've seen Craig…'

'No! Where?'

'Directly behind me and to the right standing with the *Victoria's Secret* model, who by the way needs a firm slap.'

'Always happy to oblige,' Mish says seriously trying to

spot who I'm talking about. 'Maybe when we've broken in the New Year and my bosses are too drunk to realise — oh.' She stops talking and I turn and follow her gaze to make sure she's looking at the right person. '*Huh.*' She raises an eyebrow.

'What?'

'He's a lot better looking than when we were eighteen.'

'Really?' I look at him, clearly arguing with the model.

'Yeah. Cute face without all that acne.' She looks back at the stage. 'Yeah, even cuter than the singer. But singers are nothing but trouble.'

I look from Craig to the singer feeling very odd; I've never seen Craig as any kind of sexual being before.

'I'd say you're in there, too,' Mish adds, sipping her sparkling water.

'Are you forgetting I have a boyfriend?' I ask, feeling offended and flattered at the same time.

'No.' She looks at me with all seriousness, 'But can you honestly tell me you feel comfortable with the fact you know his brother-in-law is having an affair with your sister? Say you got married — can you imagine the constant awkwardness?' I think of how uncomfortable I felt this Christmas — I don't really have the intention to do that again and I stand there dumbfounded, not quite sure where to start. She turns her head to me. 'But—' she falters. 'You know, I like Julian, he's very *um*, nice.' I frown at her. 'OK so I don't know him very well but he seems to care for you which is an upgrade from Evan isn't it?'

'Quite right,' I say and down my champagne.

'The question is.' She puts her arm around me, 'How do you feel about him? Do you want to be with him despite this situation?' I go to open my mouth but then close it when I realise, I have no idea how I feel. She gives me a slightly raised eyebrow. 'Maybe you need to start to consider this a bit? Can I borrow your phone for a moment? I've been using mine so much the battery has died already.'

'Sure.' I pass it to her and stare up at the stage while she types away quickly.

'There, done. Thanks.' I take it from her and Clive comes over to us.

'Michelle?' His tentative voice now at our side.

'Managed to blow something else up?' she asks him.

Clive smirks sarcastically, exhales and then whispers, 'He's here.'

Mish gives me a squeeze and then barks at Clive, 'Well let's go then! Lead the way!' She turns to me and opens her mouth in a silent happy, '*Aghh!*' before walking off like a professional, leaving me once again with my thoughts.

I decide to park myself at an empty table in the corner that's nearest to the entrance of the kitchen, so that I can catch the waiters first, with their trays; I sit there contentedly sampling the food, more champagne and the music.

I watch couples dancing happily with their partners and look around with amusement trying to spot Craig and Cassie. From what I remember of school discos, or more recently at Poppie's wedding, he always hated dancing; it was the one thing he wasn't very good at. I scan the dance floor and can't see them anywhere, then spot Cassie on her own dancing with Tanya and her date — who coincidentally — looks more interested in her than Tanya. I roll my eyes at her batting her eyelashes at him as Tanya looks up at the band. Getting out my phone I decide to wish Julian a Happy New Year and see I've received a few messages from Dave, Gracie, Jill and Nieve. I type away replies and throw my phone back in my bag in time to see Craig walking over to me.

'Can I sit down?'

'Well, you'll have to fight for a seat.' I gesture to the vacant table and he grins, taking the seat next to mine with his back to the dance floor.

'I wanted to apologise for Cassie.'

'You don't need to apologise.' I brush him off.

'No, I do. And while I'm at it, I want to also apologise for myself.'

'Why? You didn't forget my name.' I clasp my hands together and cross my legs the other way.

'Not for this evening...for...' he pauses. 'For the other day; for what I said at Poppie's wedding; and for always being a bit of an arse to you.'

'Being with someone like her makes you re-evaluate how you've been behaving, *huh*?'

'Something like that. Listen, I wanted to say something else to you. I....'

'Ladies and gentleman...' Mish's voice carries over the microphone and I realise that the music has stopped playing and there's a more intimate band on the stage, waiting patiently. Craig looks disappointed to be interrupted but looks to the stage anyway.

'We are so honoured that you could join us for this very special occasion...'

Curiosity gets the better of me and I tap Craig on the shoulder. 'What were you saying?' I ask quietly when he turns to face me.

'Oh, it really doesn't matter.' He smiles sadly at me then turns around again.

'So please help me give a massive warm welcome to our guest, Luke Braydon!'

He walks onto the stage and starts talking to the audience but I can't hear him. *What was Craig going to say?* I frown at the back of his head but he turns just as I'm at my deepest crease.

'I was going to ask you to dance, but I'm guessing the answer is, no?' he says, observing my face.

'*You* can dance?'

He stretches out his hand for me to take. 'Why don't you find out?' he dares me.

I take his hand and he leads me to the dance floor.

'Won't Cassie mind?' I say, looking around for her.

He points over to the front of the stage where she's practically grinding the air. 'She's probably forgotten *my* name by now too.'

We find a spot in the middle of the dance floor.

'Now.' He puts his hand on the small of my back. 'Put your hands here and here.' He moves me to the correct position and then draws me slightly closer before leading me around the floor effortlessly.

'Where was this dancer at Poppie's wedding?' I ask incredulously as we float around like Fred and Ginger.

'Well, I hadn't had dancing lessons at that point.'

'Why did you get dancing lessons?' I ask, smirking.

'Stop laughing!'

'I'm not laughing, I'm smirking,' I correct him as he twirls me around and then looks disapprovingly at me when I'm facing him again.

'I did it for my business. There's a client I want to land, who's having a party next month, and I know there'll be dancing, and I felt I needed a bit of help. What do you think?' he adds tentatively.

'If I didn't know that you used to have two left feet, I'd say you were a natural.'

His eyes twinkle at me with fake annoyance. We continue to dance and sometime later, Luke Braydon announces there's only twenty minutes left until midnight.

'Oh my God, how long have we been dancing for?' I ask, going to look at my watch in disbelief before realising I'm not wearing one.

'I have no idea,' Craig says, looking at me in a weird way as we still continue to move around the floor. 'Look, remember I was going to say something earlier…'

'*Um hmm*,' I mutter, almost afraid of where he's going with this. He's going to say I've been visiting Poppie too much or he's just going to admit there's been something sitting in my teeth for the past two hours.

'There's no need to look so worried.' He reads my face. 'There's just something that I feel you should know, I…'

My eyes look slightly over his shoulder and I spot a familiar undeniably handsome man, 'Oh my God, it's Julian,' I say, still with my arms around Craig.

'Where?' Craig turns us elegantly around so we're both looking in the direction of the door. Julian spots us and walks over, uncomfortable but strong.

'What are you doing here?' I say happily as he approaches.

'I could ask you the same question.' He nods to my posture that still hasn't moved and then Craig breaks away. 'Let's just say I owe someone a favour.'

'Hi, I'm Craig, Poppie's brother.' He stretches out his hand warmly and Julian's face drops as he accepts.

'Oh, I'm so sorry to hear about your sister. Melanie says there's been no change so far.'

'Not yet, but they say the best way to help her come out of it is to talk, so…' His voice trails off. 'Anyway, I believe I'm dancing with your partner.' Craig puts his hand again on the small of my back and gives me a little push towards Julian. 'Nice to meet you. If you'll excuse me,' and he walks out of the room.

'Hi.' I step forward and give him a kiss; I still have to tiptoe despite my heels. When I pull away, something doesn't feel right.

'You look absolutely wonderful,' he takes me in and then his eyes sadden.

'What? Is there something on my dress?' I look down and start patting.

'No, nothing to do with your dress. Can we go for a walk? Do you have a coat?'

'Yes, I checked it in.'

We stroll quietly along the fairy-lit path outside hand in hand; the music and sound of the party can still be heard.

'Quite something to see Luke Braydon live, isn't it?' he says to break our silence. 'I'll have to thank Michelle for texting me.'

So that's what she was doing with my phone. 'It's nice to see you,' I say, meaning it. Even though I'm confused, I do like this man.

'You too,' he says but his tone says something very different. 'Melanie, I feel we need to talk.'

'You're going to break up with me ten minutes before midnight?' I ask fearfully.

'No, I'm not going to break up with you; I don't ever want to break up with you...' he stops abruptly as if the last part of the sentence surprised himself as much as me. 'What I'm trying to say is that I want us to work. Very much so. But I feel that you're holding something back from me and I don't know what it is.'

Victoria Mae

He looks at me and I'm not sure what to say. I can't tell him what the problem is; I promised Keeley and Joe/Sebastian, whatever his name is, that I wouldn't.

'It's OK, you don't have to tell me now, but I just want to make sure that whatever it is, doesn't come between us, because I think we have a connection, don't you?' I smile at him but don't answer. 'And I think we might actually have a future together but I don't know how you feel about me. I know you had a difficult relationship before and that's still a little raw for you, so I know you're not exactly where I am right now…' I open my mouth to comment but nothing comes out. 'It's OK, I do understand; you don't have to say anything. I know that it's going to take a bit of time and I am prepared to wait for you. But I wanted to ask if there's any, I guess, *point* in my waiting for you.'

I look at this charming man in front of me who's wearing his heart on his sleeve; who's good with kids; who my family approve of; who's good at cooking; who has dreams and aspirations and who wants me there alongside him. I look into his kind eyes.

'You're going to break up with me five minutes before midnight, aren't you?' He interrupts my external silence.

'No, I'm not,' and I stand on tiptoes, lean in and kiss him gently. 'I think you're a wonderful man. I think you could be very good for me and yes, there is something that I haven't told you but now isn't the time to say, but believe me, it's no reflection on you, so I think we should see what happens with us and in the meantime, go back inside to enjoy the rest of the evening together. What do you think?'

'I think it's nearly midnight,' he says, looking at his watch.

We return our coats and enter the Darlington Room just as the countdown has started. 'Ten…nine…eight…!!!' We walk

hand in hand to the middle of the dance floor, 'Five...four...'
I join in and Julian yells over the crowd,

'Here's to us and a brand-new year full of happiness.'

I nod as everyone yells, 'Two...one...HAPPY NEW
YEAR!!'

He leans down and kisses me and I can't help but
acknowledge the sinking feeling that you're meant to be more
excited about a kiss. He lifts me up into a hug and from over
his shoulder I spot Craig, who's looking right at me over
Cassie's shoulder.

'Happy New Year,' he mouths at me and I mouth the same
back at him. Julian holds me even tighter and Craig is dragged
away by both Cassie and Tanya, out of my line of sight.

The rest of the evening is a blur of champagne and dancing;
I know this when I come into consciousness the next morning
as my head and feet ache equally. Still lying there, I feel very
heavy — like a weight is on me. Opening half an eye, I see an
extra arm on my stomach. I go to turn my body but realise
there's a weighty leg seat-belting me in, so I turn my head and
forcing both eyes open, I see Julian, happily asleep on the
pillow next to me.

Oh, now I remember, I smile naughtily to myself and
snuggle down a little further into the pillow and fall back
asleep.

When I wake up again several hours later Julian isn't in my
bed and I wonder if I imagined it. I tiptoe out of my room —
anything heavier might make me throw up — and I spot him
in the kitchen by the coffee machine, wearing nothing but his
boxers and white shirt; it's unbuttoned, revealing his toned
stomach.

'Good morning,' he smiles at me with longing. 'I thought
I'd make us a little breakfast. Sleep well?' He tends to the

toast that has just popped up.

'I did, actually. How about you?' I sit down before I fall down.

'Never better. I feel fantastic! I was even thinking we could go for a jog later.'

'I was thinking we could fall asleep on the sofa, in between watching some TV.'

'Oh, come on, you were telling me last night how much you'd like to go jogging today.'

'I was?' I ask, rubbing my head.

'You were,' he says, bringing over the coffee and toast. 'But your idea sounds good too.' He gives me a kiss on the cheek and then sits down opposite me, taking a bite of toast. 'You said quite a few interesting things last night.'

'I did?' My face reveals some worry.

'Yup,' he smiles smugly. 'Let's see, what were my favourites? Oh yes, you said you couldn't wait to see what my whole naked body looked like.'

'Now that you mention it, I might remember that…' I pick up some toast, thinking that my drunken babbling probably wasn't that bad.

'You said you wish you were brave enough to give up teaching and follow your real dream.'

'Did I say what my real dream was?' I ask with curiosity.

'No, you started doing shots at that point.'

I wince. 'That's why I feel so rubbish.'

'But the most interesting of all, you told me what the issue is that you've been having.'

'I haven't had an issue,' I say, wondering what I came out with.

'You told me your sister's having an affair.' I open my eyes wide. 'It must be hard to keep a secret like that — no wonder you've been a little stressed; it all makes sense now.'

'You seem very calm.' I test the waters, not sure if I told him *who* Keeley's been having an affair with.

'Well yeah, I have to say I'm a little relieved.'

'Relieved?'

'I thought it was something to do with me from the way you've been acting but it's just your sister. Now that you've told me I hope you know that if you want to, you can confide in me; I'll always be here for you.'

Oh God, I can't do this.

'Why are you looking at me like I've just announced that I've run over your puppy?'

'I can't do this,' I say out loud this time.

'Well, you don't have to tell me anything about it if you don't want to; I—'

'No,' I interrupt him. 'I can't do this.' I gesture to us. 'You're such a nice guy; you're the perfect guy, actually. You're kind and thoughtful and have said everything that I thought I wanted to hear, but I just can't do this.' *I can't always have this at the back of my mind and I certainly can't ever tell you.*

He swallows his toast and considers me. 'I know you're not telling me something.' He shakes his head. 'You're not ever going to be able to tell me, are you?'

I shake my head slowly at him, 'I'm so sorry. I really do want to be with you, but…'

'No,' he says softly and stands up, 'You *want* to want to be with me.' He bends down and kisses me on the forehead this time. 'I think you're a really special person, Melanie. And I do mean it; I will always be here for you if you want me. But I think you need to figure out what it is that you want. I'll go and get dressed.'

Chapter 22

Julian's words have rung constantly in my head since he left on New Year's Day. *What is it that I want?* Well, I haven't had a clue but it gave me a really good idea for school; I decided that for the new year my class would do a creative project, designing and making a huge 'aspiration tree.' It's taken a fortnight to plan, build and decorate and it's now standing proudly in the far corner of my classroom. Today we're making our leaves to hang onto the branches and are going to write what our biggest goal is for the future — I'm even forcing myself to join in and commit to something.

'Now, I want you to write anything that comes into your mind,' I tell my attentive class. 'Something that you'd like to achieve in your life; something you want to own or who you want to be — when you're as old as I am.' The class giggle on cue. 'I'm giving you five minutes and we're going to do this in complete silence so you can really concentrate on what it is that *you* want — not what the person next to you wants, Annabelle.' Annabelle stops whispering to Kalle next to her, embarrassed. 'And once you've finished, start reading please.'

I watch my class obediently go deep into thought or immediately start scribbling, then I look down at the leaf in front of me and play with it in my hands. *Come on. What do I want to achieve?* If I were doing this a year ago, I would have, without a doubt or a moment's hesitation, written: "To have a beautiful wedding". But now I realise, I'm not actually ready for that kind of commitment — at all. Plus, I think I've also come to realise that what I truly wanted was a *wedding,* not a marriage. Now, like Julian said, I need to decide for myself what it is that I want. *What have I always wanted to do?*

I pick up my pen and write quickly before I change my mind and then wait until everyone has finished.

'OK, shall we share what we've written down?'

Complete silence.

I change my tone and correct myself. 'We're going to share what we've written down as we hang them on the tree.'

My class is both predictable and surprising, with answers ranging from: "To marry somebody rich and famous", to the last and most outlandish: "To be an astronaut".

'What did you write down, miss?' the future Buzz asks me as he sits down.

Standing, I walk over and hang mine on the tree. 'To train for and run a marathon.' Saying it out loud is quite scary.

As the bell goes, my class file out excitedly talking about their goals and dreams; I walk out after them and over to Jill's office — now almost complete.

'Craig isn't here,' she says to me, not looking up from her laptop. 'He seems to keep running out just before the bell goes.'

'I've come to speak to you actually.' I sit on her desk. I have noticed that — Craig and I haven't had our usual after-school chats since before the Christmas break.

'Oh, OK, just give me two seconds.' She taps away.

'I've got something to ask you.'

She finishes then leans back in her wheely chair. 'Fire away.'

'How...now don't laugh,' I warn her.

'Have I ever laughed at you?' she says innocently.

'Yes. Many times, but anyway…how…do you go about training for a marathon?' I say the last part quickly before I change my mind.

'You want to run a marathon?' she asks, impressed.

'It's something I've thought about doing for years. I told Evan once but he laughed so hard at me that I put it to the back of my mind. Nieve's always tried to encourage me to run with her and then seeing Julian into it, I thought maybe I could have a go. But I have no idea where to start, so I've come to you.'

'Well, I'm flattered.' She swings from side to side in her chair, looking very powerful. 'Well, a good place to start is going for a full health check; some say this is over the top but that's what I do each time. Then getting a good pair of shoes; those silly flimsy things you have won't cut it, I'm afraid. And then getting a workout and diet plan together. I'll help you.' She gets out a piece of paper and starts scribbling.

'Wow. I'm actually going to do this.'

She looks up at me. 'It's just a plan; you haven't signed up for anything officially yet,' she reminds me. 'So, you're far too late to apply for something like the *London Marathon*, but that's a good thing; you need some warm up ones first, say a 5 or 10K? You can even do it for a charity; maybe Poppie's unit or something?'

'That's an amazing idea.'

'There's actually a 5K happening near you in April; that'll be good for your first one,' Jill nods. 'Gives you, what, twelve weeks or so to train. That's about right if you've never done anything like this before.'

'Haven't done what before?' Dave walks in so effortlessly, you'd never know anything was wrong with his leg.

'Jill's helping me plan to do a marathon,' I say standing

tall.

'Really? Wow, it's been ages since you mentioned that.'

'Well, I'm starting small with a 5K in April but it's now officially my long-term goal.'

'Long-term goal,' he imitates. 'Who are you and what have you done with the real Butler?'

'I am a new and improved version of my previous self.' Dave raises an impressed eyebrow, but says nothing further. 'Hey, you could do it with me!' I add with excitement.

'Too soon after my leg,' he says a little too quickly. 'So, I'm just here to tell you I'll be late for drinks: got a brief meeting with Dermott.'

'You've been having a lot of meetings with Dermott recently; are you planning something that we don't know about?' Jill asks him. 'I bet it's another project for the school. Definitely.' She nods at her own idea.

'I don't know what this meeting's about, if you must know,' he says, almost embarrassed. Anyway, I'm nearly late.' He turns quickly. 'I'll see you later,' he says over his shoulder.

'Whoa, what's the hurry?' Gracie says as Dave bumps into her before he makes a dash back to the main building. 'He's a bit touchy. Wonder what's got him riled?'

***

'It's probably — nothing — Melsy,' Nieve pants as we run together around Greenwich Park a few weeks later. 'He's been a bit — funny for ages, you said?'

'Yeah, there's — just something that's got his — knickers in a twist. I know he — doesn't — like Dermott anyway. Maybe — that's it,' I manage in between breathing. 'Does this get — easier?' I ask her and she laughs.

'Yes. This — is nice.' She grins at me. 'I like the new and improved Mel; she rings more and — likes something that I like doing.'

'Well — Julian said — something to me that — really stuck.'

'What was that?' We turn a corner.

'He said I need to — to decide what it — is that I want — in life.'

'And what is that?'

'Apart from — the running? *Erm* — I — haven't quite figured that — out yet but I'm — going to. Can we stop for a moment?' We slow and continue at a walking pace to get some water from the kiosk by the Observatory.

'I think you're very inspiring, you know that?' she says in between sips. 'You're very, Keeley.'

'Keeley?' I say, confused.

'Yes, look, Keeley!' She points and we see her on a bench, hugging Ava, with Henry and Lucy playing happily around her. But as we draw nearer, we see that she's crying. She spots us and doesn't even pretend that she isn't crying; her silent tears trickle down her cheeks faster and faster.

'Hi!' Nieve says, scooping up Henry and then lowers her voice. 'Oh my God, what happened?'

Keeley looks at me. 'I told him.'

'Oh no.'

'Who did you tell what?' Nieve says, in the dark.

'Auntie Melanie! Come and see my book,' Lucy says to me and I sit down on the bench and make some '*Ooh*' noises for my niece.

'He told me to get out.'

'Simon threw you out? Why?' Nieve swings Henry from

side to side.

'So, I came here; it was the first place I thought of.'

'Let's go back to mine...who wants to go back to my flat for a film!?'

The kids and Nieve all put their hands up and yell, 'Me!'

We take Keeley's car to mine — she even lets me drive. After I settle the kids in front of *Ice Age*, I join my sisters in the kitchen.

'Oh my God,' Nieve is saying as I sit down and I guess that Keeley has caught her up.

'I didn't mean for this to go so far and we have been broken up for a while now, but I had to tell Simon; it was eating me up. I've lost everything.' She looks on at her kids.

'He probably just wants a moment to breathe and take it in. You can stay here if you want. The kids can stay on my blow-up mattresses and you'll have to take the sofa? My place is a bit further from their school and your work, though — I could maybe take them before I head to work so you're not late?'

'Or I could? My work's in the evening, remember?' Nieve offers too, 'And I can watch Ava for part of the day?'

She looks at us both gratefully. 'Thank you. But I won't be in a rush to get anywhere; I haven't been working for months now. They made me redundant at the end of summer.' She puts her head in her hands. 'I didn't realise it at the time but my fancy car was part of the pay-out.'

'Why didn't you say anything?'

'I thought it was easier to suffer the burden on my own; asking for help is a sign of weakness.'

'No, it's not. It's a sign of strength because you're acknowledging that you can't do everything yourself; no one can do everything themselves.' Nieve crosses her legs on the chair and sits tall, like a wise Buddha.

'Well, I don't feel very strong. I thought I was meant to be more than just a mother and a wife — what kind of example am I setting when I'm failing at everything?' Keeley looks vulnerably from my eyes to Nieve's before sighing once more, standing up. 'I'll call Simon to tell him we're here so he doesn't worry; I hope he's a little worried,' she adds before disappearing into the hallway.

'Well, my goodness me, who knew the goody-two-shoes could do so wrong?' Nieve says, hugging her tea.

I shrug. 'I know, but she was sad and lonely, and I can't believe I'm saying this, but I can understand why she did it.' Nieve's mouth is open. 'I know. I told you I can't believe I'm saying it.'

'Well, if there's one thing to draw a family together, it's a drama. It's nice not to be the one causing the drama for a change.'

***

'What would you say to a big *Ficus* in the corner?' I wave my arms around marking the spot. 'I saw one down the road that would go perfectly here. *Ooh*, and perhaps a dream catcher by the bed?'

'That might help to brighten things up,' Michael replies in a monotone voice; his eyes have dark shadows under them and I swear his face gets more and more gaunt every time I see him.

'Let me grab something for us all to eat too while I'm out?' I say, while adding some chakra stones to my list.

He looks over at his wife. 'No, I'm fine thank you.'

'Mike, you've got to eat something.' Craig stands up and puts a hand onto his shoulder.

'In the meantime.' I rustle inside my bag and locate a breakfast bar. 'One going spare, very delicious!' He neither replies nor moves his gaze. 'Poppie would want you to eat something,' I say kindly and extend it to him.

He meets my eyes and nods, accepting it.

'I'll come with you, Mel, you'll need a hand...' Craig grins. 'Although the thought of you waddling along with a huge *Ficus* is quite the hilarious picture.'

Craig holds the door for me as we leave the hospital. 'God, he looks awful, doesn't he?' I say, doing up my coat.

'I think he looks as chipper as he can be with a wife who's lying there like a vegetable.'

'She is going to wake up, Craig,' I say forcefully.

'I want to believe that too.' The wind brushes my cheeks as we leave the hospital, stepping into the brisk evening. 'Let's just do what we can for them both and I guess the rest is just about waiting.'

'Exactly. You know, I'm...' I want to tell him that I'm raising money for Poppie's unit but I don't want him to make fun of me, '...actually very hungry. Let's get food and then the *Ficus, eh*?'

Craig nods. 'Yeah, I'm starving too, let's go to a restaurant; I'm sure Mike won't notice the time if we're gone for long. This is a nice place.' He stops outside a French bistro. 'Fancy it? I'll treat you.' We're seated at the last free table, in the corner of the noisy and warmly lit restaurant; a welcome change from the depressing walls of Poppie's room. Opening the menu, everything is written in French and I look up at Craig, whose eyes are already upon me. 'So, what do you remember from GCSE French?' He grins with a steady gaze.

I sit up tall and scan the page, confident that I can remember something. After a moment my voice, laced with smugness, declares, '*Fromage.*'

He bursts out laughing as the waiter approaches and welcomes us. Craig launches effortlessly into a conversation in French with him before pausing. 'Would you rather brie with melon and berries, or a goat's cheese tart to start?'

'Brie,' I reply, taken aback.

Craig says something else I don't understand to the waiter and pauses once more, 'A fruity Chilean Pinot Noir OK? It's meant to complement the dish.'

'Sounds delicious,' I aim at Craig before giving the waiter my best '*Merci.*'

'*Pas de probleme,*' he responds before walking away.

'You asked me what I wanted.'

'Yeah, so?' He unfolds his napkin and places it in his lap.

'Well, the last time I was in a place like this, I was with Evan and he ordered for me without asking my preference.'

'Did you tell him what you wanted?'

I contemplate this for a moment. 'No.'

He patiently lets me gather my thoughts before I continue. 'I think I got in the habit of not telling him what I wanted or what I thought because whenever I did, he would tell me I was wrong or stupid and would then laugh at me. So, I stopped having an opinion, afraid that if I did, he would break up with me. I guess I thought living that way was better than being alone.' My gaze falls and I say to my hands, 'I wanted to marry a man who I was afraid to be myself around.' I meet his eyes again. 'That's pretty ridiculous, isn't it?'

'Well, perhaps. But sometimes people can be a little *too much* of themselves around others. Take Cassie, for example; she's blunt and sometimes inappropriate but she doesn't care what people think of her; maybe she could tone that back a bit but ultimately, there's a nice person in there really.'

'I didn't realise you were still seeing Cassie?'

He nods. 'Yeah, we get along, have a good time together.' He pauses once more. 'We'll see where it goes.'

'I'd like to reach that moment where I don't care what other people think of me. But how do you get there?'

'Why are you asking me?'

'Because you've never cared what people think of you. I've never known anyone like that. I envy that about you…and *her,* I guess.'

He scratches his head. 'I do care what people think but I care more about what *I* think. One's own opinion is the most important out there. Just because someone says something about you, that doesn't define who you are unless you let it. We all have a choice whether we want to give away our power or to keep it for ourselves.'

'Your mum used to say that,' I say softly.

'She was a wise woman,' he says after a beat and seems to blink away a memory. 'Life is all about being smart and sometimes you go all dreamy and forget to be smart.'

Again, I consider this instead of reverting to my old habit of wanting to throw something at him. 'Do you remember what you said to me at Poppie and Michael's wedding?'

'Not specifically.' His voice is short but intrigued.

'Well, I do, it was something like, I live more in my head than in the real world, which I thought at the time was a little harsh, but maybe you were right?'

'Well, that's normally the case,' he says, playfully serious.

'Shut up,' I continue, with no venom in my voice, 'I've been thinking about this, and maybe daydreaming has been my defence mechanism. I'm protected in my own mind when I feel threatened in the real world.'

'Maybe you need to question if you want to live a life

where you have a default defence mechanism at all? Is that how you want to be for the rest of your life, constantly looking for reasons to escape what's in front of you?' His bottle green eyes wait for me to respond without judgement or jeering.

'I'm learning not to.'

'And the real question to ask yourself is: what are you afraid of?'

I don't speak for a long time. 'I'm afraid of being vulnerable.'

'We all are, to some extent.'

The waiter brings over our wine so we sit in silence once more until he leaves. 'Why have you become so easy to talk to?'

'You've stopped looking for a reason to be offended by everything that comes out of my mouth.'

'Maybe you used to remind me of Evan.'

'Ouch.'

'I already had one man in my life pointing out my flaws; apparently, I didn't want another.'

'Well, I'm glad you've changed your mind about me.'

I really have.

'When you change your mind, you change your experience. Take Poppie, for example — maybe this is her way of telling us that life is too precious not to grab opportunities when they come our way, or to not say things that you want to or not to do something that you've been stopping yourself from doing. Time is too fleeting to be afraid.'

'I've missed our chats after school; where do you keep running off to?'

He concentrates on his wine for a moment, swirling it around like a connoisseur. 'Well, as we're nearing completion, I've had to take care of several things in the office that I can't do on site; we'll be out of your hair before you know it.'

A few months ago, I would have jumped up and down with excitement at this prospect but a wave of unknown sadness washes through the pit of my stomach. I clear my throat, 'That's good to know. You can get on with higher profile projects now, right?' Craig nods with his attention still on his wine glass.

***

Tiptoeing back into my silent flat several hours later, I find everyone fast asleep: Henry and Lucy on the blow-up mattress; Ava in a travel cot; and Keeley on the sofa, cuddling a photo frame. Silently selecting a blanket out of the cupboard, I lay it on top of my big sister and her arms loosen slightly; I pick up the frame. It's a picture of her and Simon before they had the kids, on holiday somewhere beautifully sunny. Both of them are wearing expressions of joy and love. I put the frame on the coffee table then adjusting the blanket a little higher around my big sister, I observe her face; I didn't know you could look so tortured in your sleep. She stirs slightly and opens her glossy eyes, not saying anything.

'It'll all be OK,' I whisper optimistically.

She nods and tears up before closing her eyes once more. I kiss her on the forehead and turn off the hall light.

Chapter 23

As the half-term springs upon us, Keeley and the kids make their way to *Centre Parcs* — something that Simon booked as a Christmas present for them all. 'Well, have a great time regardless of what happens, OK?' I try to reassure her as she stands in my doorway.

'We'll see if he comes,' her small, tired voice utters.

'If he does, you're meant to work things out now, but if he doesn't, it will just be a matter of time,' I encourage.

'Maybe.' Keeley looks over her shoulder at the kids patiently waiting in the car, then back to me with hope in her eyes; for the first time in my life, I can see her barriers aren't up as high. 'If things go well, hopefully we won't be coming back here; no offence.'

'None taken.' I smile at her. 'You can stay here as long as you need to.'

She gives me a tight hug and says into my hair, 'Thank you for saving me.'

'We helped save each other; this was just my turn,' I reply, 'Now, relax and enjoy some quality time with the kids.'

I wave them off then shut the door before plonking myself on the sofa. I'm meant to be at a staff social tonight that Mish helped organise, but I've made my excuses and snuggling down a little further into the pillows, all I want is a quiet night in. Flicking through the What's On guide, I start to plan my evening, when my phone announces that Mish is ringing me;

she speaks before I even have a chance to say hello.

'How's the cold?' she asks with sarcasm.

'You and I know I'm perfectly healthy but I told you I'm not up for going; I really appreciate everything you've done to organise it, though.' Phone in one hand and remote in the other, I wiggle my happy feet in their warm slippers, with absolutely no intention of moving.

'*Um hmm*. OK, I'll be around in fifteen minutes to help you get ready.'

I scrunch up my face. 'There was this documentary I fancied watching on penguins...'

'You asked for my help and organisation, the least you can do is turn up. And trust me, you won't want to miss tonight.' I hear the jingle-jangle of keys and a door shutting.

'Like I said, I really appreciate your help, Dermott is thrilled to be going on the Thames; he said he hasn't done anything like that since moving to London. But you know me, I'm just like my dad; I don't like boats,' I say flatly, as my eyes stray back to the TV guide.

'No, you don't like your hair getting messed up in the wind,' she says reasonably, knowing me far too well. 'I'm not taking no for an answer, jump in the shower and I'll see you in a bit.' And with that she hangs up. I'll just have to find out another time how the penguins fight for their survival.

***

'What on earth?!?' I open the door in my dressing gown and turban towel hairdo to Mish with a black suit bag over her shoulder, dressed head to toe in an icy blue number, complete with a long, blonde, plaited wig.

'So, I forgot to mention one thing on the phone...' She

presses her pink lips together in a very small smirk.

'Since when did it turn into a fancy-dress party?' I cross my arms in finality.

'I thought it would be a fun Valentine's Day twist — you'd know that if you ever checked your emails or voice messages — and didn't Dave or anyone mention anything?'

I close the door in her face. 'I have been preoccupied and I am not going!' I shout through the door, but she lets herself in with her spare keys.

'Then why did you get in the shower?'

'Because you told me to,' I say, knowing full-well that I will eventually give in.

She grabs my hand and marches me towards my room. 'Let's just see how your outfit fits before we make any decisions.'

***

'I look ridiculous with a fringe and plaited pigtails, Mish,' I complain as we exit the cab and make our way to the dock.

'No, you don't, you look cute. Plus, I had to think of something, otherwise you'd be left out.'

'What d'you mean?'

'I emailed Dermott a list of character couples: fictional, real, romantic or otherwise and you were all meant to pick one; like I said, if you checked your emails, you would know that.'

'I knew I wasn't going to go so I didn't read any of them,' I retort as we walk up the jetty.

'Well, aren't you glad your fictional sister is here for you?' She grins at me and flicks her plait from one side to the other.

'Thank you, Elsa,' I smile at my best friend as I hold the

door open for her.

'You're welcome, Anna.'

'I didn't think you were coming! Well don't you look cute!' Dave greets us over his sunglasses as we make it aboard.

'See, I told you!' Mish nudges me. 'I'm going to make sure everything is sorted. Enjoy!' She flits off after giving my hand a squeeze and Dave's cheek a brief kiss.

'She's less frightening as a snow queen. I would have thought she'd come as Morticia or something.'

'Too obvious,' I grin. 'I should have come as your pair.' I play with his hat. 'It would have been much more comfortable.'

'It takes a certain type of person to pull off a Blues Brother, *Anna*.'

'Harsh.' I adjust my magenta cape. 'Well, at least I'm a princess, then.'

'The most accurate princess to match your personality,' Dave chuckles.

'Yeah, I see what you mean: devoted to mending a broken bond with my sister, well, *sisters* I guess.'

'Definitely.' He puts his arm around me, 'But I was thinking more along the lines of a bit naïve, clumsy…'

'And a hopeless romantic?' A third voice chips in.

'What is this, gang up on Mel day?' I say to the Blues Brother and now to a prince. 'Who are you supposed to be?'

'I'm the Beast,' Craig replies, standing tall.

'How accurate.' I tease. 'Why aren't you all hairy?'

'I had a shave before I came out.' He strokes his smooth and normally stubbly chin.

'He's the Beast *after* the transformation, I didn't want him to walk around with something ridiculous on his head.' Cassie glides over to us in a beautiful golden ballgown and just like at New Year, I instantaneously feel small, dumpy and unimportant.

What the hell is she doing here?

'Ah, so glad you both could make it.' Another Blue Brother joins our party. 'Your other half has done wonders for our school; what better way to celebrate than joining us!' Dermott takes Cassie's hand and shakes it gently before taking in the rest of our group. 'Melanie, glad you're feeling better! How embarrassing, Dave, I should have asked what you were wearing!' he jokes. 'Well, have a lovely time, all; it's going to be an evening full of fun and surprises! I'll be outside greeting everyone if you need me.'

'He's really fake,' Cassie snarls when Dermott's out of earshot.

'No, he's not.' Everyone else in the circle says together.

'Well, in my experience, no one is ever that happy to see people. I need a drink; come with me,' Cassie fires at Craig, before spinning around without waiting for a response, whipping my boots with her dress as she glides off towards the bar.

'Sorry, see you later.' Craig nods and follows obediently.

'Wow, who was that ghastly creature?'

'You look amazing!' I laugh at Jill, complete with a crazed short black and white wig, floor length black gown, faux fur wrap and posing with a cigarette holder.

'Wait until you see Gracie.' She steps to one side to reveal our normally reserved friend in a white corseted off the shoulder top and ruffle bottom dress, carrying a sword and wearing a long luscious dark wig; I can barely recognise her. We all woof-whistle and she blushes.

'It was Pablo's suggestion for me to dress as Elena; he

loves *The Mask of Zorro*. We even say lines from the film to each other sometimes.' Her face falls, 'Although when I tried to FaceTime him earlier, he didn't answer; guess he has better things to do.'

When the party casts off into full swing, I slip outside to take in the skyline. Sliding the door open to the front of the boat, the gentle breeze brushes a few strands of my wig's fringe away from my face; it's ever so slightly cool out here but not too unpleasant. I'm pleased to discover that I'm the only person on this side of the boat. Walking further out onto the deck, I stand by the railing and hug my arms as we sail seamlessly into the night. I take in the lights, the buzz and the moonlight glowing upon the inky black Thames. As we sail under Tower Bridge, another vessel full of people wave at me, so I happily wave back.

The door behind me slides open and Belle steps out. 'Don't you hate these parties?' she aims at me, while lighting a cigarette. 'Everyone here is so dull.'

I breathe, promise myself to behave and think before I speak. 'Where's your date?'

'Talking with Cruella de Vil, who in my opinion is nowhere *near* thin enough to pull off a dress like that.' She takes a puff and looks at me for the first time. 'Have we met before?'

I nod with a frown, 'At New Year; I'm a school friend of Craig's.'

She exhales. 'Oh, yes, Mona, wasn't it?'

'Melanie,' I correct and try to see the funny side of this. 'So why, in the nicest way possible, are you here then?' I ask, trying to sound as pleasant as possible.

'Craig didn't want to come alone, and I can see why; like I said, everyone is so dull.' I glare at this Amazonian woman looking down at me in more ways than one, and wonder just how deeply the *nice* part of her is buried.

'Thought you'd be out here.' Craig steps out to join us. 'Isn't it a great party?'

'That's just what Cassie was saying to me!' I say with sarcasm.

'I'm going to the ladies before I grab another drink.' Cassie throws her cigarette overboard and I silently wish she'd gone with it. 'Do hurry to come and find me,' she instructs him and he helps her back inside.

'She gets more and more delightful with every moment,' I laugh. 'How lucky you are to have someone so special in your life.'

'Now, now. It's challenging for someone from the outside to see into someone else's relationship.' We look at each other in silence.

'I'm sorry,' I lean on the railings with my elbows. 'Who am I to judge anyway?' He matches my body posture.

'She really didn't want to come so it's no wonder she's a bit grumpy. Dermott said no one had chosen Belle, so suggested I bring her along.'

'I see. Why are you telling me this?'

'Good question.' He looks searchingly into my eyes and we remain in silence for some time before he confesses, 'I thought you might come as Belle. She was one of your favourites, wasn't she?'

'How do you remember that?' I marvel at this man I used to hate.

'No idea; clearly you made an impression in my mind long ago. But, even though you're not Belle, I think you look adorable.'

'Thank you.' My heart beats a little faster as he tentatively inches his hand nearer to mine. 'You look very handsome too,' I dare to respond.

His little finger brushes against mine. 'Melanie, I wanted to…'

'How's my girl?' Dave interrupts whatever Craig was going to say and his hand flies away from mine.

'I'm adorable,' I grin, standing up straight and turning towards Dave, who places his arm comfortably around me once more.

'That's what I've always told you.' Dave gives me a little affectionate squeeze then looks down to a slightly disgruntled Craig. 'Did I interrupt something?'

Craig uncreases his expression and straightens up, 'Not at all.' He forms his face into a natural smile. 'See you back inside.'

'So,' Dave spins me back around to enjoy the night's skyline. 'How stunning is it this evening?' He takes in the view.

'It's beautiful,' I agree and we both wave at another party boat.

'Look, I wanted to say again that I'm sorry I've been a bit up and down with you this year.' He looks remorsefully at me. 'You really mean the world to me, you know that?'

I nod, wanting so badly for things to return to how they always were. 'I do.' He looks at me with relief mixed with something else that I can't quite put my finger on.

'If I'd known you were coming maybe I would have come as Hans or, what's the other one, Kristoff.'

'Or Olaf?' I joke and he flicks one of my plaits, jesting. The door slides open once more and an excited voice materialises. 'Come on, we're just about to start!'

'Start what?' I ask Roger Rabbit.

'Just come in and see,' he runs out, grabs my hand, I grab Dave's and we're pulled inside. A hush falls over the crowd and the second Blues Brother starts to speak,

'Good evening, everyone. I thought we'd start the evening off with a little game! As you know, I asked for everyone to choose from a list, a character. Your chosen character has a pair. The aim of the game is to find your partner for the evening and you will then go to the designated dining area and sit with your fictional significant other.'

I scan the room for Mish, who is nowhere to be seen.

'So, I am giving you, *ooh*, three minutes, to find your partner and to be seated. If you have not found your partner in said time, there will be a forfeit.' He smiles unthreateningly and I watch everyone's eyes fire all over the room, looking for their match.

'On your marks, get set, GO!!'

Dave walks casually over to Dermott as the entire party scrambles around so hard I'm surprised the boat isn't rocking from side to side. I see Fred team up with Wilma, Jill has found her Dalmatian, Roger Rabbit has found Jessica. I get shoved by Cleopatra and fly into David Beckham, 'Sorry!'

'Two minutes!!' A few couples are taking their seats around the dining table as Mish makes her way towards me. 'One minute!!' Dermott says, with Dave now beside him.

'You're not going to believe what's about to happen,' Mish smiles. 'Watch Gracie.' She points and we watch her scanning the room to no avail. Then a masked man steps out from the kitchen and makes his way over to "Elena" from behind.

'Thirty seconds!' Dermott says gleefully.

'Is it?' I say with surprise to Mish, who responds with a grin.

We shuffle a little closer to hear a sexy Spanish voice. 'Do you surrender?'

Gracie's whole body stiffens but she doesn't turn around. She says the next line from the film. 'Never. But I may scream.'

Still behind her, he places his hand on the small of her back, 'I understand. Sometimes I have that effect.' She hesitantly turns to see her Zorro. '*Mi amor*,' Pablo purrs and touches her cheek gently.

Gracie gasps and her eyes fill with tears. 'I can't believe you're here!' She pulls him into a hug and doesn't let go.

'He got in contact with Dermott, and Dermott called me to help plan the surprise.' Mish puts her arm around me. 'Love a happy ending.'

After coffees and teas are served, I sit happily in a corner with Jill and Gracie, observing the rest of the room. 'Can you believe this?' Gracie beams, gazing over at Pablo talking with Dave, Craig and Dermott. 'He said he had to see me in person and is even thinking about moving here! I mean, it's all a bit fast but it feels right. And when it feels right, it's got to be right, right? Oh my God, this is insane. I'm so happy!' She squeals, looking from Jill to me with doe-eyes.

'I for one think it's insane.' Jill adjusts her wig, 'But that's often the place where the best things happen. If I had someone fly from Spain to see me, I wouldn't let them go.'

'Me neither. We're so happy for you, hon,' I say, sipping my Americano. 'And I tell you what; seeing you with *Pablo*,' I say in a sexy Spanish accent which makes Gracie giggle with more glee, 'makes me realise,' I shrug, 'what kind of man I want to be with. Or rather, in spite of everything, *the* man I want to be with.'

'Really?'

'Who?' Gracie and Jill chorus excitedly together,

'You'll have to wait and see.' My eyes lift to the animated group on the other side of the room. *I'll have to wait and see.*

Chapter 24

I've kicked my exercise up a notch and am now jogging every day when I get home from school. Each day is not only getting easier physically but is becoming increasingly appealing, as we break into an early Spring. Today I decided to bring my gear with me and run a different circuit before heading home.

After changing in the ladies near the staffroom, I literally bump into Dave on my way out, sending the books he's carrying flying.

'Just as panoramic as always,' he says as we both bend down to gather them. 'You look good in exercise gear.' He looks me up and down. 'Suits you.'

'No one looks good in exercise gear, Dave,' I blush, 'but thanks.'

'Listen, there's something I want to tell you,' he says, shifting awkwardly. 'Can I come to yours, maybe a little later on?'

'Gracie was going to come round as soon as she's finished her after-school club, before her date with Pablo, bit of Dutch-courage; you could come too?' He doesn't answer and I realise it's something he wants to tell just me. 'Can't you just tell me now?'

'It's not really corridor stuff, Mels,' his face changes.

'Well, you got any workout stuff? You could come with me?' I suggest.

'Still can't jog yet, might throw my development back.

You go, we'll find another time, I'm sure.' He smiles weakly and goes to walk away.

'Come round tomorrow after school,' I say to his back. 'I'll be back from the hospital, maybe six-ish?'

'How's Poppie doing?' he asks, remembering.

'The same,' I exhale. 'But I'm sure my talking is helping.'

He laughs. 'It always does. OK, tomorrow, great,' and he walks off, distracted and without a goodbye. I do a couple of quick stretches, shaking off the weird feeling that something is wrong with Dave, and leave the school.

This thirty-minute loop is my biggest challenge so far, as I'm going to jog the whole way, which is something I haven't done so far. I put in my headphones and start jogging to the beat; I've found that music helps keep me distracted and motivated at the same time. It's all residential along my route and I admire the huge houses as I go, wondering if I will ever be able to afford somewhere like this. My breathing gets heavier and I concentrate on controlling it as Lady Gaga's 'Bad Romance' comes into play.

Twenty minutes in and on the final stretch, my legs are starting to feel a bit like jelly but I power through, just slowing my pace ever so slightly. Turning a corner, I see a runner coming towards me; immediately I recognise him. I slow even more as we approach each other and then stop and look up.

'You're running?' Julian says to me.

'You're running near my school?' I reply slightly out of breath.

'Well, I wanted to bump into you,' he says honestly, not out of breath at all.

'You did? Why?'

'Can we go for a coffee?' he asks, coming closer to me now.

'I don't think that's such a good idea.' I stand strong despite his handsome eyes gazing into mine.

'Please. There's something I really want to say to you.'

'That seems to be a common theme today.'

'I'd really like to, Melanie; something needs to be said.'

'Well, we're not too far from the heath, we could go somewhere near there?'

We go to the same cafe we went to on our second date and the only table free is the one that we sat at before; if he notices this too, he doesn't say anything.

'You look really well.'

'Thanks, so do you.' I mean it; he looks very handsome.

'How's school?' He tears open a sugar and pours it in his cup.

'Fine. How's work for you?'

'Good. I'm really glad I *ran* into you actually. I'm not going to be in the country for that much longer.'

'You're going travelling again?'

'I finally took the plunge and decided to open up a restaurant — in Perth.'

'Wow. Congratulations! So, you're moving to Australia?'

'Yeah, that's the plan. Tylor and I are going in on it together. But, you know, I couldn't have done it without you.'

'Me? I didn't do anything.'

'When we broke up, I asked myself: what do I want? This is what I came up with.' We sit there in silence, tending to our drinks and as I look up, I can see he's considering his next words, 'And I understand why you couldn't be with me; I know.'

'You know what?' I say slowly, promising myself never to tell him unless he really does know.

'About Joe's affair with your sister; Charlotte told me,' he adds and my heart drops.

I come out with, 'I'm so sorry,' even though I know I didn't cause anything.

He shakes his head. 'Look, if I were in your position, I couldn't have been with you either. Having something like that hanging over you isn't fun.' We look at each other finally with understanding but with a hint of sadness too. 'They ruined what could have been perfectly perfect, didn't they?'

I nod and sip my green tea. 'How is Charlotte?' I dare to ask.

'Very calm, actually. Although when Joe told her she went into early labour,' he says, a little too casually.

'Oh my God. Is everything OK?'

'Yes.' He smiles. 'Penny Rose was born completely healthy. Charlotte had to stay in hospital for a few days but was fine after that.'

'Cute name.' I smile. 'So, how are Joe and Charlotte?' I naïvely hoped that having a baby would bring them closer and everything would be OK.

'Well.' He exhales. 'Charlotte is letting him see the kids and everything, but she made him move out. Only time will tell but honestly, it doesn't look too good.'

'Oh, this is such a mess,' I say and look out of the window. 'Simon made Keeley and the kids move out too. They've been meeting up and talking more, but in the meantime, they're staying with me.'

'In your flat? No wonder you're out running!'

I smile at him. 'It's a little snug,' I admit. 'But not that bad, really. I sort of feel like I'm making up for lost time. I like helping Henry with his homework, reading with Luce, and playing with Ava. And Keeley and I haven't been this close since we were kids, so...'

'Charlotte doesn't blame Keeley, by the way.'

'Really?' I say with surprise.

He shrugs. 'She's not the first one it happened with.'

My phone interrupts my response and I answer it. 'Hi Gracie.'

'Hey! Just wondering when you're heading back; you've really been going for it, I'm impressed!'

'What? Oh, no, I bumped into *um*, someone.' I look and smile at Julian. 'Meet you in like fifteen, twenty minutes, maybe?'

'Sure, sure, take your time!'

I hang up and place my phone on the table, 'Sorry about that, I forgot I'd made plans.'

'Well, I don't want to keep you. But I just really needed to tell you that, for what it's worth, I do think you're a special person, and that there are no hard feelings between us. And even though I know we aren't meant to be together as a couple, and that I'll be in a different time-zone soon, but I would very much still like to have you in my life as a friend.'

A weight feels like it's been lifted off of my shoulders. 'I'd really like that. But can you ever really be friends with someone you've slept with? I certainly haven't been able to in the past; have you?'

'No. But I haven't wanted to be friends with anyone else that I've slept with. Plus, as we've done *that* already, we can focus on being friends.' I blush, smile and nod at the same time. 'So, you're running now?' He changes the subject and gets out his wallet.

'Yeah.' I nod. 'I've even signed up for a 5K next month!'

'Well, I'm not leaving until September so if you'd like company or a bit of support or whatever on the run, I'm your man.'

273

We walk back to my school chatting effortlessly and he leaves me at the gates with a hug, rather than his usual kiss on the cheek. I've no idea if this friendship can last, but I'm willing to find out.

***

I tell Poppie the next day about the developments with Julian as I tend to the *Ficus* that Craig and I picked out. The graze on her face has healed and she looks completely normal now — just like she's sleeping — something that I've convinced myself that she is and that one day she will just reply.

'So, I'm going to meet Dave now,' I tell her. 'He said he's got something to tell me.' I pause as Craig flashes into my mind and I look at Poppie, whose expression obviously hasn't changed. 'Your brother has been really nice to me since your accident; you wouldn't believe it. You have to wake up and see it for yourself,' I say to her sadly. 'Please wake up, hon, I miss your madness and I'd really like your unique opinion on a few things.' My eyes start welling up and I decide I need a bit of fresh air. 'I'll be right back, OK, I'm just going to get a drink; do you want anything?' I ask hopefully. I nod at the silence and head out the door.

When I return, I can hear Craig's voice coming from Poppie's room.

'And I never thought I would want to be with someone who was so stubborn and strongly opinionated.' I decide to knock on the door before I hear more than I want to and I make him jump. 'Oh, hi, I didn't realise you were here.'

'Just went for some fresh air and some water.' I gesture with the bottle in my hand and then offer it to him. 'Did you want one? I can go and leave you to tell Poppie more about

Cassie.'

'What?' He shakes his head. 'No, thank you. No, I—'

I cut him off. 'It's none of my business Craig. Although I have to say, I do think that you deserve better than Cassie.'

'Is that so.' He leans back in his chair amused.

'Well, I wouldn't have said that a year ago, but I think since we've started to get to know each other more, I've seen a different side of you — a side that I didn't think existed. And that side certainly shouldn't be wasted on the likes of her.' I stop vocalising my thoughts as a nurse comes in.

'So, are you both doing the run?' she says, picking up the chart at the end of Poppie's bed.

'I'm sorry?' Craig asks. 'What run would this be?'

She looks up, horrified, at me, 'Oh, I'm so sorry, was it a surprise for your husband, miss?'

I laugh. 'He's not my husband...'

'Oh, awkward.' She bites her lip. 'Boyfriend, then?' she ventures.

'Friend,' I confirm.

'Well, I'm sorry but I must say I'm surprised. Apart from Poppie's husband, you're the only two that visit and I just assumed...ah well, can't be right all of the time.'

'No problem, but no, it's not a surprise; I just haven't told him yet.' She leaves us to it and I swallow.

'Told me what?' He furrows his brow.

'That I'm raising money for the war; Poppie's ward — running.' I wait for him to lay into me but he just sits there looking at me. 'Aren't you going to make fun of me?'

He shakes his head. 'When are you doing this?'

'End of next month.'

'Why running? It would make more sense for you to do a bake sale or something with your skills.'

'Because it's a challenge for me. We are actually having a *Bake Off* kind of thing at school but I wanted to do something that steps me out of my comfort zone.' He stares at me blankly again. 'I know, it surprised me too. I don't know, I think when I broke up with Julian…'

'You broke up with Julian?' he says, surprised. 'When?'

'New Year's Day,' I shrug.

'But I saw you two together yesterday, looking really happy,' he says confused.

'We bumped into each other and had a catch up, but there's nothing there.' I look at him pointedly with big eyes. 'But like I was saying, he said to me I need to decide exactly what it is that I want. And I thought about it and I've always wanted to run a marathon, so, here we are. First step on the ladder, but at least I'm on there.'

'Well, aren't you full of surprises.'

'And you, with your dancing from New Year's; I never told you how much I enjoyed that,' I add bravely.

'I did too. You're easy to lead.' A small sideways smile escapes from his lips.

'What's that supposed to mean?' I put my hands on my hips.

'I meant around the dance floor.'

I exhale. 'Right, I have to go, I'm meeting Dave at mine.'

'Juggling two men and training for a run? My goodness, you're busy, aren't you?'

'I told you I'm not with Julian anymore and I've never been with Dave.'

He shrugs. 'If you say so.'

***

An hour after Dave has arrived and told me what he couldn't say in the corridor, I'm left with my mouth well and truly wide open. We sit there in silence and he looks at me, worried.

'So, what do you think?' He cowers back in his seat on the sofa.

'I can't believe it,' I say in shock. 'I mean, a few things make a bit of sense now, but, wow; I just didn't see this coming. Why didn't you tell me sooner?'

'I've wanted to tell you how I felt for ages but couldn't quite believe it myself. That's why I pushed you away.'

I sit, taking everything in. 'I'm really glad you told me, Dave, but you're one of my best friends and I...'

'That's exactly why I felt I couldn't tell you; I didn't want to ruin our friendship. I love what we have and I knew this would change everything as soon as I said it.'

'It's not going to change anything,' I reassure him. 'You'll always be my Dave.'

Chapter 25

The following Sunday I go to my parent's for lunch, with Nieve and Marcus. Keeley, Simon and the kids are meant to be here but they're moving back in today — Keeley told Mum that they've been invited to Simon's sister's. And Nieve was right, if anything positive has come out of this affair, it's that it has brought us siblings very much closer together. Keeley and Nieve actually go for lunch now or Nieve will babysit whilst I take Keeley shopping. Nieve has even suggested that we all go to a spa for the day. All in all, I'm grateful for the amount of positivity that has come out of the family drama. Plus, even though Simon hasn't completely forgiven Keeley, she said they're facing everything that's been brewing up for years; I actually think that they will pull through this.

'So, your mother tells me you've been running?' Dad says with half an eyebrow of interest.

'Well, jogging is more accurate. It's something I've always wanted to do.' I try to brush him off but before I change the subject I add, 'I'm raising money for the hospital wing Poppie's in and achieving a goal at the same time I guess.'

Dad looks at me straight-faced. 'Well, I'm very proud of you,' he says with no emotion and then goes back to his chicken.

I look at Mum in shocked gratitude and she nods at me. *My dad's proud of me.* He's never told me he's been proud of me. I look at Nieve who's smiling at me too; she knows just how long I've waited to hear that; she's still waiting.

'So, what's new with you two,' I ask the happy, hand-holding couple.

'Well, Marcus and I have booked a bit of an adventure,' Nieve starts telling us. 'A friend of his is getting married in Mexico so we're taking three weeks off work and travelling around; it's going to be amazing…' Marcus sits there quietly and obediently, gazing at Nieve in her commentary as if she's the most beautiful thing on this planet. He's her one, I know it. 'And when we get back, we're going to start looking for our own place; finally put Nana's money to good use, eh?'

***

'Look, stop pestering me. I know exactly how to do this, OK?' Gracie flaps as Jill instructs her on how to make the perfect meringue.

'We are a team and what you're doing isn't going to help us win,' Jill retorts, attempting to grab the bowl.

'Would you back off?' Gracie bites back and flicks some egg white at her.

'Do you want to switch partners?' Jill says to me and Dave from the adjacent workstation.

'What do you reckon, Dave, want to go with Jill?' I ask him, trying not to laugh.

'We're really baking up a storm over here, thanks Jill; maybe next time,' Dave says before she turns in a huff and he mouths to me, 'No way!'

'You all wowed us with your twenty-four identical mini desserts and now have just over forty minutes left, ladies and gentlemen, for your show-stopper!' Dermott says to all the teachers.

'Go Miss Butler!' I hear a member of my class cheer from the audience that is positioned in the school hall opposite the canteen kitchen, watching on pull-down screens from a live camera that's with us in the kitchen.

'You really are a genius, you know,' Dave says to me as we work around each other perfectly in sync and I put our carrot cake with pineapple in the oven.

'I know, a charity team teacher bake-off is definitely going to become a yearly thing. Although,' I lower my voice, 'I didn't think of it showing off your bad side to the students.' We look over to Jill and Gracie who are arguing loudly and Dermott has had to come over to intervene.

'Well, I've got dibs on you as my partner from now on, deal?' Dave grins at me.

'Deal.'

'And I'm not just saying that because we won the first round,' he adds as we clear our station. We have time to walk around the audience before we have to ice and decorate, so we thank several rows for coming. When Dermott calls time, Dave and I have finished with five minutes to spare and are trying not to laugh at the *mess* that Jill and Gracie have made of their Eton Mess.

'Ladies and gentleman, please give your teachers a big hand!' Dermott says to the camera and joins in merrily with the clapping. 'We have ten teams of talented bakers here but only one will be declared the winner! So, without further ado, can I welcome back Mr Foster, Head of the PTA and Dylan Michaels, the winner of our raffle for a student judge, to take their places again at the judges' table please.' The audience breaks into a clap again and Dave leans over to me and whispers,

'Of all the bloody kids in this school, that brat was chosen as the winner?' He shakes his head. 'Unbelievable!'

Dylan is sitting there looking very pleased with himself but I'm sure he will continue to behave since his parents are sitting in the front row watching. Mr Foster is a funny looking man with eyes that are slightly too close together but all the same, he's a very nice chap. Each of the teachers take it in turns to bring up their creations to the front — something that fills me with horror while watching the actual *Bake Off* — what if you drop it?! Luckily here though, everyone manages to make it to the front successfully and receives a critique.

'Thank you, everyone. Now Dylan, Mr Foster and I will discuss, vote and decide who will be the McCarthy Primary's Bake Off *Judges* Winner but whilst we're doing that, we require your help.' The audience stir, as this is a surprise to them all. 'We want you to sample each of these delicious cakes and if you could then vote by way of a donation, whichever cake you think is the best. Please give as generously as you can. The team that makes the most money will be declared as the McCarthy Primary's Bake Off *Audience* Winner!'

Dave looks at me and mouths, 'Like I said, you are brilliant.'

I grin like a Cheshire cat and feel very proud of myself.

'If we could start from the front row.' Dermott sections off part of the audience. 'And ask you to rotate in a clockwise fashion, please.'

The audience make their way into the canteen and walk around excitedly, chatting and praising while they go, getting out their wallets and placing money in jars on each table before taking their seats again.

'Fantastic! Now Dylan and Mr Foster are going to count each jar and while they are busy doing that, I'd like to ask

Miss Butler to the mic to tell us a little more on why we're all here today.'

I walk to the judges table and thank Dermott before clearing my throat and looking directly at the audience. 'Good afternoon, everybody. I'd like to thank you all so much for taking the time to come here today and also for giving so generously.' I gesture to the table full of cash. 'Today we're not only here as a fun end of term, and Easter celebration, but we are raising money for an intensive care unit at our local hospital. Just before Christmas a dear friend of mine was in an accident and the funds today will go towards her unit — maintaining and improving facilities, buying much needed equipment for research and development — which will help better the lives of so many patients and their loved ones.' It's not until that moment I realise Craig is sitting at the back. He smiles at me and my line of thought completely wavers. 'So—' *I swear there was more I was going to say,* 'thank you again from the bottom of my heart.'

The audience burst into applause and Dermott takes back the mic from me. 'Miss Butler, everybody.' He asks Dylan to stand up and gives him some instructions off mic to which he nods and stands proudly. 'Now the moment you have all been waiting for. Dylan, if you could make the announcement, please.' He hands Dylan a piece of paper and the mic.

'Hello everyone, thank you for your contributions today and for your vote.' I smile at this little man, a complete natural on the mic. 'So, without further ado, I will announce in reverse order the totals of the *Audience* vote. In tenth place is Miss Evans and Miss Moore, with their Eton mess raising a total of £4.06.'

Gracie puts her head in her hands while Jill hits the table and gets a stern look from Dermott. Dylan continues to read until we get to number two; Dave and I still haven't been called.

'That leaves two teams: Miss Butler and Mr Wright; and Mrs Dagmire and Mrs Sheen.'

We've got this in the bag, I think to myself and Dave nods at me, thinking the same thing.

Dylan passes the mic to Mr Foster. 'The audience winner was also chosen as the judges' winner; the PTA have agreed to double what has been raised for that creation.' I clap as loudly as I can; I had no idea.

Mr Foster returns the mic to Dylan and he continues, 'The team in second place raised an impressive £97 but in first place, with a whopping £378.45...' the audience gasp and he pauses for dramatic effect, 'is my teacher Miss Butler and Mr Wright with their carrot and pineapple cake!'

Dave and I burst into a huge hug and our classes whoop and cheer. We go up to the front together — Dave with his hand on my back — and receive two certificates from Mr Foster, which I hold in the air.

'Ladies and gentlemen.' Dermott's back on the mic. 'The combined total of the audience vote; the PTA's kind donation; the auction of all of the twenty-four identical mini desserts, plus our school bake sale from last week, is a fantastic £4,072!'

I look at Dave. 'That doesn't even include my running sponsorship!'

He gives me another hug and over his shoulder I see Craig clapping slowly, but not smiling; I watch as he heads out of the door.

Later that day we're all called to gather in the staffroom by Dermott as he says he has an announcement. We all wait patiently and I look around at the end of term exhaustion spreading across the faces of my colleagues, but I have to say, with all the training combined with my *Bake Off* buzz, I actually feel completely energised. If someone had told me that exercise would give you more energy, I would have told them they were mad, and gone back to my wine.

'We've made it, everybody!' Dermott says as he comes in and sits down on a blue tub chair. A hush falls over the staffroom and he adjusts his seat so he can see everybody in the room. 'Now, I've called you all here because I have finally been given permission to tell you something.' The hush increases. 'So, as you may have noticed, when I started here, I made a few changes.' He gestures to the room and some people nod in reply. 'My job was to come in and make some substantial differences — making the school better resourced for the students and more comfortable for the staff. And I think that there may have been some rising suspicion as to how all of this could have become possible.' I look at Dave, who is looking intently at Dermott. 'The governing body and the PTA have finally given me the go ahead to explain to you all, but if what I'm about to say could stay in this room for the moment, we would all be very grateful.' He pauses, making sure he has everybody's attention before continuing. 'Ms Crawley made a very brisk exit at the end of last year as it was found that she was using school funds — almost all school funds — for her own personal use.'

My mouth flies silently open and I look around to see my face matches that of most teachers here, apart from Shirley, who's a little pale in the cheeks.

'An investigation started in January last year as there seemed to be financial irregularities. Simply, the figures Ms Crawley was giving the governors weren't adding up. The police were contacted at the very beginning by the governors with an allegation of financial misuse and fraud. An investigation is still underway, but Ms Crawley was instructed by police to repay everything that she had taken out of the school budget — most of which has now been recovered.' He pauses for breath. 'Hence our new room here and the new sports suite.'

We sit in bewildered silence and I start to think of what the total cost of everything must come to. Dermott breaks our thoughts. 'I'm sure you all have a million questions so let's open the floor.'

By the time I get back home that evening my mind is racing. Tens of thousands of pounds, Crawley stole. How could we, as her staff, not have noticed that? Maybe her bullying was a distraction technique? She was constantly telling us that the school at the last Ofsted wasn't doing well because of *us*, when really, we were declared as 'inadequate' because of *her*. It just goes to show that you should always believe in your ability and not let the words of others dictate how you live your life or establish your sense of self-worth. *Well,* I nod at myself in the bathroom mirror, *I'm in the process of trying.*

Chapter 26

The next few days, I split my time between planning baking a cake for my parents' wedding anniversary party and training for my run, that happens to land the day after. I would have never thought that exercise and baking could go together but I've got into a rhythm and feel so inspired that I've created something beyond anything I could have imagined.

I've based it on a recipe that my nana used to make but I've updated it and given it my own twist. When I was six my nana won first prize at a county fair for this recipe; a local paper interviewed her, took her picture and sang her praises. If I become even a tenth of the baker she was, I'll know I haven't done badly.

My creation for Mum and Dad is an extravagant three-tiered cake of different flavours, complete with jade coloured sugar flowers cascading around from the top to the bottom, complete with a '35' on the top tier. For one of the first times in my life I believe I am truly awesome.

Mum sweet-talked the venue that's hosting their party into me using their kitchen; something I am very grateful for, as my plan was to bake at mine and then borrow Dave's crusty old Fiesta before assembling the cake here.

I stand back to admire its pure awesomeness.

'Knock, knock! Oh, wow, Melanie, you've just outdone yourself.'

I hear her voice before I see her face. 'Thanks, Mum.' I

beam at her as she walks slowly around my masterpiece.

'It looks *almost* too beautiful to eat.' She winks at me. 'But I think you need a freshening up, darling.'

Glancing down, I observe I'm a rather messy cook. Dusted in flour, I pat myself down, creating something of a cloud.

'And you've got a little frosting on your right cheek.' She grins.

'Saving it for later,' I justify, find it with my finger and take a lick.

'Oh, I must take a picture of you and your creation,' she whips out her small point-and-click and snaps before I'm ready. 'Perfect! I love the natural shots.'

'Mum, I was licking my finger!'

'Fine, one more then.'

I stand a little taller and smile as wide as possible.

'I bet Nana would be very proud that you are treading in her footsteps.'

'Thanks,' I sigh, gazing at my creation, 'I wish she was here to see it.'

'Well, I am here to see it, my darling, so I shall say on behalf of my mother, I am very proud of you. You have gone above and beyond and I'm so glad that you are finally showing the world just how talented you are — in every area of your life. And I can't wait to eat it.' She smiles and goes to give me a hug before remembering that I'm covered in most of the ingredients. 'Perhaps I'll save that hug for after you've changed, darling?'

***

The melodious sound of a string quartet floats through the corridor as I make my way back downstairs from the room

Mum and Dad have booked for the night, all freshened up. The room that my parents have hired for the party is now completely decorated with balloons and banners and coral. I walk through the open sliding doors onto a veranda, where all the tables are set up outside, to enjoy the beautiful day.

Nieve and Marcus are sitting on the ground playing with Lucy and Henry; Keeley and Simon are laughing at something Ava has just said.

'Well, look at you!' Nieve lifts her head.

'Look at us all,' I say, beaming at my family. 'I think we all scrub up quite well!' I give Keeley and then Nieve a kiss on the cheek.

'Oh, my beautiful family,' Mum appears behind us. 'You are all my greatest achievement!'

'She hasn't even started drinking yet.' Dad takes his hand from his pocket and puts it around his wife's shoulders.

'Mum and Dad, I want you to open my present now so we can use it before the guests arrive.' Nieve jumps up and grabs a long, thin, badly wrapped gift from one of the tables. They open it and stare with no idea what it is or how to use it.

'It's lovely, Nieve! I've always wanted a — *um* — long walking stick?'

We all laugh. 'It's a selfie stick Mum,' Keeley says, shifting Ava from one hip to the other.

'Oh, of course it is…' Mum says, rotating and trying to figure it out.

'May I?' Marcus takes the stick out of Mum's hands and attaches his phone to it.

'Oh, I see, how lovely! Yes, let's get a group shot!' She waves us all to stand by them.

'OK,' Marcus says, extending the length. 'Everybody in.' I pick up Lucy and Nieve grabs a squirming Henry; we all squeeze together. Everyone starts giggling apart from my dad but maybe he'll loosen up soon; I feel so grateful for each and every one of these people. 'Say cheese!'

'Cheese!!' We all reply obediently.

'Wonderful!' Mum cheers as Marcus shows us the photo. 'That's definitely one for the wall.'

As the party goes into full swing, I enjoy chatting with some of my parents' friends who I haven't seen in years; all interesting people with an abundance of stories to tell.

After food, toasts and speeches, a band replaces the string quartet and everyone moves onto the dance floor. I stay in my seat, happy to people-watch as always. I laugh as Mum practically throws Dad around the dance floor in a bit of a tango.

'Can I have this dance?' I turn to find a familiar face standing there looking down at me with warm eyes.

'Evan. What are you doing here?'

'I had this written in my diary before we…parted ways. You look sublime.'

'Thank you,' I say, feeling quite numb.

'So, how have you been?' He stands awkwardly, putting down the hand he's had out, which I haven't accepted.

'Good. You?' I realise my arms are folded.

He bites his lip, 'Not so good as it happens, actually.' He attempts a small smile and seems to have lost his words.

'Well, I'm sorry to hear that,' I say and find I actually mean it. We continue to look at each other and I gaze into the eyes of the man I thought I was in love with for so long. 'Why are you here, Evan?'

'I want to dance with you,' he says and holds out his hand once more for me to accept. 'Come on. For old times' sake.' Hesitantly, I take his hand; it's warm and familiar and he guides me effortlessly to the dance floor. We move together perfectly, like we always did and for a long while neither of us says anything. Finally, he breaks the silence. 'I meant it, you know, you really look sublime. And, I don't know what it is but you look unrecognisably happy.'

'Always prepared with a compliment,' I say.

'No, there's like, a…a spark about you.'

'Well.' I consider this. 'That's probably because I've been doing some things for me. Putting myself first. Maybe that's it.'

'Maybe,' he says sadly as he spins me around before we return to silence.

'So, how's Daisy?' I ask, not sure if I really want to know the answer.

'I have no idea. We broke up a few months ago.'

'Oh. Right.'

'It turns out she wasn't the one for me.' His eyes fill with remorse. 'I've been doing a lot of thinking and I've come to some conclusions.'

'Is that so?' He turns me again then draws me in closer and rests his head on mine. We dance silently again and my heartbeat quickens as the band strikes up into Elvis' 'Always on my mind.' Evan holds me even closer and then whispers the lyrics into my hair.

He breaks apart and looks intensely into my eyes. 'I've realised just how stupid, *so* incredibly stupid I was to betray you and to let you go. I miss you and after thinking about what it is that I want, I realise that,' he shrugs, 'it's you, us, that I want. I want you there beside me always. I guess I just panicked when we were together because you were so perfect for me and I thought it was too good to be true. So, I ran scared, away from you. But I want to build a life with you, I know that now.' He looks as though he may burst into tears at any moment. 'I'm very sorry that I hurt you and I never want to do that again. Please say you'll take me back, Melanie, because I am truly nothing without you.' He holds me at arm's length now, sorrow covering every inch of his face. 'I love you, Melanie Butler, I always have; I was scared of how much before but I'm ready now to make that commitment to you, and I want to spend the rest of my life, making it up to you and making you happy, so…'

Oh my good God, this is not happening now. I catch Nieve out of the corner of my eye, tapping Keeley on the arm to watch this scene unfold.

Evan bends down on one knee and takes a small square box out of his left breast pocket. 'Melanie. You are the person I was always meant to be with. I want to always be there for you, supporting you and loving you. You are beautiful and I would like to spend the rest of my life giving you everything you will ever need.'

Evan opens the box and a huge diamond solitaire sparkles at me, shiny and tempting; a circle of promises and dreams.

'Melanie, will you do me the honour of forgiving me and becoming my wife?' His hopeful eyes glisten up at me and I know there is only one answer I will give. What has truly been in my heart always. I smile at him, butterflies fill my stomach and I've never been so happy, determined, or sure of anything else. I take a deep breath, giggle and bend down, cupping his face in my hands and I kiss him lightly on the lips. Pulling away I look deep into his eyes,

'I will forgive you, Evan,' and I kiss him again before lowering my voice. 'And thank you for what you said, it really means a lot to me. But there is no way on this planet, or any other, that I will ever marry you.' I smile at him broadly as I hear my sisters cheering.

His face falls. 'You're saying no?'

I nod. 'No,' I say resolutely. 'I will never marry you, Evan. Particularly not with the ring that you bought for Daisy. And I'm so glad you,' I put my hands into air quotes, '"ran scared" from me, because you running into the arms of another woman has given me the greatest gift I could have imagined. I don't need someone to *give* me everything, because if I want something, I can go out and get it myself. So, thank you for breaking my heart, forcing me to take a good long hard look at myself, and start building a future that I actually want, with someone who I actually love and I know loves me back.' I stand up. 'And thank you for coming to see me for this much needed closure, but I'm afraid I have to leave now. Have a nice life, Evan.'

And with that, I walk out of the hall and into the sunshine, finally closing the door on that chapter of my life. I quickly fumble in my bag to find my phone. I need to meet him, where is close to here that we could meet? Stopping in my tracks, I dive in with both hands — *did I forget my phone?* Suddenly I hear it ring and when I've grabbed it, I see he's ringing me.

'I was just about to ring you. There's something that I really need to say; can you meet me? I don't mind where, I—'

'My God, would you stop talking for two moments so I can tell you something!' Craig's excited voice yells at me. 'Poppie's awake!'

'She is? Oh my God, I'm coming there now; tell her I'll be there soon!'

We hang up and I decide I'll tell him face-to-face how I feel.

'Melanie!'

I look up and see Dave, but he's not alone.

292

'Dermott, Dave, how are you both?'

They stop holding hands and Dave gives me a huge hug.

'First time we've ventured out,' Dave says quietly to me and then looks back adoringly at Dermott.

'Hi, Melanie, you look very lovely,' he says, slightly embarrassed, but stands with his professional air.

'Thanks. Dave told me about you two the other day; I'm very happy for you both. But I'm sorry I can't stop; Poppie's just woken up!'

'She has?' Dave says with joy, 'That's amazing! We have to drive you.' He looks at his new other half.

'Yes, of course we do. My car's this way, Melanie; come on.' Dermott points and we all run towards Dermott's Mazda.

***

'Thank you,' I yell at them both as I run into the hospital and towards her wing.

I slow as I near the corridor, deciding to compose myself slightly. When I'm two doors away I hear Poppie's voice excitedly talking. 'How long have I been out of it for this to happen? This is huge! When are you going to tell her?' My ears prick up and my heart beats faster — *I knew he felt the same about me.*

'When I see her later today. I didn't ask for it to happen, it just did. We've spent more and more time together and I don't think either of us expected it.' I shake my head and go to walk in.

'Does Cassie have any idea?' My heart falls into my ankles and I creep back to my eavesdropping position.

'She hasn't got any idea at all; I'm a little nervous about telling her actually.'

'Don't be. I'm sure she's felt the same way after everything you've said. But, oh my goodness, my little brother has decided to settle down.'

'Don't get too excited, I haven't got a ring or anything. Will you help me decide what to say to her?' *I've heard enough.* I slap on a smile and knock on the door. Poppie's bright face shines at me as I walk in; I ignore Craig completely.

'Melanie!!' She stretches out her arms, 'Apparently I can't get up yet,' she explains.

I give her the biggest hug and burst out crying. 'It's so good to *hear* you.'

'You too.' She squeezes me back and I don't let go of her. 'Oh come on now, there's no need to cry. Craig's just been telling me about how much you've been here and everything that you're doing for the hospital.'

'Oh, it's nothing.' I bat her comment away, wanting to focus on her. 'So how are you feeling?'

'Rested,' she nods. 'It's most bizarre; I have what I think are memories and snippets of conversations — they could be dreams of course — but they could have been people talking to me.' She flicks a look at Craig. 'Craig was just saying something that sounded very familiar.'

Craig interrupts her. 'Well, we're just glad that you're here.'

I look at him, 'So Cassie's on her way, is she?'

He looks confused. 'What? No, I'm seeing her later to…well, it doesn't matter…I meant *we* as in you and I.'

'Of course you did,' I say sarcastically. Uncomfortable silence falls on the room. 'Pops, I think I should leave you two to it. I'll be back tomorrow after the run.' Giving her another hug, I then head towards the door; I can feel myself welling up. I turn, 'Plus it will give you both time to plan how Craig's going to propose to Cassie. I'm so happy you're here, Pops,' I add before I dash to the lift and burst out crying.

Chapter 27

All ready to go, I open my curtains and the day greets me with a burst of blue sky and a touch of clouds — which according to Julian — is perfect running weather. Walking over to my mirror I look at my reflection and see a strong, confident, ever so slightly broken but brilliant woman staring back at me. This wasn't the perfect ending I'd hoped for, but maybe that's just it: it's not the end, it's very much the beginning. Going to grab a hairband from my dresser, I notice a box. Tentatively my fingertips touch it, like it's going to snap at my hand or burn my skin. *Just pick it up.* I'd forgotten all about this until about a month ago. Craig's present from Christmas was a puzzle he'd had made of a photo of him and me that Poppie insisted on taking at her wedding. I look at the photo that he'd stuck to the top of the box. My smile is ever so slightly disgruntled to have Craig's arm around my shoulders but Craig looks really rather handsome. I put my feelings away in the box with the photo, grab the hair band and head out the door.

As I walk out of my street and onto the main road, I'm greeted by other runners, casually also on their way to register; you can sense the anticipation and excitement and it's contagious. Taking my place in the queue, I'm ahead of a group of giggly girls dressed in matching pink and black outfits and behind a chicken and an egg debating whether the new manager of their local football team lives up to the expectations of the last. Looking around, I spot Julian where we said we would meet. He's doing quad stretches with all seriousness, then spreads his legs apart and reaches down to grab each ankle with his hands, sticking his bum in my direction. I sign in, press my unique number to stick on my top and walk over to Julian. Upside down, he spots me but doesn't move, he just talks to me through his legs. 'Well, hi there! How are you feeling this morning? Eaten and drunk, yes?'

'I did exactly as instructed.' I begin to stretch too.

'You look nervous.' He's now bouncing up and down in a Miley Cyrus sort of twerk.

'I am. But I'm excited, too — it's all adrenaline really. What exactly is that meant to stretch?' I smirk at him while I'm doing much more reserved ankle circles.

'It has nothing to do with stretching; it's for the benefit of the ladies.'

'It's a wonder you're still single.'

'And I might say the same for you!' He straightens up and takes me in.

'Well, I've decided to sideline myself.' I shrug. 'I'll just focus on me and maybe when the time is right, I'll meet the person I'm supposed to be with.'

'So it's a no-go with the brother, then?'

Ironically, Julian has been the only person I've told about my feelings for Craig. 'So it would seem,' I say, stretching my right calf muscle. 'I was clearly misreading his actions and making up my own signals; ever the "romantic vacant dreamer" as he would put it.'

'Easily done when it's something that you want to happen,' he says, looking at me sadly for a moment before breaking into a dazzling smile. 'Well, let's kick some arse for Poppie's hospital wing, shall we?'

'Yes, let's do it,' I say and we head towards the start line.

We take our places in between the chicken and egg and some more serious looking runners; there must be a good couple of thousand people here today.

'Go Melanie!!'

'Woo!!'

I look around and see Mish, Dave and Dermott, Jill, Gracie and Pablo in the crowd, holding up a big banner with my name on. I wave frantically at them all and start to feel a little calmer after seeing my little support system.

'Welcome, everyone!' A voice booms out of nowhere and I stretch my neck to see where it's coming from. Julian points at a small man standing on a platform with a microphone. 'Today's run is for you and for numerous charities and causes out there! I don't think we've ever had this kind of a turnout before or as good weather for it! So good luck to you all, have fun and we'll see you at the finishing line!'

The crowd cheers and Julian and I join in with gusto. Putting my head down, I shut my eyes, gathering myself and take a deep breath. *I'm really doing this.* When I open my eyes, I see my left shoelace is undone so I bend down to do it back up; the last thing I want is to fall on my face at the starting post.

'Now, on my whistle, you will beg—, excuse me, the general public are not allowed up here, please leave the platform.' The crowd murmurs and I try to hurry to do up my lace to see what all the fuss is about.

'Look, this won't take long...' another voice sounds over the microphone and there's a bit of a loud kerfuffle and some feedback. 'Thank you. Melanie Butler!? Where are you?' I freeze, still crouched down. *It can't be.* Suddenly I'm lifted up by the armpits and thrust into the air like a prize.

'Here she is!!' cries Julian before putting me down again. The crowd parts and a thousand curious faces are on me.

'Julian?' Craig's put-out voice says. 'What are you doing here?'

'Running,' he says pointedly. 'What about you?' Julian grins from ear to ear and folds his arms. I feel my face burning as I look at Craig.

'What am I doing here?' He looks directly at me. 'Melanie, you are a complete moron.'

'*Boooo*!!!' A few people in the crowd, and I'm pretty sure my friends, shout at him.

'Let me finish!' he continues and the crowd quiet their heckling. 'Yesterday I'm guessing you overheard something?' I nod. 'I wasn't talking about Cassie.'

'I heard you say you didn't know how to tell her.'

'Yes, I didn't know how to tell her that I don't want to see her anymore.'

'You don't?' I say, surprised

'No. I don't,' he says calmly. 'I broke up with her yesterday.'

'But I heard Poppie saying you're ready to settle down.'

'Yes, but not with her.' He looks pointedly at me. 'You seemed to have missed that part of the conversation.' The small man seems to have had enough and tries to grab the microphone back; the crowd hear the odd word during their tug of war. 'Look, I'm trying...gesture...just...on two minutes...would you...' Craig barks at him then snatches the mic back. 'Melanie. You are impossible, slightly ridiculous and so stubborn that you often miss what is right in front of you. *I* have been in front of you for twenty odd years. I never knew how to tell you how I felt so it was easier to tease you. But you need to know a few things: how much you helped me when my parents died, and when things got tough with my sister; and that I chose to move to Greenwich because I knew you weren't too far from there; and I didn't need to be at your school every day during the sports project, I could have done most of it from my office; I took dancing lessons because I thought you'd be at that ball and I wanted to impress you; I'd get excited at the thought of seeing you at the hospital and I'd be crushed when you weren't there, and if that doesn't show you how I feel about you, you know how much I hate crowds and making speeches but I'm here today because I knew nothing short of a grand gesture would be able to show you that I'm actually serious.' His bottle green eyes pierce into mine just like they did at Poppie's wedding. 'You're inspiring, beautiful inside and out and despite the odd interest in puzzles and smelly foods, the person I was talking about was you.' He smiles at me, embarrassed but happy. 'I want to settle down with *you*. If you'll have me,' he adds. Everyone in the crowd shushes and waits for my answer. My eyes sparkle with happy tears and I smile so broadly I think my face might burst; I nod at him.

'She nodded!' Julian announces to the crowd, who burst into applause.

Craig beams at me, relieved. 'I'll see you at the end,' he says to me before turning to the small man. 'Thank you, good sir,' and then faces the crowd again. 'And thank you everyone for letting me delay your race. So…on your marks, get set, GOOOO!!' he says quickly before handing back the microphone to a disgruntled host who watches as the runners set off.

'Not imagining signals after all!' Julian says to me as we start.

If I was buzzing before, I'm not sure what I'd call this

feeling, but it floats me effortlessly all the way to the one-mile mark.

'LOOK!' Julian points to our right.

Craig is there holding up a sign; I squint to see it:

> *"I always liked teasing you because you're even more beautiful when you're angry."*

Who would have thought that the person I thought I liked the least, was the person I wanted to be with the most. He's always seen the real me, even before I knew who that person was.

At mile two, he's there waiting again with a new message:

> *"Every time you fell, I fell even harder for you."*

My heart beats faster and leaving Julian behind, I pick up my speed to the final mile, where the man who is so far beyond my original idea of a prince charming, is waiting for me with one final confession:

> *"I like puzzles too."*

I laugh loudly and he drops the sign, running parallel with me on the other side of the barrier to the finish line.

My support system is standing just beyond the finishing post, cheering away, making me run faster and faster, and with one final push, I break through the finish line and the small man from the beginning of the race puts a medal around my neck.

I look down at my medal and think of everything it represents; I literally ran out of my comfort zone. *If this is possible, what else is out there?* I look up still holding my medal, spot Craig, feet from me and think, *I can't wait to find out.*

Epilogue

A year and a half later

Standing on the spot, I take everything in and feel the beat of my heart, drumming with anticipation; my whole life so far feels like it has led to this moment. Poppie stands next to me and takes my hand. 'You ready?' I nod as she strokes the shining diamond ring on my left hand.

'Let's do this!' A whistle blows and we start running with everyone else. I feel strong, confident and so blissfully happy, because I know that after running the 26.2 miles, there will be someone waiting for me; someone who has always been waiting for me. Who knows what my flaws are and loves them because they're a part of me. Turns out I don't pity the girl who ended up with him; she's actually, well, rather brilliant.

Acknowledgments

Before my thank-yous, here's a little story…

The book you're holding in your hands is my first 'book baby'. Back in 2010, after I finished reading another rom-com novel from my collection, I heard myself saying out loud, 'I think I could do that'. I woke up one day, not long after, with an idea for an opening scene, which led to me scribbling down whatever flowed in between teaching kids how to play the violin and the piano.

Back then, I was writing for myself, with no intention of releasing it to the world; it was my hobby. Cut to numerous re-writes, seasonal procrastinations, and the thought of, 'Why not?', brings us to October 2019, when I released 'Behind the Clouds' as an e-book. I'm so excited to finally be holding her in my hands after all this time.

Thank you to every single person who has rallied alongside me on this journey, and supported me when I needed it most; you know who you are, and I am forever grateful.

Thank you to my editors and proofreaders:

Suzie Bird, thank you for wanting to know what happened next; Helen Foley, I'm so very grateful that I moved to Form C, and you will always be my Cameron Diaz; Ann Jones, thank you for continuing to ask…; Joan Bullingham, thank you for your insight; Emma Webb, thank you for your sharp eye and weekly chats; and Faye Thomsit-Ireland, thank you for your attention to detail, as well as your kind words.

Next, thank you to all of my wonderful readers and Rockies for enjoying my stories, and for asking when the next one is out. I am so thankful to each and every one of you.

And last but never least, thank you, James. You are so much more than my partner; you're my rock. Neither of my books would exist without your help, encouragement, but most of all, faith in me. You make me believe that I am capable of anything. Even before I moved to Wales, you asked me what I wanted to do, and I said, 'I want to sing and I want to write.' And that is exactly what I do.

Here's to forever choosing to follow your dreams…

Victoria Mae

Victoria Mae was born in London and moved to the beautiful Welsh Valleys for love. When she's not writing she's a musician, world traveller, and mindfulness enthusiast. She loves country music, salsa dancing, and espresso martinis — not necessarily in that order. Victoria is the author of two rom-com novels:

Behind the Clouds
Between the Lines

Victoria Mae loves hearing from her readers and you can follow her on:

Facebook and Instagram: @victoriamaeauthor
Twitter: @VictoriaMAuthor
Goodreads: Victoria Mae

Also available from Victoria Mae

Wedding columnist turned travel writer, Liv Bennett, has been left at the altar.

A year to the day later, in a bid to save the magazine she works for, Liv is asked to do the seemingly impossible: attend and write about a conveyor belt of weddings that will take her around the world.

Replacing the lead writer for the international best-selling bridal magazine, Blush is no mean feat, yet, Liv packs up her feelings and embarks on this unexpected adventure with three strangers: hair and makeup specialist, Sarah; wedding stylist, Hugo; and the rude and impossible, photographer, Dom.

An around-the-world trip might be just the ticket for a broken heart. Across Europe, Asia, and North America, could this journey of a lifetime be the catalyst she needs to venture inwards, move on, or find some closure?

Before Liv can rewrite her own story, she's got to practise reading Between the Lines.

Printed in Great Britain
by Amazon